PRAISE FOR THE
CLAIMED BY THE HIGHLANDER NOVELS

When a Laird Takes a Lady

"The magnetic attraction between Aiden and Isabail is intense and sensual, culminating in sizzling love scenes. Keats's ability to re-create medieval Scotland adds authenticity to this novel, which is rich with multidimensional characters and an engaging story."

—*Publishers Weekly*

Taming a Wild Scot

"Get ready for a rich, exciting new voice in Scottish historical romance! Rowan Keats captures all the passion and heart of the Highlands as she expertly weaves a wonderful tale of passion, intrigue, and love that you won't want to put down. I'm already looking forward to the next book in what is sure to be a must-read series."

—Monica McCarty, *New York Times* bestselling author of *The Raider*

"Keats's debut sets the stage for a rising star of medieval romance. She seamlessly weaves an unusual romance with the intrigues and power plays associated with the era, greatly enhancing the story's emotional power." —*Romantic Times*

"Lyrical writing . . . and a strong cast of characters will keep the reader engaged." —*Publishers Weekly*

ALSO BY ROWAN KEATS

Taming a Wild Scot
When a Laird Takes a Lady
To Kiss a Kilted Warrior

WHAT A LASS WANTS

A CLAIMED BY THE HIGHLANDER NOVEL

ROWAN KEATS

A SIGNET ECLIPSE BOOK

SIGNET ECLIPSE
Published by the Penguin Group
Penguin Group (USA) LLC, 375 Hudson Street,
New York, New York 10014

USA | Canada | UK | Ireland | Australia | New Zealand | India | South Africa | China
penguin.com
A Penguin Random House Company

First published by Signet Eclipse, an imprint of New American Library,
a division of Penguin Group (USA) LLC

First Printing, May 2015

ISBN 978-0-451-47441-4

Printed in the United States of America
10 9 8 7 6 5 4 3 2 1

Chapter 1

Cambuskenneth Abbey
Near Stirling Castle
October 1286

Caitrina de Montfort scurried down the darkened corridor of the abbey, a candlestick gripped tightly in one hand and a bowl of lemon brined herring in the other. The queen had awoken in the middle of the night with a fierce desire to eat fish. Given that Her Grace was only weeks away from birthing the future king of Scotland, Caitrina had happily volunteered to fulfill her request. But the timing was inconvenient. And a wee bit disquieting. The graceful stone columns and carved oak crucifixes she admired by daylight were havens for eerie shadows at this hour.

A shiver ran down her spine as she passed an unlit archway.

The circle of light cast by her flickering candle barely

held the gloom at bay. Perhaps it would have been wiser to rouse one of the maids. The chambers provided to visiting nobles were in a separate tower of the abbey, more than a scream away from the sleeping quarters of the Augustinian monks . . .

Caitrina grimaced and slowed her pace to a more ladylike walk. *Dear lord*. Why did she insist on letting her foolish imaginings give wings to her feet? What reason would she have to scream? Monks lived here. These were hallowed halls.

She climbed the stairs to the third level, where a single, brave torch fought—and lost—a battle against the shadows. The dim outlines of several arched doorways were discernible along the corridor, but little else.

The queen's quarters were at the far end—a grand set of rooms that included an antechamber, a stone hearth, and a large platform bed. Just beyond the iron-studded door ahead, a pair of armed soldiers faithfully stood guard, protecting the queen and the half dozen women who served her.

Safety was a mere twenty paces away.

She stepped forward.

A faint smile was curling her lips when a hand snaked out of the dark. Big and brutal, it grabbed her by the throat and slammed her against the stone wall. She attempted to shriek, but the only sound that escaped her lips was a strangled whisper. Her candlestick toppled to the wooden floor and the flame was snuffed as it rolled, leaving her in the dead of night with a hot-breathed monster.

Heart pounding, Caitrina squeezed her eyes shut.

"You," growled the monster, "try my patience."

She recognized the voice, but it was no less monstrous for its familiarity. It belonged to Giric the Bear—henchman and loyal knave to Edward Longshanks, the King of England. Even with her eyes closed, she could see his large, misshapen left ear and the puckered scar some failed assassin had drawn upon his cheek.

"Every move the queen makes must be reported."

A flush of shame seared her cheeks. Did he think she could forget, even for one moment, the horrid task demanded of her? Caitrina attempted to respond, but his hand was still too tight, still choking. Impossible.

Hearing her sputter, he eased his hold, and a sweet rush of air filled her chest. He leaned in close, his breath thick with ale and rot. "If the queen shares a meal with the abbot, you tell me. If she eats haggis instead of venison, you tell me. And if she chooses not to return to Stirling Castle for the evening, *you tell me*. Every move. Am I clear?"

"'Twas a belated decision," Caitrina said hoarsely. Miraculously, she had managed to hold on to the bowl of fish, and she cradled it to her chest. A flimsy barrier, to be sure, but a strange comfort nonetheless. "She felt poorly."

"Were she already confined, as a woman of her station ought to be, such discomfort could have been avoided."

"And had her husband not perished on the eve of her birthday," Caitrina responded, "she might well be resting at Kinghorn instead of seeking out every holy monk in the land. But she is convinced the unfortunate timing of Alexander's death is an ill omen, and she fears for the soul of her unborn child."

Giric snorted. "She's a madwoman. All the more reason I should know what she is about."

The insult chafed her already raw conscience. "I'm in service to the queen. I cannot be sending a messenger every hour."

"It is King Edward you must please, not that French bitch." Something feather soft slid along her cheek. "Honor the bargain you struck with him. Find a way to make him happy."

Caitrina grimaced. Bargain? That made it sound as if she'd had a choice. "I have given him every insight into the queen's affairs that I am privy to. My only lapse has been this delay."

"A delay that might have had serious consequences." Giric tucked the soft object into the neckline of Caitrina's gown. "Fail him, and the king will make good on his promise to brand you and your sister as traitors to the crown."

A vision of her sister sprang into Caitrina's mind—the last time they'd seen each other, at Dunfermline Abbey in early April. The day after King Alexander's state funeral. She would never forget the bewildered expression on Marsailli's young face as Edward and his soldiers escorted her off to Uxbridge Priory. Nine years separated the two girls in age, and Marsailli had not understood that when a king offers his protection, he cannot be denied. Even when that protection was merely a mask of kindness. "I have not failed."

The hand about her neck tightened again. "I will be the judge of your success," he snarled. "Not you. Make your reports with more diligence, or you will not enjoy the consequences."

Her family had been stripped of land, wealth, and title, but noble blood still coursed through Caitrina's veins—her grandfather had been the Earl of Leicester and her grandmother had been the daughter of a king. Allowing Giric to believe she was without power would be a mistake. She opened her eyes. The henchman's face was only inches away, and she could vaguely behold the rippled flesh of his scar. "I am cousin to the queen. Punish me without just cause and I'll see you hang for it."

The Bear chuckled in her ear. "You and your sister are the spawn of an excommunicated murderer. Who do you imagine will leap to your defense?"

His words sparked a bitter fire in Caitrina's chest, and she struggled against his hold. "He was *not* a murderer. My father simply did what honor demanded. He avenged his kin."

"There was no cause for vengeance. Your uncle and grandfather died on a battlefield. Henry of Almain had his throat cut in a church."

"You paint Henry as an innocent," she said. "But he was not. He stole Leicester's colors and then slaughtered every man who flocked to his banner."

"King Edward does not tell the tale the same way."

"Of course not. Henry was obeying Edward's orders!"

Giric's thumb pressed deeply into her throat. "Your father's sins are not worthy of debate," he snarled. "All that matters is the babe. Do as I say, or your sister will pay the price. Understand?"

Caitrina's desire to argue vanished along with her air. She understood the stakes all too well. Spying on her cousin upset her, but imagining the life Marsailli would live if they were branded as traitors made her physically ill. Their father had died a penniless pauper in some unknown land. She could not allow Marsailli to endure the same fate. She nodded.

"Is the birth imminent?"

She shook her head.

Giric eased his hold again. "The midwife in my employ suggests it could be any time in the next month. I must know the moment she is confined."

Caitrina's gut knotted. What need would Giric have for a midwife? She had been spying on the queen for several months and she had long known King Edward's interest lay in the bairn—the future monarch of Scotland. But what was the king's ultimate intent? "The monks have offered the queen the hospitality of their fine manor at Clackmannan. We travel there on the morrow."

"Good."

"I assume that once the bairn is born, Marsailli will be free to leave the priory and take up residence with me in the queen's household?"

A short silence followed her question.

Finally, he released her and stepped back. "She will be free to depart once your task is complete."

"And when is that?"

"After you snatch the babe and bring it to me."

"What?" Caitrina stared at his murky outline in horror, her stomach heaving. Steal her cousin's babe? The only child Yolande would ever have with her now dead husband? "No word was ever said about stealing the bairn. I was asked to spy, nothing more. I cannot do such a thing."

"Did you truly believe a bit of spying would be enough to earn you forgiveness for your father's evil deed?" the Bear jeered. "Surely you are not so witless as that."

Head spinning, Caitrina slumped against the stone wall. If not witless, then certainly naive. It all made a sick sort of sense now—why King Edward had approached her personally at the funeral, why the meeting had occurred in an abandoned bothy behind the abbey, and why he had taken her sister into his care. This had been their plan all along. Her sister was more than a simple prisoner. She was the means by which King Edward would bring a proud and independent nation to its knees.

"Is my sister safe?"

"Well enough . . . for now. She is no longer at the priory. She is here in Scotland, with me."

Caitrina died a little at his words. It had been dreadful enough imagining her sister alone with a group of strange nuns. But with Giric? God only knew what horrors Marsailli was enduring at this mongrel's hands. At ten and five, her sister had developed into a willowy beauty with a gentle soul. She would not fare well under abuse. Not that Edward Longshanks spared a thought for the lives of innocent young lasses—he cared only for his own plans.

And those plans included hammering the Scots into submission in any way he could. He'd revealed his true colors in his negotiations with Caitrina, openly deriding his neighbors to the north. But she'd never imagined he would stoop so low as to steal Yolande's bairn. *Dear lord.* "Kidnapping the heir to the throne of Scotland will be no easy feat."

"You are cousin to the queen," he reminded her.

"Cousin or no," she protested, "what you ask is impossible. The bairn will never be alone."

"Find a way," he said softly. "Or lose everything you value."

Then he took another step back and disappeared into the darkness.

As his footsteps faded and silence took over the corridor, the stiffness in Caitrina's shoulders eased. Echoes of the Bear's threats still rang in her ears, but she darted for the big oak door at the end of the corridor with the bowl of herring clasped to her bosom like a stolen treasure. She'd been gone far too long. The queen would be weak from hunger.

Inside the antechamber, the two armed guards draped in red and gold tabards stood silent and purposeful, completely unaware of the incident in the corridor. Not that they would have come to her defense had they known—they were members of the royal garde du corps. They would die before leaving the queen's side.

She pushed on the inner doors and entered.

A waft of soft heat from the fire greeted her. Five ladies-in-waiting, clad only in their white linen night rails and silk slippers, were loosely gathered around the huge platform bed in the center of the room, chatting in quiet undertones.

Gisele de Noyon, the mistress of the robes, scurried to her side. She snatched the fish from Caitrina's hands, irritation evident in the deep creases on her brow. "*Mon dieu!* You lazy wench. Did you stop to stare at the moon? Martine was right. I should have sent a maid."

"The kitchens are on the far side of the abbey," Caitrina reminded her.

But she need not have bothered. Gisele had already spun about and sailed for the bed. The heavy velvet draperies hung open on one side, revealing the young queen, reclined upon a sea of embroidered pillows. A broad smile spread across Yolande's face as she spied the fish, and she eagerly accepted a silver spoon with which to eat. She had the spoon poised above the bowl, about to partake, when she suddenly lifted her gaze and stared across the room.

"Caitrina," she called. "Come."

The informal summons earned Caitrina a glare from Gisele. Ladies-in-waiting were typically addressed by their titles, and the queen rarely strayed from that etiquette. Except with her cousin.

Avoiding the censure in Gisele's eyes, Caitrina crossed to the bed with as much speed as decorum would allow and curtsied. "How may I serve you, Your Grace?"

"Lady Gisele has assured me that no food would be brought to me without being tasted," Yolande said, gently caressing her mounded belly with her free hand. "But I need to hear that assurance from your own lips. For the sake of my prince."

Her fears were not groundless. Some months before, a fiend had attempted to poison the queen and her unborn child—and very nearly succeeded. "You have my word," said Caitrina. "I woke the cook, and he tasted the fish himself, right before my eyes."

Satisfied, the queen's spoon dipped into the bowl and scooped up a small portion of the flaky fish. It went into her mouth, and Yolande's eyes closed briefly as she savored her midnight meal. "Perfect," she murmured after the mouthful was consumed. Then she emptied the bowl in a series of delicate but eager bites.

Gisele removed the bowl to a side table and one of the other ladies offered the queen a lavender-scented cloth to wipe her lips. Now replete, the queen laid her head back. "I wish to rest."

Caitrina was about to step away when the queen's eyes popped open and she grabbed Caitrina's hand. "Tomorrow, we will talk, my little cousin. You have been a true comfort to me these past months since my Alexander's death."

"I live to serve you, Your Grace."

"We will require a lady of the nursery," the queen said, her eyelids drooping. "Someone who will put the needs of the new prince above all else. You have proven your loyalty time and again, and I can think of none better to entrust my babe and his future."

Caitrina felt, rather than saw, the stabbing glance from Gisele. "Would you not wish to appoint a woman with more experience, Your Grace? A woman with children of her own?"

"Nay," the queen said, allowing her eyes to close on a soft sigh. "An unwed woman is best. The lady of the nursery should have no other claims on her attention." She released Caitrina's hand. "But we will speak more on this tomorrow."

Bowing deeply, Caitrina stepped back.

The other ladies closed in, tucking the sheets around the queen and lowering the drapes.

Lady of the nursery. How incredible. She'd never

imagined the queen would honor her with such an appointment. Especially now. If Yolande had any inkling of the conversation in the corridor, she'd have Caitrina wrapped in chains and thrown into the dungeon. And rightly so. Disloyalty and treason should never be rewarded, no matter how fine the intentions were.

With her heart beating a heavy march, Caitrina reached into the neckline of her gown and pulled out the feather-soft item Giric had tucked there. It was a lock of hair, bound with a piece of hemp. Gleaming, nut-brown hair, with a slight curl. Caitrina's breath caught in her throat.

Marsailli's hair.

It had been hacked roughly from her sister's head, the shorn edges uneven and varied in length—a rather obvious threat: steal the bairn, or your sister will suffer. Giric probably intended the hair to be a mild warning, but the sight of it stabbed Caitrina deep in the chest. It was one thing to shear a man's hair, but a woman's? Giric might just as well have laid Marsailli's cheek open with a blow or broken her nose. Her sister's beauty would be marred for some time to come.

Giric was truly a monster.

And he now had control over her sweet, innocent Marsailli.

Caitrina lifted her gaze to the queen's bed. The ladies-in-waiting were blowing out candles and returning to their pallets. As fearful as she was to defy the Bear, the time had come for action. She could not allow Marsailli to remain in that wretch's clutches. Nor could she bring herself to steal Yolande's precious babe.

Nay.

She must find her sister and determine some way to outwit Giric.

As Bran MacLean urged his mount over the ridge and down into the glen, he stole a glance over his shoulder. Rolling hills of brown grass and faded purple heather filled his gaze. No visible sign of pursuit. But that didn't mean they weren't there. The band of MacCurrans on his tail were very determined. And skilled. They had successfully navigated his every effort to shake them thus far, and he'd be a fool to assume he'd lost them.

The night before, under the light of a full moon, he'd caught a glimpse of their camp about a league distant. In the hours since, they would surely have gained ground.

He bent lower over the horse's neck as the mighty beast galloped down the hill, the wind whipping its mane into his eyes. In hindsight, stealing this charger had been an error. He had allowed its worth to blind him. Aye, it was a magnificent animal with a deep chest and heavily muscled legs, but it was bred for war, not speed. The MacCurrans had given chase on fleet-footed coursers.

Any hope of reaching Edinburgh ahead of the Mac-Currans and disappearing among its familiar streets had been dashed. They would catch him long before he reached the city. A new destination was in order. Stirling, perhaps. It was nearly as large and crowded as Edinburgh. But could he reach the walls before the MacCurrans ran him down?

He spared another glance over his shoulder.

A flash of white at the crest of the ridge sent a shot of ice water through his veins. They were almost atop him. He was about to lose the treasure in his pouch . . . and quite possibly his life. Unless he did something bold and unexpected.

With a tug on the reins, he veered south toward the heavy forest that hid the Black Devon Burn from view. He entered the woods at full canter, ducking to avoid low-hanging tree branches. Aware that his mount was weary and eager for water, he urged the horse toward the stream with his heels, then untied his pouch from the saddle and waited for the right moment. It came upon him swiftly—a moss-covered fallen log to the right. He dove off the horse, hitting the ground so hard he could barely draw breath. But that served him well. He had no sooner rolled into the musty lee of the fallen tree than his eager pursuers thundered past, following the hoofprints his mount had left in the loam.

Bran leapt to his feet, aching from head to toe.

He had only a few minutes to save his skin. Once the MacCurrans caught sight of his riderless horse, they'd swiftly backtrack. The village of Clackmannan lay a short distance west. The manor was held by the holy monks of Cambuskenneth, and with any luck, he'd find sanctuary there.

Tossing his satchel over his shoulder, he wended his way through the bracken, taking care not to bend the withering fern fronds in his direction. When he reached the burn, he waded through the water for thirty paces. A temporary measure at best. The MacCurrans were Highlanders—they would soon pick up his track. He reached the bounds of the forest and found himself at the edge of a fallow field. Across the field lay the small village, and beyond that, the dark stone walls of the manor. But 'twas not the sleepy town he'd expected.

A large party had arrived at the manor house; at least twenty horses, two carriages, and several carts piled high with goods stood in the close. A crowd of villagers had gathered to watch the servants unload. Bran swiftly scanned the scene, his gaze halting when he reached the banner held by a young soldier—a split shield: gold with three red lions rampant on one side, azure with three argent fleurs-de-lis on the other.

The arms of Yolande, the dowager queen of Scotland. Bran smiled.

A busy scene would serve him well. Where there were many hands in the work, there was also confusion, and confusion almost always brought opportunity. His best chance of eluding the MacCurrans would be to hide where they least expected to find him: in the thick of the queen's retinue. His gaze lifted to the top floor of the manor house. But it would not be easy to gull the sort of men who surrounded a queen.

He opened his pouch and stared at the silver and sapphire crown within.

Then again, nothing worth having ever came easy.

He circled around the village and approached the manor from the north, where activity was the greatest. Head low, stride purposeful, he headed directly for the caravan of carts. To blend into a royal household, he would need finer garments than the simple lèine he currently wore. With a swagger that suggested he was exactly where he belonged, he sauntered up to a cart stacked with personal effects, seized a brass-banded chest, and hefted it over his shoulder. Then he did precisely what the other carters were doing—headed for the interior of the manor house.

But as he passed the seneschal and his clerk, who stood at the wide-open gate guiding the unloading, he was hailed. "You there," the seneschal said. "Halt."

Bran paused, keeping his head bowed. The seneschal must not get a good look at his face.

"Who told you to gather that chest?"

An excellent question. For which he had no truthful answer. "One of the queen's ladies," he lied. "She feared that some of their clothing had gone astray."

"Nonsense," the seneschal said. "I accounted for all of the queen's chests myself. This one belongs to Chevalier Francois, who will be occupying a chamber on the second *étage*. Third door on the left. Take it there immediately."

"Aye," he said, nodding.

Bran mounted the stairs, but did not stop on the second floor. He climbed to the third level and ducked into the first empty chamber he found. Then he set the chest down, closed the door, and rummaged through the contents. Unfortunately, Chevalier Francois must be a knight overly fond of rich food. Everything inside was too large for him.

Abandoning the chest, he left the room and made his way back down the stairs, merging with the other servants returning to the carts.

"Did ye lay eyes upon the queen?" the heavyset carter in front of him asked of another.

"Aye," his friend replied. "But only a wee look. She and her ladies went straight to their rooms."

"Is it true she's got the face of an angel?"

The other man snorted. "I canna say. All I noted was her swollen belly."

"A shame Marshal Finlay is off to his cousin's wedding in Oban." The stockier man strode to the cart and hauled a chest atop his shoulders. "He'll be right fashed to learn he's had a royal guest."

"He'll have chance enough to pay his respects when he returns."

"Aye?"

"Aye. Fearchar says the abbot will play host to Her Grace until the bairn is born."

Bran selected another well-appointed chest and repeated his effort. It took him three tries to locate the attire he was seeking—simple, elegant tunics crafted of the finest wool and light linen sarks that drifted over his skin like warm water. Dressing swiftly, he exchanged his lèine for a dove gray tunic and a black belt.

The chest gave up several other useful items—two additional tunics, one blue and one green, and a hooded cloak, all of which he stuffed into his satchel. Near the bottom, he found a pair of soft leather gloves—just the sort a man of means would use for riding. He tucked those into his belt.

Now came the difficult part.

Carving out his place.

Having spent the better part of a lifetime observing the wealthy in order to rob them, he knew a great deal about looking the part of a noble. But successfully playing a role, even for as short a time as he intended to remain in Clackmannan, would require more than just the right look. It would require him to think swiftly, act without hesitation, and dance the very fine line between truth and lie.

Descending the stairs, Bran waited just inside the manor until the seneschal and his clerk were engrossed in deciding the fate of two more items from the carts, and then he slipped past the pair and headed for the stables. Once inside the dim confines of a horse stall, he donned the cloak and tied his satchel to one of the saddles slung over the stall walls.

As he applied dirt from the stable floor to the hem of his cloak to acquire a well-traveled look, a one-eyed tabby cat entered the stall, her belly heavy with a litter of soon-to-be-born kittens. She rubbed her body against his legs with an arched back and a plaintive mewl.

"Hey there, lassie," he said, crouching to scratch the cat under the chin. The tabby was leaner than he would expect a village cat to be, so he dipped a hand into the small purse at his belt and found his last piece of dried herring. He offered it to the cat in the palm of his hand and waited patiently as she nibbled. Not that he could afford to wait much longer. The MacCurrans would descend upon the village forthwith.

Standing in the shadowy interior of the stables, Bran eyed the seneschal. Thin faced and heavily browed, he was poring over his clerk's list with an unrelenting frown. A man with a ruthless attention to detail, it would seem.

Bran glanced down.

Was he missing anything? Cloak, gloves, dirk, purse. All good. His boots were a wee bit shabby, but if he properly held the seneschal's attention, that shouldn't be a problem. He spread his hands. Och, *there* was the hole in his plan. Jewels. A well-born man would wear at least one ring. Digging into his leather purse, he found one of the other items he'd filched at the MacCurran wedding. A gold ring set with a small ruby.

He slid it over his middle finger. Perfect.

He stepped into the sunlight and marched toward the manor house.

"Where is the master carter?" he demanded as he approached. "Someone must collect my satchel."

The seneschal looked up, frowning. "And who might you be, sir?"

Bran met his gaze easily. "Giles Gordon, marshal of Feldrinny. Feldrinny is a liege estate to Cambuskenneth, bordering the abbey to the west. Abbot Michael insisted that I journey to Clackmannan in Marshal Finlay's absence to ensure all is well tended for the queen's sojourn. It is the marshal's deepest regret that he be absent at this time, but we shall do everything in our power to ensure the queen's comfort."

The seneschal stared at him, hard.

The wool cloak was lightweight, but it still brought a flush of heat to Bran's cheeks. He wasn't accustomed to wearing so much clothing, even on a cool autumn day. But he ignored the discomfort, facing the seneschal with a slight sneer. "And you, sir?"

"Roger de Capelin, the queen's seneschal."

Bran nodded. "Excellent. Have someone collect my satchel from the stables. I got word only this morning that Her Grace would be confined here and, by necessity, I left without my man."

Then, without waiting for de Capelin's response, he entered the manor.

"I wish to see the constable, Clackmannan's seneschal, and the priest," he said loudly to those going about their business in the great hall. "Immediately."

"Brother Torquil and Seneschal Amos accompanied Marshal Findlay to Oban."

Excellent. The fewer people he had to convince, the better. "Fetch me the constable and the seneschal's clerk, then."

The trick to a good ruse was to mix as many truths with the lies as possible. Feldrinny was indeed an estate belonging to the monks at Cambuskenneth. He knew that because his father had once been the marshal to Laird MacLean, who held the land bordering Cambuskenneth to the northwest. Of course, his information was twenty years old, dating back to the years before his da stole from the laird and was banished in disgrace. But surely things had not changed much in that time?

"I understand Marshal Finlay's seneschal and the priest traveled with him to Oban," Bran said to Dougal, the constable, when he appeared. A big, brawny man with long red hair and a wiry beard.

"Aye." The constable's tight, distrustful face eased with Bran's command of the facts.

"Did they leave you with the keys?"

"Aye."

"And what of the supplies? Do we have good measure of the foodstuffs on hand? Can we provide for the queen in the manner she deserves?"

Dougal shook his head. "We've no venison, and birds we have on hook will not last long with forty additional mouths to feed."

"Organize a hunt, then," Bran said. "And have our cook speak with the queen's cook about Her Grace's preferences."

"Marshal Gordon?"

Bran looked up. A young lad had come in through the big front door, his hair disheveled and smudges of dung upon his lèine. "What is it?"

"There are three men in the close. MacCurrans, they claim. They say they're on the hunt for a thief. They spied him traveling in this direction and they wish to search the grounds."

Bran tossed a look at the constable. "Do you know these MacCurrans?"

"Nay."

Proper etiquette dictated he greet the visitors—but that would spell disaster. "I must see to the queen's needs. Check their credentials and, if all is satisfactory, have your men-at-arms offer all due assistance to these lads. We cannot have a thief at large while the queen is in residence."

Dougal nodded and departed.

Bran tasked the clerk with reviewing the accounts to ensure they had sufficient coin to weather a lengthy stay by the queen, and then climbed the stairs to the third floor. He knocked upon the door to the queen's rooms and was greeted at the door by a dour-looking woman in a white headdress. "Giles Gordon, milady. The marshal. I respectfully request an audience with the most senior of the queen's ladies."

"Lady Gisele is tending to Her Grace."

He nodded. "Please inform her that for the moment all travel beyond the manor walls is curtailed. There is a thief on the loose. My constable and a contingent of our soldiers are on the hunt for the cretin, but until he is found, no one leaves the safety of the manor."

She nodded and withdrew.

Pleased with himself, Bran went in search of a room to claim as his own. Forbidding travel would ensure word of his arrival in Clackmannan did not get back to the monks. Now all he had to do was avoid the Mac-Currans until their search of the grounds was complete, give them a day to move on, and then he could steal a horse and head back toward Edinburgh.

Caitrina stared at the very plump Lady Etienne with a sinking feeling in her gut. "We're not permitted to leave the manor? Not even to take a ride accompanied by soldiers?"

"*Non.*" Etienne scowled at her embroidery needle, which was buried awkwardly in the linen backing close to the wooden frame. "Why do you care?"

Normally she wouldn't. But Giric was out there in the woods somewhere, holding her sister captive. And Caitrina needed to find them. "When the new prince is born, I will be tending to his care night and day. Until then, I would like to enjoy the waning days of autumn."

"It will take them no more than a day or two to find the thief."

To the other ladies-in-waiting, a day or two meant nothing. Another silk lily sewn onto their samplers, perhaps. To Marsailli, it could mean another shorn lock of hair . . . or worse. "Two days is too many. I wish to be outside. The air is crisp and bright."

Etienne shrugged. "Only a heathen raised in this godforsaken land would think thus."

Caitrina ignored the slight. They actually forgave her father for his crimes. He had been a French nobleman bent on avenging his family honor. But her mother had been a Scot, and to the other ladies, that meant she was a lesser being. "Who is this man who decreed we stay locked inside?"

"The marshal. A man sent by the monks to ensure we are well cared for."

Lifting the hem of her blue satin bliaut, Caitrina made for the door. "I will speak with him."

"What right have you to interfere?" asked Etienne. "You are a commoner."

The barb stung and Caitrina wilted a little, but she still halted and spun around. Her mother had suffered greatly when she was stripped of her title, and she had been forced to beg her cousin, the Earl of Atholl, for a place in his household. But what happened to them could happen to anyone. And she was still the queen's cousin. "I am a lady of the queen's court, as are you. I have every right."

Etienne had no response to that.

Caitrina left the room with her head high and descended the stairs into the great hall. "Where is the marshal?" she asked a passing gillie.

He pointed to a tall figure standing before the hearth. The marshal was younger than she'd expected, a stalwart fellow with a full head of dark gold hair and a strong, beardless chin. He was also handsome. And something of a charmer. The slow smile he gave the serving girl who brought him a fresh horn of ale bordered on inappropriate.

"Marshal," she said, crossing the room.

He faced her as she approached, his deep brown eyes taking a brazen inventory of her every feature, from the tip of her beaded slippers to the top of her braided hair. Then he offered her a short bow. "Good day to you, Lady . . . ?"

"Lady Caitrina."

"How might I aid you?"

"I fear this decision to contain us might be a bit rash."

His eyebrows lifted. "Are you aware, my lady, that there is a thief on the loose?"

"I am aware," she acknowledged, trying not to look him right in the eye. My goodness, the man was as forward as the devil. "But one thief is hardly an army of invaders. I cannot see any risk in riding with a proper escort."

"I disagree."

Caitrina cut short her study of his broad chest—which filled the fine wool of his gray surcote to perfection—and shot him a frown. His dismissal of her opinion was cavalier. "Really? Why?"

He seemed surprised that she would question his decision—his eyes narrowed and his nostrils flared a bit—but he addressed her comment without rancor. "The lads who hunt this fellow say he's both dangerous and sly. Willing to go to any lengths to get what he wants. To ride outside the manor walls with such a maligner nearby would be an invitation to misfortune."

That certainly did not sound like any man she would care to encounter. But she could not allow anyone to stop her from finding Marsailli. Dangerous or no. "Give me four men. Surely even the slyest of thieves cannot best four armed soldiers."

"Nay."

Caitrina stiffened. "Are you refusing to give me the men?"

"Return to your rooms," he said. "There'll be no riding today."

Had she truly thought this man a charmer? He was a cad. "You cannot simply dismiss my request."

"I can, and I have. My duty is to keep all within these walls safe, and I'll not abandon that duty to please a lass." He smiled. "Even as bonnie a lass as you."

Caitrina glared at him. Did he really think a smile would appease her? The wretch had no idea how dire her circumstances were—nor could she confess the reality in an effort to sway him.

"And if I choose to take a horse and leave of my own accord?"

The smile left his eyes. "It would be an error to test the bounds of my good nature, Lady Caitrina."

All hint of gentleness had vanished, leaving a hard, intense man whom she had no difficulty imagining hauling her up the narrow steps of the keep and locking her in her rooms. "The queen will hear of this, sir."

He shrugged. "Share my edict with anyone you must."

Teeth on edge, she gave the marshal one last bitter stare, and then turned on her heel. Damn the man. And damn the thief who'd chosen this direction in which to travel. Between the two of them, they had ruined everything.

She mounted the stairs to the third floor. But she could not be so easily stymied. If riding out the front gate was out of the question, then she'd find another way to search the forest.

Chapter 2

Once Lady Caitrina had disappeared into the stairwell, Bran released the breath he'd been holding. A very determined lass, that one. He'd fully expected to have to drag her up the stairs, kicking and screaming like a wildcat. But apparently, ladies-in-waiting didn't resort to such antics.

He gave the lady a reasonable lead, then followed her up the stairs.

The queen had appropriated Marshal Finlay's rooms, so the seneschal had offered Bran a smaller room at the opposite end of the third-floor corridor. Any room would do, frankly. He'd be here only a night or two. All he needed was a wee bit of privacy . . .

He opened the door to his chamber.

The young lad bent over a small oak chest by the window abruptly straightened. "Marshal! My apologies. I thought to be done afore you returned."

"What in the bloody blazes of hell are you doing?" demanded Bran. His satchel lay at the young man's feet, the contents open to view. The fine wool of the two purloined tunics spilled out onto the plank flooring.

"Unpacking your belongings."

Was that a glint of silver he spied in the corner of the satchel? Lord. If the lad but touched the bag once more, the crown would be revealed.

"This is how you mind my effects?" he asked coldly, pointing at the satchel. "Allowing my clothing to wipe the mud from the floor?"

A flush rose in the lad's cheeks. He immediately bent and reached for the spilled cloth, but Bran halted him.

"Nay," he snapped.

The young man straightened. His lips were twisted with regret, but Bran could not allow a moment of sympathy to undo all his hard work. He'd paid a high price to acquire that crown.

"Do not touch my things again. Get out."

The lad bobbed his head and scrambled for the door.

Bran watched him flee down the corridor, then closed the door and sighed. A thousand ways for this ruse to go astray, and he'd just tripped over one of the simplest. He had forgotten that well-born men had others unpack their bags. Fool. And sending one lad running would not save his treasure. With the queen in residence, there would be gillies constantly underfoot, sweeping cobwebs and delivering firewood and lighting candles. He could not continue to keep the crown inside the manor.

The safest place was the stables. He'd noted several dark spots up in the rafters.

But he'd have to wait for nightfall to move the crown.

Bran placed his clothing in the chest and looked around for a temporary hole to hide the crown. Not in the bed—gillies might warm the sheets before he retired for the night. Not under the bed—the bed stood on a platform. He slowly spun around. A cushioned chair, a small table, the hearth . . . Not a lot of choices. His gaze tilted upward. The bed hangings were really his only alternative—there was a chance the gillies would ruffle them to rid them of dust, but he suspected that was not a frequently performed chore.

A sharp rap sounded on the wooden door. "Marshal?"

Bran shoved the crown under the bed pillows. "Aye?"

The door swung open. The cook stood there, a white cloth wrapped around his substantial middle and a worried frown upon his brow. "Murtagh, sir. The cook. I wonder if I might have a word regarding this eve's meal?"

"Have you consulted with Her Grace's cook?"

The man's frown deepened. "Oh, aye. That I have. And there lies the root of my difficulty. The wee Frenchie's demands are quite unreasonable, Marshal. He's asking for delicacies we've no hope of acquiring."

"What sort of delicacies?"

"Almond paste and sea bream." Murtagh wrinkled his nose. "Apparently Her Grace is particularly fond of fish at the moment, but the salmon from our rivers will no satisfy her delicate needs. She'll only eat white-fleshed fish. And where am I to get almonds? Or the spices her cook is insisting upon? The man is a witless knave. We've only—"

"Haud your wheesht." Bran folded his arms over his chest. "Hosting the queen at Clackmannan is the greatest of honors. I'll not allow Her Grace to suffer whilst under our roof. You will find a way to satisfy her cook, or die in the attempt. Is that clear?"

"Aye," said Murtagh, flushing. "But I cannot conjure items I do not have."

"There are always options." Bran nodded at the open door. "Collect the queen's cook and meet me down in the manor stores."

"I will also need several fire pits dug. The kitchen hearth is not large enough to feed the queen's retinue. I must put a boar, two lambs, six geese, and forty capons on the spit."

"Consider it done."

Murtagh nodded. "Thank ye, Marshal."

Bran said nothing, just stared at the cook, hard.

And Murtagh got the message. He backed out of the room. "I'll fetch the queen's cook."

When the door was shut and Bran was once again alone, he retrieved the crown. Boot to the bed platform, he lifted himself up and tucked his prize in a swath of cloth draped over the forward bedposts. A discerning eye might notice the lump, but not in the next few hours. Satisfied, he leapt down.

Now all he had to do was organize a feast fit for a queen and stop two opinionated cooks from killing each other in the process.

He grinned.

Or perhaps their battle would serve as entertainment for the festivities. So long as they did each other in *after* the meal was cooked, all would be well.

*   *   *

Supper was an interesting affair.

Queen Yolande chose to eat in her rooms, citing weariness from the day's travels, which left Caitrina and the other ladies to join Marshal Gordon and the most senior of the queen's courtiers at the high table. As the most recently appointed lady-in-waiting, Caitrina ended up at the far left end of the table, next to the elderly and hard-of-hearing Chevalier Artois.

Lady Gisele claimed the spot next to the handsome young marshal and the pair appeared to find no challenge in making pleasant conversation. Indeed, Gordon proved quite the raconteur—he drew many a smile from the countess. Quite a feat, as the lady rarely displayed any signs of amusement, even in the company of some of the queen's most seasoned courtiers.

Caitrina focused her attention on the food.

The cooks had quite outdone themselves. 'Twas simple fare compared with the queen's usual meals, but it was well prepared and tasty. There was a fine selection of meats, including roast boar, capon with ginger and cinnamon, and herring served with parsley sauce. Ale flowed freely, the pages frequently filling all cups to the brim.

Perhaps if the conversation with Chevalier Artois had been easier, Caitrina would have spent less time looking down the table. But even the simplest comment, be it about the food or the bard's choice of song, was a chore. Everything had to be repeated. Several times. After a few struggling efforts, their talk fell silent and Caitrina was left to listen to the laughter emanating from Gordon and Gisele's end of the table.

She was relieved when supper was over.

In the midst of the dancing and piping that followed the meal, it was surprisingly easy to slip out of the manor. It was a quiet moonlit night, with plenty of stars scattered across the late-October sky. Caitrina pulled her soft woolen brat over her shoulders. Several guards stood atop the manor walls, but all were looking out at the surrounding countryside, not inward. No one stopped her as she made her way to the stables.

She ducked into the dim confines, not entirely certain of her plan. Was she truly going to leave the manor unattended and ride off into the night? It hardly seemed wise. But how else would she find Marsailli? Perhaps it was a moot point. To have a hope of succeeding, she had to first locate a suitable mount. Not an easy task. Horses were huge beasts, capable of crushing a wee thing such as herself. What she needed was a placid mount of short stature. She made her way from stall to stall, peering at the animals within. Surely the monks would own such a beast? She stared up at the massive dapple gray destrier standing in the stall before her.

It snorted, and she took a quick step back.

By the heavens. Its head was as large as her entire body.

The sharp rap of a boot heel striking the wooden threshold shook her from her reverie. Someone was coming! She ducked into an empty stall and buried herself as best she could in a pile of straw. Who would be entering at this hour? The stable lads and the grooms were partaking of the ale up at the manor—she'd made certain they were well into their cups and enjoying the festivities before heading out the door.

Peering through her blanket of straw, she watched a tall shadow make its way to the back of the stables. A man, with a lean build and broad shoulders. All other features were obscured by the dim light. One of the grooms, perhaps? Although he held himself a little too cocky for a mere stable hand. And he wore a cloak, which suggested a degree of furtive behavior. This man had something to hide.

Quite literally, it appeared.

As she watched, he tucked a leather-wrapped bundle in the rafters above the darkest corner of the stables. He positioned it quite carefully, neatly between two posts, ensuring that it would not be seen even in the brighter light of day. When he was satisfied that it was well hidden, he turned and scanned the narrow confines of the little wooden building. Caitrina shrank back a little. Was any piece of her skirt visible in the hay? She prayed not.

Her prayers were answered.

He marched past her, unaware of her presence. But as he passed by, Caitrina caught a glimpse of a strong chin and a long, thin nose. It was a face she recognized. Marshal Gordon. But why would the marshal be hiding something in the stables? Especially in the dead of night?

Perhaps a better question was, *what* was he hiding?

Caitrina stood and shook the straw from her clothing. There was only one way to find out: take a peek inside the bundle. The only problem was, she wasn't quite tall enough to reach it. Searching the stables, she found a small three-legged stool that gave her just enough added height. But getting the bundle down was harder than she'd thought. He'd wedged it tightly in place, and she had to wriggle the package to get it loose. Fortunately, it wasn't heavy, and she soon held it in her hands.

Aware that time was swiftly passing, Caitrina leapt down from the stool and peered inside the leather pouch. The object inside was shiny and hard, but she could not make out exactly what it was. Something valuable, no doubt.

But still, why was the marshal hiding it in the stables?

The marshal had many resources at his disposal, including the keys to the manor coffers. Why would he not place his valuables there? Under key and under guard would seem to be safer than a darkened corner of the stables. Unless he was hiding an object he did not want discovered by other souls among the manor staff.

Caitrina clutched the pouch to her chest.

But that suggested the marshal was not the honest man he portrayed. And it made her hungry to know exactly what it was that the pouch contained. Better light would be useful, which she would find only up at the manor. It was risky to take the pouch, but she had a feeling its contents would prove useful. She needed help to rescue her sister, and the marshal—honest man or no—might be just the aid she required.

Tucking the pouch under her brat, Caitrina scurried back to the manor.

It was time to discover the marshal's secret.

Bran was about to turn in for the night when a soft knock sounded on his door. Although he was bare chested and clad only in his braies, he bid his guest to enter.

The door creaked open.

He raised his brows. Not a maid with linens, nor a gillie with firewood.

"Lady Caitrina," he said, waving her into the room. "This is quite unexpected."

"I'm certain that it is," she responded, stepping through the portal and shutting the door behind her. The silver ribbon in her brown hair had come loose, allowing several dark curls to escape, but she was still fully dressed in a blue gown with white lace trim. Which left him at something of a disadvantage.

Not that he minded. "You've something to discuss, I take it."

Her gaze dropped from his face to his chest and then glanced away. "I do. But I would prefer to discuss it with you fully attired."

Bran grabbed his linen sark off the bed and slid it over his head. "I apologize if I've offended you, my lady. But I was not expecting company at this late hour."

She nodded, a flush rising in her cheeks. "Quite understandable."

"What is it you wish to discuss?"

She took a deep breath, straightened her shoulders, and turned to face him. "I would like to strike a bargain."

"What room is there to bargain? My reasons for keeping you within the manor are sound."

She pulled something from beneath her brat and held it out to him. "I believe this is yours."

Bran stared at the leather pouch, his heart beating like a drum in his chest. The large scrape across the front flap was recognizable from his leap off the horse—the satchel was his. The one he'd just hidden in the stables. But now it was clearly empty. He lifted his gaze to her face and gave her a hard, cold stare. "What is it you want, Lady Caitrina?"

When he didn't take the pouch, she lowered her hand. "A bargain, I told you."

"Be more specific."

The tone of his voice clearly unnerved her—her bottom lip quivered a wee bit—but she didn't back down. She tossed the leather pouch onto a nearby chair and faced him squarely. "I have the crown stored safely in my rooms. If you would like to have it returned, you will do as I ask."

Bran briefly considered denying that the crown was his, but the look in her eyes told him that would be pointless. She was far too certain. She must have seen him in the stables. Very unfortunate. "Nay, madam. You'll return the item, or I'll have the constable arrest you for theft."

She tilted her head. "Truly? You're going to pretend that an honest marshal would hide valuables in the stables?"

Bran said nothing.

"Well, then." She crossed her arms over her chest. A perfectly lovely chest that rose and fell with every shaky breath. "I suppose I must call your bluff. Call the constable."

Bloody hell. The lass might be bonnie, but she was

as difficult as they came. He could no sooner call the constable than he could walk off without the crown. "I cannot have the constable searching the queen's rooms, and you know it."

She nodded. "I do know it. Just as I know that your reasons for hiding a valuable item in such an odd place amount to no good. I suspect that you're the thief those MacCurran men came looking for. But you may rest easy—I'll not reveal your secret unless you force me to."

She spoke gently, almost kindly, but sugar-dusted coercion was still coercion. Bran closed the gap between them and took her chin in his hand. "We return to my original question, Lady Caitrina. What is it you want?"

The faint flush in her cheeks deepened. "I want you to search the woods around the manor."

"Why?"

"A man, who I believe is a danger to the queen, is hiding there."

He ran his thumb lightly along her jawbone. Such delicate skin. Softer than the finest velvet purse. "Why would you not have the queen's guards search for him?"

She took a sharp step back, freeing herself from his grip. "I have my reasons."

"Reasons that are as shady as my own, I suspect." Lady Caitrina was an intriguing paradox. She possessed plenty of courage, but it was a reluctant courage. The awkward stiffness in her shoulders said that she would rather be anywhere but here, confronting him. But she was here nonetheless, driven by some internal need. And he found himself curious to know what that need was. "What is this man to you?"

Her lips tightened. "All you need know is that he's a fiend."

The bleak look that swept across her face as she uttered the word "fiend" sparked a burn in his chest. Men who threatened lasses were a special breed of blackguard. "Has he harmed you?"

"Nay," she said, turning away. "Nor do I care to explain anything further. Who he is and what he's done are none of your concern. Your task is simply to find him."

Although her back was to him, he could see her small fists clench and unclench in her skirts. Whatever the man had done, it *had* harmed her—whether she would admit the truth or not. And that bothered him. "And if I provide you with the information you seek, do I have your word that you'll return the crown?"

She grew still. "Aye."

Her hesitation told him more than her response did. She had no intention of giving him the crown until she had *everything* she needed. Whatever that might be. And the man in the woods would be instrumental to a satisfactory ending. "How shall I know if I've found the right fellow?"

"He has a large scar on the left side of his face."

"Have you any sense of where he might be hiding?"

"Nay. I only know that he won't be alone."

He crossed the room to the small table by the hearth, picked up the jug of wine that the gillies had left him, and poured a cup. "My men and the MacCurrans are searching every inch of Clackmannan land. I'll know soon enough where he is." He offered her the cup. "Would you care for some wine?"

She shook her head. "I'll drink when I have cause to celebrate."

Another dark curl slipped free, falling to her nape. Bran's gut knotted. She was a beautiful lass, one of the loveliest he'd ever seen. And the soft halo of hair around her head gave her an air of vulnerability that belied the unyielding cant of her shoulders and steely look in her eyes. But the desire he felt for Lady Caitrina was inconvenient at best and a huge mistake at worst.

Bran shrugged and downed the contents of the cup himself. The dark red liquid slid smoothly down his throat. "Being alive and free are always cause to celebrate."

"Not everyone is free." The words came out quickly, on an impulsive huff of breath, and it was obvious that she immediately regretted them. Her lips tightened and she looked away.

A part of him wanted to go to her, fold her in his arms, and kiss away her worries. The foolish part. He drowned it with another cup of wine. Chivalry would not win him back the crown. Why should he care if someone she knew was imprisoned? Would she care if *he* were the one in gaol? He placed the empty cup on the table and turned to face her. His gaze trailed over the jeweled pin in her hair, the tiny pearls sewn onto her gown, and the silk slippers on her feet. Nay, she would not.

"Let us be very clear, lass. The deal is this: I find the man, you give me the crown. Attempt to cross me, and you'll discover that I'm not a very pleasant man."

Her eyes widened, but she nodded.

He pointed to the door. "Now go, before I give in to my scurrilous past and teach you a lesson about entering a man's bedchamber without proper escort."

No further encouragement was needed. She ran for the door. After briefly checking the corridor for witnesses to her poor judgment, she scurried away.

As the door shut softly behind her, Bran allowed his frustration to surface. With a low growl, he snatched the leather pouch from the chair and tossed it into the blazing hearth. Damn it. Why had he not searched the stables thoroughly before hiding the crown? He could have avoided a great deal of trouble had he only taken a little more care. Now he was trapped in an arrangement with a lass who, as brazen as she was, had no experience with dangerous men.

Had anyone else stolen from him, he'd have exacted his revenge with a pointed knife.

But Lady Caitrina was no thug he had to battle on the streets of Edinburgh. She was an innocent noblewoman, mixed up in affairs beyond her comprehension. She had no idea what he was capable of, or the things he was prepared to do in order to survive.

For now, he would play her game. Because it suited him.

But the moment the MacCurrans gave up the chase and freedom beckoned, he would take back his prize—willing lass or no.

Marsailli labored over the stew for hours. Using only the small knife at her belt, she skinned and gutted two fat hares, chopped the firm neep into tiny squares, and cut up the onions. A handful of herbs and some salt added flavor, and a bit of flour thickened the gravy. For a lass who'd never cooked afore today, the result was as fine as she could have imagined.

But her efforts did not please Giric. The mountain-like warrior took one spoonful of the stew and tossed aside his bowl with a howl of rage. "Bah! Who dares to feed me this dredge?"

His men pointed to Marsailli.

"Bring her to me. Now."

A shudder ran through her. The last time the Bear had demanded to see her, he'd cut off a hank of her hair and she'd wept all night. What would befall her now? Would he shear off the rest of her hair? Beat her sense-less? She squeezed her eyes shut. Or would he plunge his dirk into her chest and bury her in the woods—as he'd done with that old tinker who'd had the misfor-tune to cross their path a sennight before?

Two of his men marched into the tent she shared with the midwife, grabbed her by the arms, and dragged her across the muddy clearing, their fingers digging into her flesh. When she stumbled, wrenching her right knee, they paid no mind, continuing to pull in spite of the sharp cry she emitted.

Giric seized her chin in his brutish hand and forced her to meet his gaze. A painful tilt upward. "Are you trying to poison me, girl?"

"Nay," she cried, tears springing into her eyes. "I did the best I could, but I'm no cook."

He shoved her away so roughly that she would have fallen had his men not still held her arms. "The best you could? I would feast better at the midden heap, you feckless wench!" Unsheathing his dirk, he pointed it at her. "Have I not made your position here clear? You are at the mercy of my good graces."

Marsailli stared at the sharp tip of the blade, unable to look away. This was it. He was about to stab his dirk into her. She would die alone in these strange woods, without ever seeing Caitrina again. A violent tremble shook her legs, and her head grew faint.

But, to her great relief, he stepped no closer, apparently content to rage from a distance. "Your sister abandoned you—have you forgotten that? She sent you off with King Edward to waste away with a bunch of nuns. Had I not come to claim you, you would be there still. I've brought you home to Scotland and cared for you at my own expense—but even my generosity has its limits. If you are to remain in my camp, you must serve a purpose. Do you understand?"

"Aye." Marsailli blinked back her tears.

"Then serve a bloody purpose," he snarled. "Learn to cook a meal worth serving or you will find yourself serving me in ways you will find much less comfortable."

Marsailli stared at the ground, her shoulders bowed. She was doomed, then. Without an experienced cook in camp, who would teach her? Her next effort would surely give rise to the same anger and disdain as this one.

The Bear's hand cupped her chin again. "Perhaps that would be the best solution, eh?"

She lifted her gaze to his scarred face.

"You're a pretty enough girl," he said, his voice suddenly soft and gentle. "No breasts or hips to speak of, but fair skinned and bright eyed. And you did a fine job of arranging your hair to hide your baldness."

A heavy sense of uneasiness flooded Marsailli's body. The look in his eyes was dark and expectant, and a strange smile curved his thin lips. She stiffened in his hold, resisting a powerful urge to leap away, to run as far and as fast as she could.

"Would you prefer to serve me in my bed, little dove?" He rubbed his thumb over her bottom lip. "That might be a better use of your talents."

Marsailli swallowed a mouthful of sour spit. *Serve him in his bed?* Even without knowing exactly what that meant, she knew the suggestion was horribly inappropriate. A woman did not lie with a man outside of wedlock—and it was quite clear he wasn't offering to wed her. "Nay," she said, choking on the word. "I'd prefer to cook."

His smile vanished. He stared at her lips for a long moment, all suggestion of warmth and kindness gone. "So be it. Return to your cauldron. But disappoint me with your offerings again and your desires will bend to mine." He released her and walked away.

Marsailli breathed a deep sigh of relief.

She still had no idea how she would produce a meal that would satisfy Giric, but she was happier dealing with that problem than resisting the man's troubling interest in her lips. If she could learn a few simple recipes, she might be able to keep him at bay. The challenge was finding those recipes. She slowly scanned the camp, eyeing the faces of the Bear's men one by one. Someone had done the cooking before she was assigned the duty. But who?

She rubbed her aching right knee.

Was it the barrel-chested soldier with the missing thumb? He'd shown her how to start a fire and where to find the cauldron and cooking utensils. Or perhaps the fair-haired lad with the large front teeth? He'd helped her sort through the selection of herbs and spices, ably identifying each by its smell. Or perhaps it was the tall, thin man with the balding pate and shoulder-length dark hair? She regularly found him spying upon her with his arms folded over his chest and a frown upon his face—very disapproving of her every action.

The same way that he was staring at her now.

Of course, he glanced away the moment she met his gaze.

He didn't look the least bit friendly, and she had no reason to believe that he would help her, but she had to start somewhere. Marsailli straightened her shoulders, lifted her skirts so they wouldn't drag in the mud, and limped across the camp toward the tall, thin man.

What did she have to fear?

Anything would be easier than facing an angry Bear.

Chapter 3

Bran unrolled the parchment map and spread it across the table. With a corked inkpot in one corner and a pewter cup in another, he held it open while he studied the thin black lines that represented the boundaries of Clackmannan. "The northwest forest, you say?"

"Aye," Dougal said, pointing to the map. "Right here. We found a dozen Englishmen camped in a small clearing."

"Was the thief among them?"

Dougal shook his head, his thick red beard swinging with the motion. "Which sorely disappointed the Mac-Currans. There was no sign of the wretch. They now believe he entered Black Devon Burn and headed west."

"Are they bound for Stirling, then?"

"Aye." The constable grimaced. "I invited them to return to the manor and feast with us, but they declined. They're keen to find their man."

Bran resisted a smile. The departure of the MacCurrans was excellent news, but sharing his joy would be inappropriate. "And what reason did the English give for being in Clackmannan?"

"They are riding north to Fort William, but broke a cartwheel in the mud."

Moving the inkpot and the pewter cup, Bran allowed the map to curl up. He handed Dougal the rolled parchment. "Did we offer them our assistance?"

"Of course," said Dougal, scratching his chin beneath his beard. "But they were no interested. Said they had their own wheelwright."

"Was there anyone of note among them?"

"I saw only soldiers, but they had several tents."

He could ask Dougal about the man with the scar, but that would suggest he knew more than he should about the men in the forest. Better that he look for himself. Alone and discreetly. "Were it only a small party, I'd leave them to make way on their own. But twelve Englishmen? We can take no chances, not with the queen in residence. Post guards in the forest."

"Aye, Marshal. I'll see to it right away." Dougal offered him a short bow and then marched off.

Bran looked up and met Lady Caitrina's gaze across the great hall. She and another of the queen's ladies were consulting with the two cooks, but she had been casting quick glances in his direction the entire time Dougal had been making his report. She raised a single eyebrow, and he nodded in response.

Had he believed it feasible to keep Caitrina at a distance, he would have. But he knew she would not be easily dissuaded.

Upon excusing herself to her companions, she crossed the room to his side. She walked with a natural grace and sway that held his attention every inch of the way. "What have you found out?"

"There is indeed a party of men in the forest," he confirmed, lifting his gaze to her face. An equally entrancing view. Especially that pert little nose. "I can't be certain it includes the man you seek, but I'll verify that when I ride out to see for myself."

"I'll ride with you."

"Absolutely not." His stealth skills did not include hiding a lass in skirts, especially skirts of pale purple satin. Caitrina would be a beacon in the dark green of the woodland. A very lovely beacon, but a beacon just the same. "You'll remain here in the manor, where it is safe."

"There is only one way I'll be convinced you have the correct man," she said, "and that is if I see him for myself."

"Don't be difficult, lass. There is real danger in approaching these men."

"I'm well aware of the risks." She cocked her head. "But I doubt that you intend to march openly into his camp. Spying on him from a distance would seem to be the wiser course."

"Be that as it may, I've no intention of bringing you along."

"I'm not giving you a choice," she said quietly. "If I cannot confirm that the man you've found is the man I seek, then I'll not return the crown."

He sighed. How quickly he'd forgotten. Bonnie as a

bluebell, to be sure, but also prickly as a gorse bush. "Fine. Accompany me if you must, but find another gown. Something less . . . obvious."

Caitrina glanced down at her dress, a thoughtful frown creasing her brow. "Of course," she said. "Browns and greens would be far more suitable. I'll make the change immediately. When do we leave?"

"As soon as you're ready."

"We won't wait until nightfall?"

"Nay," he said. "Our objective is to see, and seeing in the dark is near impossible."

"Our objective is also secrecy," she pointed out. "How do you intend to leave the manor and approach the men in the forest without being seen?"

"Leave that to me."

Her eyebrows soared. "You expect me to simply put my faith in your abilities?"

"Aye."

"Why? Are you conveniently a woodsman in addition to being a thief?"

Bran briefly closed his eyes. As tempting as it was to bend the lass over his knee and teach her a thing or two about respect, he dared not. The great hall was full of curious eyes. Instead, he pictured the wealthy young lasses he had often charmed on the High Street in Edinburgh, and he produced a lazy smile. "You'll discover soon enough that I'm a *very* capable man, lass."

Her gaze met his, and a rosy bloom spread across her cheeks.

The color softened her features in an unexpected way—fine and delicate became warm and sensual. Less sharply cut diamond and more sultry pink pearl.

"Go," he said, pleased with his efforts. "When you're ready, meet me at the postern gate."

She hesitated, clearly not used to being dismissed.

"Go," he repeated. "We must make the most of the day."

Perhaps it was the suggestion of passing time, but she finally let go of her misgivings and nodded. "The postern gate," she confirmed. Then she headed for the stairs.

Bran watched her until the last bit of purple satin had disappeared into the stairwell. Now all he had to do was find a way to secrete the lady out of the manor. Slipping out on his own would have been easy enough, but Caitrina would pose a challenge. She was hardly the sort of lass who could move about without drawing notice, even if she rid herself of the brightly colored gown.

He tapped a finger on his chin.

Unless, of course, she wasn't a lass.

Caitrina dug through the chest until she found the gown she was looking for: a dark green kirtle with a brocade bodice of brown and cream. Much more subtle than purple. She shook out the gown and laid it on the bed. "This is the one," she said to one of the young maids who had accompanied them to Clackmannan.

The lass fingered the dark material with a frown. "Are you certain, my lady? A trifle dull this is, for a day gown."

"It is indeed," Caitrina agreed. Not that she'd always thought so—it had been one of her favorites back in Atholl, before she'd been chosen as a lady-in-waiting.

There had been few occasions to wear satin and lace there, especially after her maither took ill. A much simpler time, requiring much simpler attire. "But if I'm to venture into the cellars, then I'll not risk one of my better gowns."

The maid unlaced Caitrina's purple gown and tugged it gently over her head, taking care not to muss her braided hair. "And why must a lady enter the cellars?"

"To find furniture for the nursery." Caitrina ducked into the dark green gown and helped the maid smooth the material over her white linen sark. "The queen has commissioned the master carpenter to craft an oak creidle worthy of a prince, but there'll not be time to hew everything we will require. I've been assured there are numerous items in the storerooms below the manor that might prove suitable."

The maid wrinkled her nose. "May I suggest, then, that you don boots instead of slippers? There'll be all manner of dust and dirt below the stairs."

"A fine idea." And just what she would need for her ride into the forest.

But she had to make the exchange swiftly—left to his own, Marshal Gordon might depart without her. He wasn't a real marshal, after all. He was a thief. A contemptible wretch. How could she have any faith that he would honor his word? Caitrina waited impatiently for the maid to lace up her boots and then scurried downstairs.

The postern gate was a narrow wooden egress behind the stables. It was used mostly by the huntsmen and the gardeners to perform work outside the manor walls, but they typically left at first light and returned at sunset. In the middle of the day, the portal saw little movement. Indeed, when Caitrina arrived, it was closed and there was no one about.

Not even her thief.

She slowly pivoted, scanning every shadow. Where was he? She hadn't entirely taken him at his word—she'd hidden the crown where he'd never think to look—but she *had* believed this was the easier option for him. With the constant flow of ladies and servants, entering the queen's rooms would be a challenging feat. But what if he didn't come? She knew roughly where the men were camped. Was she prepared to go alone?

"Hallo, lass."

Caitrina spun around. Her wayward thief stood immediately behind her, holding a small bundle of cloth in his hands. How could a man living a lie look so calm and worry-free? Not a single line marred his handsome brow. "Where are the horses?"

He smiled that smile again. The slightly crooked one that made her pulse leap and her belly tighten in anticipation. "We'll get to the horses soon enough. First, I've had another think on your attire. I need you to wear these."

She accepted the bundle of cloth, fingering the rough-spun material. "Are these trews?"

"Aye."

Her gaze shot up to meet his. "Are you mad? I cannot wear such a garment."

"If you want to accompany me, you must." He nodded to the soldier visible on the wall just to their left.

"The guards will think nothing of two lads departing the manor. But a lass—even one dressed in a dark gown—will be cause for comment."

"The comments will be far more damning when they find me in a man's clothing."

His smile deepened. "Then let us not be caught."

"You jest," she said. "But there is nothing amusing about being hauled before the magistrate, or muddying my reputation beyond repair."

The twinkle left his eyes. "I'll not allow that fate to befall you."

He spoke with such confidence that she almost believed him. But unfortunate events had a cruel way of coming true. Caitrina's fingers tightened around the coarse twill trews. Discovery was a very real risk, but not enough of a risk to walk away. Not when Marsailli's life hung in the balance. "Fine," she said. "Where shall I dress?"

He pointed to the stables.

She took a step in that direction and halted. "This is uncomfortable enough without adding to my worries. I struggle each time I call you Marshal Gordon. Can you offer me another name?"

"Bran."

An uncomplicated name that was a little at odds with such a complicated man. But she liked it. "Well, Bran. Please keep the stable hands at bay while I don my disguise."

He nodded. "Just be swift, lass. The daylight hours are passing."

Caitrina found an empty corner of the stables and, with several nervous glances over her shoulder, exchanged her gown for the clothing he had given her. The attire was simple and it didn't take long to lace up the sark and belt the trews about her waist. But the slide of the rough material between her legs and over her rump made her face burn. Even fully dressed, she felt naked. No, worse than naked—exposed. And the sark did nothing to hide her very feminine bosom.

Hugging the wall of the stables, she made her way to the door and quietly called out to Bran, "Your plan is flawed. These clothes will fool no one."

"Let me be the judge of that," he said. "Step out."

Caitrina wanted to step outside; she truly did. Marsailli was counting on her. But the very thought of anyone spying her in this scandalous attire made her light-headed. Imagine what she must look like. A harlot, no doubt. Or some other type of fallen woman. She gripped the door frame with both hands and stared at the patch of sunlit dirt swimming just outside the entrance. "I cannot," she admitted breathlessly.

"You're a truly difficult lass," he said, marching into the stables with a scowl. "And given some of the lasses I've met—" He halted as he caught a look at her face. Without hesitation, he folded her into his arms. "Are you ill?"

"Just having . . . a wee bit of trouble . . . breathing."

"So I see." He pushed her head down. "Head between your knees. That'll set things right."

"I'm already top over terve," she protested. But she didn't resist the gentle push, and to her amazement she almost immediately felt less woozy. "What a curious remedy."

"Aye," he agreed. "But it does the deed."

"How did you learn such a trick?"

He shrugged. "My da. The first time I went to battle at his side, I very near emptied my spleen on his boots. Training in the lists does not prepare you for the moment when you must stare into the eyes of the lad you've impaled upon your sword."

It was hard to imagine him as a trembling, pale-faced young man. If his tale was true, that lad had been long lost to experience. The man who held her in his warm, unwavering embrace was anything but weak. Steadfast and secure came to mind.

"Can you stand now?" he asked.

"I think so."

He released her and stepped away. "Let's have a look at you, then."

Grateful for the dim interior of the stables, Caitrina straightened. "I do not look like a lad."

He stared at her for a long moment—such a long, uncomfortable moment that Caitrina wished she had something hard to hit him with.

"Well?"

"You've the right of it," he said slowly. "I'd never have believed it possible, but you look more like a woman in those clothes than you do in your own."

A wave of heat rolled up her neck and into her cheeks. Was that a hint of admiration in his eyes? Surely not. "Then we're in agreement," she said, pushing past him and reaching for her gown. "I'll wear the gown I came in."

"Nay," he said. "You'll go as a lad, or not at all."

Caitrina spun around to face him. "But we both agreed this disguise was a poor choice."

"It needs some adjustment," he admitted.

"Don't be daft. No amount of *adjustment* could possibly make this work."

A slow smile spread across his face. " 'Twill be a challenge, indeed, to hide such a lovely feminine form. But it can be done. With these." He handed her two long panels of linen.

She blinked. "How, exactly?"

"Wrap one loosely about your bare middle to give it a wider appearance. Wrap the second about your bosom, tight as you can. Draw the sark over the top and belt it at your hips, not your waist."

Heat flooded into her cheeks again. Dear lord. The man threw out words like "bare" and "bosom" with complete nonchalance. As if they were discussing the weather, and not the intimate details of her body. How could she ever look him in the eye again? "Fine," she said sharply. She pointed a finger at the exit, wordlessly instructing him to leave.

He headed for the door. "Hail me if you require assistance."

Her cheeks scorched with embarrassment. What kind of assistance did he imagine he would offer? The man was a miserable cur. A handsome cur, but a cur nonetheless. The moment he disappeared, she shucked the sark and wrapped the linen about her body as he had instructed. It took several tries before she got the linen secured about her bosom in a satisfactory manner, but within a few minutes she was once again fully dressed. She tucked her long braid into the back of her shirt and then called to Bran.

"You may return."

Surprisingly, with the addition of the linen, she felt much more comfortable. When he entered, she was able to meet his gaze with only a slight warming in her cheeks. Until his stare once again lengthened beyond appropriate. "How does it look?"

He nodded. "Excellent. With a brat over your hair, you'll do just fine."

"You truly think I'll pass for a lad?"

"Not under close inspection," he said, taking her arm and leading her deeper into the stables. "But you'll gull the guards on the wall, sure enough. How well do you ride?"

Caitrina peered into the stall before them. A long-legged roan mare stood quietly inside, her rope halter tied to a large iron ring on the wall. Not the short and placid mount she had hoped for, but certainly calm. "I can stay a horse well enough, as long as it maintains a smooth, unhurried gait."

"So, if she breaks into a trot, I'll be picking you up from the ground?"

She frowned. Her riding experience was limited to occasional hunts, and they were generally done at a leisurely pace. "What reason would we have to trot? Surely we have enough time to reach the camp and return before dark?"

"I can think of several reasons we might need to ride fast and hard," he said, shaking his head. He stepped to the next stall. "I think it best we take one mount, not two."

"I don't understand," she said, following him. "Where will I ride?"

"With me."

Caitrina stared up at the huge dapple gray stallion, her heart pounding. "Surely you jest."

He laid a blanket over the horse's back and then picked a saddle from the selection of tack hanging on the wall behind them. " 'Twill be much safer than riding apart."

"Safer for whom?" she asked, aghast.

"For both of us," he replied, cinching the saddle with two sharp tugs. "Discretion is our ally in this endeavor." Unhooking the destrier's rope halter from the ring, he led the horse out of the stall.

Caitrina took several steps back. The beast was even larger than she'd first thought.

Bran completed his preparations and then leapt upon the horse's back. Leaning down, he extended his hand. "Let's have at it, lass."

Oh, lord. The moment of truth was upon her. She wiped her damp palms on her thighs. "I'm still not certain how this is to be done."

He pointed his thumb over his shoulder. "You'll ride behind me."

Her heart skipped a beat. "Are you mad? I'll surely fall off."

"Not if you hold on."

"To what?" she asked.

He grinned. "Me."

A picture rose in her mind and she gasped. "You expect me to ride astride?"

"Aye," he said. "Just behind the saddle. A lad does not ride like a lady."

Well, of course not. But that realization had been very slow in coming. Caitrina ignored the heat rising in her cheeks and held out her hand. "Let's get on with it, then."

"Brave lass." He took hold of her arm. "Leap up."

She bent her knees and sprang, not remotely hopeful that she would reach her seat. But with his strength behind her, she swung easily onto the horse's back. She barely had time to lift her brat over her hair and grab his waist before Bran urged the great horse out into the close.

Caitrina kept her face hidden as they made their way to the postern gate. No one stopped them, but they passed several stable lads mucking straw—lads who might well recognize her, given the chance. She was so fearful of being hailed a charlatan that she gave little thought to the placement of her hands until they were well clear of the manor walls.

When the guards on the walls were some distance behind them and the shadowed edge of the forest loomed several hundred paces ahead, Caitrina relaxed her fisted hold on the front of Bran's lèine. The warmth of the skin beneath his clothes had leached into her fingers in a very pleasant manner. *Too* pleasant. Pulling away suddenly seemed like a good notion, but not if it meant falling off. Which was a very real risk—the big horse had a rather jarring gait. Still, there seemed to be no proper place to put her hands. If she let them fall loosely, they would end up in his lap. Definitely not appropriate. If she splayed them across his chest, she would swiftly map every hill and valley of his firm body. Enjoyable, perhaps, but hardly acceptable. And try as she might, she could not clasp her hands together—his chest was too broad. So where, then?

"Cease your squirming," he said gruffly.

Caitrina glared at the nubby linen weave of his lèine. An easy admonition for him to make. A thief would not concern himself with propriety. "This is not my usual mode of travel," she said. "So forgive me if I can't settle."

"You're forgiven," he said. "But I'm a man, you ken? And despite your fine wrappings, I'm very aware that you're a woman."

She grew still. Although she was yet a maid, talk among the queen's ladies tended toward the salacious. Conversation frequently turned to affairs of the heart, and as such she was quite familiar with the ebb and flow of desire. Especially as it pertained to the male form. "Perhaps you need to focus your thoughts on our objective," she said, moving her hands to his sleeves. It was still a fascinating terrain to explore, but safer, somehow. "The man I seek is a very dangerous sort."

"Some detail would be welcome."

How much could she tell him about the Bear without revealing the bitter truth? "I've seen him kill a man with his bare hands. He beat the fellow near to death, then broke his neck."

"An assailant?"

They entered the woods to the raucous caw of a protesting jay. The canopy of leaves above their heads cooled the air and returned a faint echo of the horse's plodding hoofbeats.

"Nay, simply a man who dared to insult the king." It had been a deeply offensive slur, involving Longshanks and a goat, but in the end, only words. But to Giric, the punishment had been justified—a worthless

Scot did not malign the King of England and live to tell the tale.

"Why did no one stop him?"

Caitrina had tried to stay his hand and had earned a bruised cheek in the process, but no man in the street had interfered. And she understood why. The Bear stood a head taller than most other men and had shoulders as broad as a barn door. He was a formidable foe, and the scars on his face were a warning to any who dared oppose him—even a sharp blade wielded by a sure hand would not prevail.

"He was surrounded by six armed men." True, but even his own men had been uneasy with the justice Giric had meted out. Not enough to challenge him, of course.

"And how did he escape the constable?"

"He accused a traveling merchant of the crime and his men stood witness."

At a fork in the trail marked by a large pine, they turned west.

"Why do you believe him a danger to the queen?"

Caitrina had given some thought to the story she would tell if he pressed her for details. Sticking as closely to the truth as she dared, she said, "The queen has traveled the width and breadth of Scotland these past several months in search of spiritual guidance, and I've spied this man in almost every burgh we've stopped. Were he a Scotsman, I'd be less concerned. But he's a Sassenach, and I've no love for the English."

He tossed a frown over his shoulder. "Scotland has been at peace with England for many years. What reason would this man have to harm the queen?"

"I don't know," she lied. "Save that these are turbulent times, with the king dead and his son yet unborn. And as I said, he's a dangerous man."

Bran lifted a low-hanging branch to ease their passage. "The party up ahead may not include the man you seek. Dougal says they're soldiers on their way to Fort William."

Caitrina ducked as the branch swung back into place. "I hope you're right."

But it was unlikely. Giric was out here somewhere, and this was the only party reported by Dougal and his men. Her heartbeat fluttered. If it *was* Giric and his men, Marsailli would be among them, and she could make real plans to set her sister free.

"How do you plan to approach them?" she asked.

"Quietly."

She waited for him to say more, and frowned when nothing was forthcoming. "Surely you have a plan?"

"Plans have a way of going awry," he said. "I prefer to think on my feet."

Caitrina blinked. He thought to engage a brute like Giric with nothing more than his wits? Was he mad? "Do not mistake this man for a fool. His actions may imply a certain rashness, but he is far from simpleminded."

"We're not completely without resources," he said. "I had Dougal post guards in the woods around the camp. They have orders to keep their distance, but if we run into trouble, they'll be within easy reach."

That was reassuring. But it was hardly a plan. "Will we seek a high point from which to spy upon the camp?"

He shrugged. "Perhaps."

"When will you decide?" she asked, frowning.

"I'll know when I get there."

Caitrina clenched her fingers on his arms. He had no idea what sort of monster they were up against. "Stop. That simply won't do. We cannot approach this man unprepared."

Bran tugged on the reins and brought the horse to a halt. He twisted in the saddle and favored her with a narrow-eyed look that instantly wilted her resolve. "Lass, I've expended great effort to bring you this far. But make no mistake. I'll not hesitate to unhorse you right here if you insist on challenging me further."

Caitrina swallowed tightly.

He would do it; the chill in his eyes made that very clear. Having come this far, being so close to seeing Marsailli, she was left with no option. Bran might well be underestimating Giric, but it made no difference. She had to go on. Dropping her gaze, she said demurely, "I understand."

"Good." He settled back into the saddle and urged the horse forward. "It's not much longer now. I see one of Dougal's men in the trees up ahead."

Caitrina peered around his shoulder. "How do you know it's one of Dougal's men?"

He pointed. "They all wear a white band painted with a black cross tied about their right arm."

"That's quite inventive."

"Aye," he agreed. "Pull your brat close and cease your blether now, lass. I'll do the talking to the guard."

Caitrina did as he bade. She did not entirely cover her face—that would have raised the suspicions of the guard—but she made sure that her hair and her rather feminine chin were hidden in the folds of the cloth. Her belly was knotted, but she did her best to sit on the horse with a casual confidence as they rode up to the guard.

Dougal's man was a grizzled fellow, bowed slightly by his advancing years. Bran did not recognize him, and judging by the suspicious frown he wore as they approached, the guard knew naught of him, either.

"*Latha math,*" he greeted the old man in Gaelic.

The wariness in the guard's eyes eased. "A good day to you, as well."

"I'm Marshal Gordon," Bran said. "Late of Feldrinny. Did Dougal mention me to you?"

"Aye, he did," responded the old man. "But he said naught of you traveling in this direction." His gaze slid over Bran's shoulder. "Nor did he say anything aboot this young laddie."

"The lad is just a stable hand I've brought to care for my horse," Bran said dismissively. "My aim is to take a closer look at our English visitors. Their tale of a broken wheel rings false to me."

The guard's gaze lingered on Caitrina for a moment before returning to Bran. "Should we hasten them away, then?"

"Not the now," said Bran. "But keep your sword sharp and your wits about you. With the queen at Clackmannan, we must be especially diligent."

"True enough."

"I'll pass this way on my return and relay all that I discover." And with that, Bran nodded his good-bye and prodded his horse into a walk. When they were far enough away that he was confident the guard could not overhear, he said to Caitrina, "He's a canny old fellow. I'm not certain he believes you are a lad."

"Will he report my presence to Dougal, do you think?"

"Not likely," he assured her. "But if he does, his description of you will be sorely lacking."

She relaxed against his back, both hands loosely clasped about his middle. There was plenty of linen padding between them to disguise her shape, but the soft press of her face and the warmth of her breaths through his lèine stirred him with remarkable ease. The fault lay with his imagination. One solitary moment in the stables had done him in. Despite his determined efforts to think of something else, the vision of her body draped in nothing but a sark and trews kept resurfacing. He'd never seen a lass so beautiful, so sweetly curved, so unaware of her own charms.

He closed his eyes.

Why did he insist on torturing himself? Nothing could happen between Lady Caitrina and himself. She was a noblewoman and he was a common thief. No amount of hard work or ingenuity would change that. And he had plans that did not include a woman at his side. Dangerous plans. Plans that he could execute only once he had the crown.

Bran took a deep breath, opened his eyes, and reined in the horse. "We walk from here."

Caitrina stared at him as he dismounted. "Are we close?"

"Another three hundred paces, mayhap a bit farther."

"That's yet a distance. Why would we travel afoot?"

He jingled the bridle. "Sounds carry all too well in the forest. Unless our desire is to announce our arrival, we must leave the horse behind."

"Oh." She allowed him to help her down, sliding into his arms with a faint blush and quick smile. "I hope my boots are up to the task."

He glanced at her feet. The boots were well made—the leather smooth and supple, and the stitches evenly placed. They probably cost more than he pocketed in a week. "They'll do."

Shaking his head at the direction of his thoughts, he led the way between the trees. A thick layer of moss covered every root and rock along their path, ensuring a muted passage. Bran showed Caitrina how easily the moss could be disturbed, and encouraged her to place her boots gently and carefully. As his father had been fond of saying, no sense leaving a trail if one could be avoided.

Bran held up his hand, halting their progress briefly to allow a family of woodland grouse to scurry by. Curious. He hadn't thought about his da in quite some time. He'd believed the man's influence buried with his body. But here in the countryside, where they'd lived as bandits for several years, old memories were sprouting with a rather relentless prevalence.

Gordon MacLean had been the bane of his existence.

If not for his witless da, his mother and his brother might now be alive. They might yet be dwelling on

MacLean land, serving the laird and raising honest families. Instead, his maither had been forced to watch her husband swing upon the gibbet, her heart broken, and his brother had died in gaol.

But his da had taught him a few very useful lessons.

Like the proper way to approach a camp to avoid making the horses restless. And how to disarm a guard swiftly and silently.

"Stay here," he whispered to Caitrina as they halted once more. "I'll return anon."

He didn't give her a chance to argue, just darted through the trees toward the helmeted Englishman patrolling the woods in front of him. A beefy fellow with arms like tree trunks. But even the largest man can fall, if taken by surprise. And Bran was an expert in surprise.

He slid up behind the hapless guard, wrapped an arm around the man's throat, and with a tight hold cut off his air. The man thrashed a bit, but Bran held him firm until the flailing slowed and then ceased entirely. As the guard went limp, Bran lowered him gently to the ground and allowed him to breathe once more. Thievery could cost you a hand if you were caught, but murder meant the gibbet.

He bound and gagged the guard, then headed back to the spot where he'd left Caitrina.

To his dismay, she was no longer there. He scanned the woods left and right but could see no sign of her. A few bent fern fronds told him where she'd gone, however. Straight toward the camp.

Bollocks.

Chapter 4

Caitrina had every intention of following Bran's directive until she caught a glimpse of several colored tents through the trees. Fluttering sheets of blue and green stripes. There was obviously a clearing up ahead—quite possibly the very place where Giric was holding Marsailli. The woolen brat she wore was a loose weave of green and brown. If she kept to the forest and moved carefully the way Bran had taught her, perhaps she could peer into the camp and find her sister.

She chewed her lip and stared into the woods where Bran had disappeared.

He had told her to stay here. No doubt for her own safety.

But wouldn't it be best to catch that first sight of Marsailli while she was alone? If she waited until Bran returned, he might glean the personal connection she had to the English soldiers—a disaster by all accounts. She would lose her leverage over him, and with it, his aid.

Drawing the brat tightly around her shoulders, Caitrina ducked under the arching branch of a holly bush and made for the clearing. If she was quick, she might make it back before Bran realized she had gone. Moving swiftly and hugging the trees for protection, she approached the edge of the forest. The clearing was long and narrow, with a small burn running through the middle. Four tents were pitched on the west side of the stream where the ground was flatter, the blue one directly in front of her. Unfortunately, it blocked her view of the campfire, which was in the center, based on the thin ribbons of greasy smoke rising into the cloudy afternoon sky. Even when she stood on the tips of her toes, she could see only three men, none of them Giric. Two were chopping wood for the fire and stacking split wedges. A third was seated on a fallen log avidly cleaning mud from his boots. If there were others, they must be gathered around the fire.

She sighed.

To have a hope of spotting her sister, she needed a better viewpoint. Like the top of that boulder twenty paces to her right. It was partially hidden behind a drooping pine bough, so she wouldn't risk discovery should one of the soldiers look up.

Caitrina scrambled through the brush toward the rock. There were a number of smaller rocks at the base of the boulder, and she used them to help her reach the top. She was just about to sweep aside the pine bough and take a peek at the camp when a hand grabbed her ankle. She only barely restrained a shriek.

"What do we have here?"

It was one of the soldiers, a tall, gangly fellow with a scattering of blemishes across his chin.

She kicked at him, determined to get free. If Giric found her here, there was no telling what he would do. But despite his youthful appearance, the soldier had a manly grip. He yanked her to her rump and then pulled her down from the rock. Bitter tears sprang into Caitrina's eyes.

Satan's beard. Her impatience had ruined everything.

Why hadn't she waited for Bran?

The soldier grabbed a fistful of her sark and began to drag her through the bracken. "The Bear ain't too fond of stinkin' Scots," he said. "You'd best pray he's in a merciful mood."

Nothing Caitrina did gained her freedom—not kicking, not scratching, not biting. The soldier did not seem to care that her nails and teeth dug into his flesh; he continued on his merry way with a smile on his face. No doubt imagining a pleasant reward for capturing a spy.

Caitrina was just about to slump with despair when a rock the size of a small neep hit the lad neatly in the temple, and he fell headfirst into the bracken with little more than a sigh. She tore free of his limp grip and scrambled back into the trees, where she came face-to-face with a rather stony-eyed Bran.

"I know," she said morosely. "I'm a fool."

He folded his arms over his chest and continued to stare at her.

"I made a grievous error in not minding your direction, and I sincerely beg your pardon," she said. He still did not look appeased, so she added, "I'll not do it again."

"Did he harm you?"

"Nay." A wee lie—her arse hurt like the devil—but it eased the icy glare in Bran's eyes.

He nodded sharply, then pointed to the boulder. "Good. Since you were so determined to climb, let us take advantage of your eagerness. Up you go."

Her bruised rump protested as she clambered back atop the boulder, but she dared not complain. "You're a very good shot with a rock. Where did you learn such a skill?"

"On the streets of Edinburgh."

She tried to image how or when he might have thrown a rock in town, but failed. Thieves apparently led interesting lives. "Why did you not slay him?"

He shrugged. "Never draw your dirk when a blow will do it. What can you see?"

Caitrina peered between the long needles of the pine tree. As she had guessed, the bulk of the soldiers were seated around the fire, eating soup from wooden bowls and quaffing horns of ale. "A dozen men in all, most of them half in their cups."

"Can you spy the man you seek?"

She could not. None of the men in sight had a misshapen ear and a scar across his cheek. But what did it matter? The soldier had mentioned the Bear by name— this was definitely Giric's camp. And if she was not mistaken, the slim woman bent over the cooking cauldron was none other than Marsailli. Caitrina smiled.

"Aye," she said. "The one I seek is standing right before my eyes."

"Excellent," Bran said. "Then let us return to the manor. I have fulfilled my part of the bargain. It is now time for you to fulfill yours."

Her heart sank. It was true. He'd met his obligation—he was due his prize.

But *she* would not be satisfied until Marsailli was free. Until she could be certain her sister was beyond Giric's grasp. How was she to accomplish that? Caitrina watched the woman by the fire chat briefly with a tall, thin man with a balding pate and then limp across the muddy field to the green-striped tent. It was definitely Marsailli. The gentle tilt of her head, the way she lifted her skirts as she moved, and the curl of her nut-brown locks were all familiar. But she was hurt—she favored her right side as she walked.

A bittersweet ache filled her chest.

Seeing her sister, even from a distance, was a joy beyond imagining, but witnessing her pain was unbearable. She had to set Marsailli free. And soon. The task would not be an easy one, however. The tent she had entered backed onto the burn, and the only way to reach it was straight through the camp—right past all the guards.

With a grimace, Caitrina turned away from the view and joined Bran at the base of the boulder. She'd been so sure that a route to success would become obvious once she saw the layout of the camp. But she had nothing. Bran offered his hand as they stepped over a rotting log and she slid her fingers into his warm palm. Not even an unwilling ally. Bran would disappear the moment she handed over the crown. Now that the MacCurrans had ridden for Stirling, he had no reason to remain.

"What will you do with the crown once you have it?" she asked.

He glanced at her. "What does it matter?"

"I'm simply curious."

"You've no need to know," he cautioned her. "And as you can personally attest, curiosity can sometimes lead you to dangerous places."

She raised her eyebrows. "Do you threaten me?"

He tossed her one of his charming smiles, and she melted a little. "Nay. But the less you know of me and my troubles, the safer you'll be from those who might come looking for truths."

"Fair enough," she said. "But would I be off the mark to suggest your troubles are the sort that are influenced by large quantities of coin?"

"That's none of your concern."

But it was. She needed to find some way to keep her ally-cum-thief in her pocket. Coin had seemed an obvious enticement, but he had barely blinked at her broad hint. If Bran was not driven by greed, then what *was* he driven by?

They reached the horse, and Bran gave her a leg up.

The sun had finally broken through the clouds and bright splashes of sunlight littered the forest floor around them. As he checked the cinch on the saddle, Caitrina studied the play of light on his golden hair. "The MacCurrans are Highlanders," she said thoughtfully. "I believe their clan seat is deep within the Red Mountains. The crown must hold great meaning for them if they chased you this far south in an effort to reclaim it."

Bran lifted his gaze. His expression was calm, but

there was an unusual stillness to him that told her she had hit the mark. "Wounded pride," he said with a shrug. "They'll give up soon enough."

"I am acquainted with the Lady of Dunstoras, Isabail," Caitrina said. "I attended her wedding to Andrew Macintosh a number of years ago."

"She's wed to Aiden MacCurran now."

"So I've heard." She waited until he had gained the saddle before adding, "I've been quite remiss in sending her my good wishes. I must remedy that."

He said nothing, just urged the horse into motion and followed their trail back to the old guard. "I saw no sign of a wheelwright," he informed the gray-haired man. "The cart is still stuck in the mud."

"So they might be here a while yet."

"Aye. Give them a day or two to settle their own affairs. If they've made no progress by then, send someone to repair the wheel." Bran sat back in the saddle. "You should be aware that we ran into a spot of trouble."

The old guard frowned. "What sort of trouble?"

Bran explained what had happened, sticking very close to the truth. "The young Sassenach will have a wee sore head come morn. If they complain about a lack of hospitality," he said, smiling, "fetch me. I'd be pleased to address their concerns."

Dougal's man snorted. "Serves the bloody fool right."

"The lad here," Bran nodded over his shoulder, "will meet the rewards of his poor judgment back at the manor. I'll make certain he can't sit for a day."

The old man's gaze met Caitrina's over the edge of her brat. "As it should be, I suppose."

They left without further ado. When they had been plodding along for a while, she asked, "I trust you weren't actually thinking to take a switch to my behind?"

"Nay. I've no desire to be arrested for striking a lady."

"That's good to hear. You sounded quite convincing to the guard."

"One of my many talents," he said dryly.

The horse stumbled in a rut and Caitrina slammed against Bran's sturdy back. Only for a moment, but long enough for her to take the measure of every masculine sinew she'd glimpsed in his rooms the night before. He was the very opposite of the sort of man she should desire. A cad. A bounder. A rogue. But her body reacted to the press of his flesh without care, sending a hot sizzle to the very core of her being. There was something delightfully reassuring about his strength. He was magnificent, really. "So, when we reach the manor, you'll just collect your prize and be on your way?"

"Aye."

Caitrina tightened her grip around his waist. Well, then. There it was—he was leaving. Unless she found some way to stop him. As they left the woods and followed the path across the meadow toward the postern gate, she sighed. Cruelly, she could think of no other option but to betray him. "What if I choose not to relinquish the crown?"

"You won't make that mistake."

A shiver ran down her spine. His response was icy cool and edged with steely promise. Exactly the sort of response she might expect from a dangerous criminal. If it had been a matter of personal gain, Caitrina would have shut her mouth and pursued her cause no further. But Marsailli might even now be enduring another beating. Especially if Giric had cause to believe it was she who had spied upon the camp.

"I'm afraid I must," she said bravely. He wouldn't attack her in full view of the guards on the manor walls. Nay, of course not. That would be madness. "I will only give you the crown if you help me with one more task."

He halted the destrier and stared at the sunlit manor for a long moment. Then he sighed heavily. "What task would that be?"

"There is something I need to retrieve from within the English camp."

He twisted in his saddle. "Something? Or some*one*?"

Caitrina stiffened. How had he guessed?

"The time has come for complete honesty, Lady Caitrina. I've had my fill of lies. Now I want to hear the truth. All of it."

The *whole* truth? Impossible. She was a spy for King Edward. Even half-truths would condemn her as a traitor.

Caitrina mulled over several possible stories in her head, seeking one that did not make her look like a fool or a faithless Sassenach-lover. Sadly, none of them met her requirements. And as she hemmed and hawed and debated exactly what to tell Bran, he dismounted the horse and strode off down the path toward the manor. Leaving her alone astride a massive beast that she had no hope of controlling.

"Wait!" she cried.

He stopped but did not turn around.

"They are holding my sister," she said. "Her name is Marsailli."

He pivoted. "And what could they possibly hope to gain by threatening your sister?"

Caitrina's shoulders slumped. "Details about the queen."

Bran marched back to her side. "Why do they do this? What is their aim?"

"They are henchmen of Edward Longshanks," she told him. "I do not know their precise aim, but rest assured, with Giric the Bear as their leader, they can be up to no good."

He frowned up at her. "Giric is the man who beat a man to death for insulting the English king?"

"Aye."

"Saints be." He raked a hand through his hair. "Why force *me* to help you? Why not enlist the aid of the queen's guard?"

"Because her guards have only one goal: to protect the queen. They care naught about Marsailli." And the moment Giric was interrogated, he would point the finger at Caitrina. She would hang right alongside him, branded a traitor like her father. An utterly unbearable thought, especially as it would leave Marsailli alone. "And I would prefer the queen never know of my failings."

"As a man with many failings myself, I well understand." Bran put a gentle hand on her leg. "Were this a different time and place, I might be persuaded to aid you. Regretfully, I must decline. I never intended to play the role of Marshal Gordon for more than a day or two. People talk, and it won't be long before someone questions my credentials."

"But without your help, I have no hope of freeing Marsailli."

He let his hand drop. "My apologies. I am not the man you need."

"Please," she begged.

"Nay," he said, taking a step back. "You must find another ally."

His reasons for walking away were logical, full of wisdom even. But Caitrina could not accept his decision, not if it meant she would be forced to steal the queen's babe. Not if it meant Marsailli had to suffer. She straightened her shoulders. "Then you will forfeit the crown."

He smiled. "I am a thief, my lady. I make my living snatching items from unwilling hands. You may think you've found a clever hiding spot, but I assure you, by this hour tomorrow, I'll have it safely tucked in my pouch."

The unshakable confidence in his eyes deflated her. "Why did you agree to find the camp, if you were so certain you could reclaim the crown?"

His smile turned rueful. "I'm easily swayed by a pretty smile."

"Not any longer, it would seem."

He shrugged. "All good things must come to an end."

"Indeed," she said silkily. "Including the politeness of our banter. The gloves have come off, as they say in the lists. If the crown is not incentive enough to keep you at my side, then perhaps this will be: Unless I have your pledge of aid, I will send a messenger to Stirling the moment I return to the manor. The castle is less than a day's ride away. I'm certain the MacCurrans will make haste to Clackmannan and apprehend you—*before* you can locate your precious crown."

Bran folded his arms over his chest. He should be angry that his bonnie young lassie was once again attempting to coerce him. Especially since Wulf MacCurran had pledged to separate Bran's head from his shoulders if he ever dared to steal from Dunstoras. But despite the genuine concern he had regarding the MacCurrans' return, he could summon only a mild amusement. "You run a great risk telling me of your intent before you are safely within the walls."

"You'll not harm me."

He lifted his eyebrows. "You think not?"

"Nay," she said. "Spilling blood is not in your nature. If it were, that English guard we encountered would be lying in the sod. Instead, he's merely nursing a lump on the head."

"I don't have to spill blood to harm you."

She put her hands on her hips. "Do your worst. Nothing short of a mortal injury will stop me from sending that messenger."

He glared at her for a long moment, trying his damnedest to cower her. But her bright red cheeks and bristling posture won him over. She might be tiny, but she was definitely fierce. A grin broke free. "I admire a woman of determination. Fine. I will stay an additional sennight—but no longer. If Marshal Finlay returns from Oban to find me masquerading as a nobleman, I'll be tossed in the oubliette."

Caitrina sighed. "That's fair. Thank you."

He gathered up the reins and vaulted back into the saddle. They rode in silence up to the open postern gate, both lost in their thoughts. As Bran ducked under the stone arch, he asked, "Did you happen to note the tent your sister was residing within?"

"The green-striped one next to the burn."

"Good," he said. "We'll return to the camp tonight and determine our best course of action."

She stiffened against his back. "It can't be tonight. My maid believes I've spent all day in the cellars looking for goods to appoint the nursery. I cannot show up empty-handed."

Bran resisted a snort. Empty-handed? She was hardly that. Caitrina's hands were splayed across his belly in a most disturbing way. He felt the play of her fingers with every breath he took. "Then by all means let us see what the stores have to offer."

He helped her slide off the horse at the rear of the stables, then continued on to the front alone. With a series of crisp demands, he made certain the stable lads were fully occupied, allowing Caitrina to change her clothing undisturbed.

Agreeing to rescue her sister was likely a huge mistake.

But he understood the gut-deep worry of having a sibling imprisoned. Especially a younger sibling, one with less skill and knowledge. One who looked to his elder sibling with faith and surety. Bran handed the saddle to a lad, removed the horse blanket, and began to brush the destrier with a woven straw whisk. Eight years had passed since he lost Neasan to the damp chill of Edinburgh dungeon, but the bitterness still chewed at him. He had failed his brother—left him to die, instead of risking all to free him—but saving others was still within his power.

So he would do his best to free the girl.

Out of the corner of his eye, he saw Caitrina sneak off toward the manor house, attired in her brown and green gown. There was an added benefit, of course: more time in the fair lady's company. He found her charming, despite her propensity to blackmail. He grinned. Or perhaps it was her willingness to do so that appealed to him. He definitely admired her resolve.

He tossed the brush aside and led the dapple gray destrier into the stables.

Whatever the source of his interest, he intended to take full advantage of his time at her side. Even if that meant crawling through an endless number of dusty storerooms to find whatever the lady was looking for. He tied the big warhorse inside and gave it a pat on the neck. A short dalliance could prove enjoyable—as long as he remembered that he traveled light and fast.

As the hard rap of boot steps echoed in the passageway, Caitrina pulled her woolen brat tight around her shoulders. The cellars were dark and rather disquieting. She spun around, lighting the passageway behind her with the torch, and immediately breathed a sigh of relief. It was Bran. "Were you able to procure the keys?"

He shook the key ring before her eyes. A mismatched

collection of iron bones—some new, some rusted, some large, some small. All capable of unlocking secrets.

"Did you steal them?"

"There was no need," he said, with a faint smile. "Dougal is quite convinced I am who I say I am."

"However did you manage that?" She pointed to a door and waited for him to unlock it.

"Certitude," he said. He swung the oak portal open to reveal a small room stacked to the rafters with bolts of cloth. "And a few basic facts. Are the contents here of any use?"

"Aye," she said, squeezing into the room. "I need several bolts of white linen. The softest we can find. To line the creidle and to serve as swaddling."

Together, they dug through the bolts, stacking and restacking, until they found three that met Caitrina's finger test for fineness. Only the softest of cloth could be allowed to touch the skin of a king. When Bran had wrapped the bolts in a tarp and set them aside, she pointed to a second door. "This larger room should hold fittings. Tables and chests and the like."

He tried several keys before finally locating the one that worked.

"What need does a babe have for a table?"

The door creaked loudly. Using the torch, Caitrina burned away a cobweb that spanned the entrance and then stepped inside. "I'm seeking a bath basin. The child must be washed in rosewater and anointed with oil of myrrh immediately upon its birth. For the sanctity of his soul."

"And those of us who were bathed in the village pond? Are we doomed to hell?"

She tossed him a frown. "The pond? Surely not. Where were you born?"

"Perthshire."

"Oh?" Clackmannan was in Perthshire. "Not far from here?"

"Perth is a large county," he said, his expression neutral.

"It is indeed," she said. The boundaries stretched north and west to great length. "Are you a Murray?"

"Nay."

"A Menzies?" She stepped over a tipped barrel of old brooms and shone the light into the farthest corners of the storeroom.

"Nay."

"Aha!" she cried, spying a rounded shape in a pile atop an armoire. "Hold this."

He took the torch and followed her around a battered trestle table. "Take care. Some of these items are poorly placed."

Flipping a wooden bucket and using it as a stool, she gained just enough height to grab the lip of the basin. She tugged, but could not get it free. Glancing over her shoulder, she asked, "Is it stuck on something?"

"Aye. There's a basket and some sort of wooden frame in the way. Step aside, lass. I'll get it down."

Happy to relinquish the task to a man a full head taller than she, Caitrina turned and leapt off the bucket. But as she spun, her brat snagged on a stick protruding from the pile of items atop the armoire and yanked the entire mess down upon her head.

She ducked, expecting to be pelted by falling debris.

But, in a display of very impressive reflexes, Bran threw his body forward and shielded her from harm. The basket, the basin, and a number of other wooden objects crashed to the dirt floor. An empty spool from a spinning wheel bounced off her boot and rolled into the darkness.

"Are you injured?" Bran asked.

"Nay," she said breathlessly, peering out from the umbrella of his body. Miraculously, the only casualty was a faded banner that had fluttered into the torch and burst into flame. But for some reason, her heart continued to pound long after it became clear that the danger had passed. It took her a moment to identify the cause: the warm strength of his body, pressing against her in a dozen different places.

It was a body she knew quite well, after their lengthy ride in the forest. But there was something new and tantalizing about touching him here, in the dark, with the musky male scent of him filling her nose. She lifted her gaze to his.

His eyes glittered with intent, and she knew long before he closed the gap between them that he was going to kiss her. He leaned in slowly, giving her plenty of opportunity to run, but she held perfectly still. Waiting. She *wanted* him to kiss her—wanted it like she'd never wanted anything before. It was like the entire day had been a prelude to this moment. Every teasing comment, every grazing touch, every hot stare had been leading here, to this room, to this kiss.

As their breaths mingled, Caitrina closed her eyes, determined to savor the experience from beginning to end. This would be her first real kiss, and she wanted it to be perfect. Well, as perfect as a kiss from a dangerous thief could be . . .

Bran's lips met hers, warm and firm and frankly demanding. He nibbled at the corners of her mouth, then pressed deep and hard. Caitrina was a little shocked. This was not the perfunctory peck of a gentleman admirer; it was an intimate meshing of lips that had no match in her imagination. But it was wonderful. Her entire body came alive to his touch, every inch of her skin atingle.

She eagerly pressed back, needing more.

And he gave her more. Taking her chin in hand, he deepened the embrace, opening his mouth and sucking on her bottom lip. Caitrina nearly swooned. Her hands clutched the front of his lèine as an unexpected ripple of delight shot from her mouth to the very tips of her fingers and toes.

But the best part wasn't her reaction; it was his.

As the kiss continued and she mewled her approval, his breathing grew harsh and ragged. The hand that held the torch shook and a flush rose on the crests of his cheeks. The extent of his desire for her was obvious. Which was why she was amazed when he gently pulled away and took a step back.

He tossed her a rueful smile.

"You should slap my face for taking such liberties."

"When I enjoyed them as much as you? I think not." She put her hands to her lips, which were still tingling. "And in any case, I owe you my thanks for a timely rescue. That wooden basin would surely have left a dent in my skull."

He bent and picked the basin up. "Aye. It looks to be hollowed from a single piece of wood."

"More important," she said, "the pattern of tiny lilies carved around the lip is just the sort of detail the queen will admire."

"Then it seems you have what you came for," he said.

"Indeed I do." Caitrina's eyes met his and she smiled. "Precisely what I came for."

The sun had set and Giric was partaking of his eventide meal when three of his soldiers approached the tent. Two senior men, half dragging a young lad with dried blood on his brow. He knew by their grim expressions that their tale would not be to his liking, so he took another leisurely sip of his wine before he acknowledged them.

"Well? What is it?"

"We found Davie here lying in the gorse with a bump on his noggin. It took us some time to wake him, but eventually—"

Giric sighed. "Get to the point."

"He caught someone spying on the camp."

Giric lumbered to his feet, shaking his head. The tent was barely tall enough to contain him, and his hair brushed the drooping folds of blue canvas. "That's not precisely true now, is it? What you mean to say is that he caught someone and then let him go."

"Nay," young Davie protested. "I never let him go. I was attacked! Hit with a rock the size of a melon."

"Is the spy in custody?"

"Nay."

Giric raised an eyebrow. "Then I was correct. You let him go."

"Not willingly," Davie said. "I was doing my duty, all proper-like."

"All proper-like," Giric repeated softly. "Truly?"

The lad nodded.

"Take a look at your two companions and tell me what you see."

Davie glanced to either side of him. "Soldiers."

"And how do you know they are soldiers?"

"They're wearing mail hauberks and carrying swords."

Giric nodded encouragingly. "What else?"

For a moment, Davie looked confused. He glanced from side to side with a heavy frown. And then the clarity of enlightenment washed over him. All expression left his face. "Helms. They're wearing helms."

"They are indeed." Giric stood toe-to-toe with the boy, towering over him and peering down at the blooded mark upon his brow. A good-size lump. "Why?"

"To protect their heads," the lad said morosely.

"And where is *your* helm?"

"In my tent."

Giric waved to one of the other soldiers. "Fetch it." Then he smiled at Davie. "Describe the spy to me. Every detail you can recall. Leave nothing out."

"He were a lad. Short and dark haired, wearing breeks and a woolen brat."

"You're certain it wasn't a woman?"

"What?" Davie's eyebrows soared. "A wench? Nay. Not a tittie in sight."

Giric sat back on his heels. It was not the first time

Davie had been brought before him. The lad was not particularly observant and errors in judgment were his forte. The spy might well have been Caitrina de Montfort. "Shoulder-length hair? Or longer?"

Davie shrugged. "I couldn't tell. He had his brat over his head."

"Of course he did."

The soldier jogged back to the tent and handed Giric Davie's helm. Giric turned it over in his hands, studying the craftsmanship. A basic raised dome with a nosepiece. No riveted reinforcements, no painted finish. Simple but solid, it offered reasonable protection to a fighting man.

"Put it on," he ordered Davie.

The lad grabbed the helm and plunked it on his head. "I'll wear it faithfully, Sir Giric. That I swear."

"As you should." Giric put his hands on either side of the helm. Hands that were, like the rest of him, large, scarred, and brutal. But reassuringly capable. "I don't tolerate failure."

He pinned the lad's gaze with his own, then began to press.

Davie released a low, agonized moan.

A moan that quickly escalated into a bloodcurdling shriek as Giric squeezed his hands together with greater force and slowly bent the helm. It took every ounce of his strength to bend the metal, but bend it he did—until it cut into the boy's flesh. When the lad began to thrash and tiny rivulets of blood were running down both sides of his neck, Giric thrust the screaming boy aside. "If I ever see you without a helm again, I will crush your skull like a grape. Understand?"

He glared at the two senior guards.

"Get him out of here."

Returning to the table, he snatched up his goblet of wine and downed the contents in a single swallow. It would seem that Caitrina had not taken his threats at the abbey seriously. Perhaps it was time to send a stronger message.

"Bring me the girl!" he snarled.

Chapter 5

Caitrina was greeted at the door to the queen's ante-chamber by a very worried Gisele. "Where have you been?" the older woman cried in French. "Her Grace has been feeling poorly all day. Tired and listless, barely able to sit before the fire. I had to call for the midwife."

"I was in the cellars—"

"It no longer matters," Gisele snapped. "She has been asking for you. Wash the filth from your hands and see to her." Then she flounced off in the direction of the kitchens.

Caitrina nodded to Bran. "Just leave the items here. I'll collect them later."

"Is all well?" he asked.

"I'm not certain," she confessed.

He arched a brow. "Are you in need of a champion?"

"Nay," she said, with a light laugh. "My worries are not so dire as that."

Setting his armload down, he offered her a crooked

smile. "If you change your mind, seek me out. I'm off to revisit the English camp. I'll report back with my plan to rescue your sister."

She watched him leave, entranced by his every move. He had a natural grace that was a pleasure to watch, and a smooth charm that left smiles in his wake. The young maid he passed in the hall beamed when he but nodded in her direction. When he had disappeared into the stairwell, she pushed open the inner doors and entered the queen's chambers.

Yolande was lying abed, her long auburn hair spread across the pillows, her eyes dark pools in her pale face. She was surrounded by a small group of people that included the royal midwife and her confessor, William Fraser, the bishop of Saint Andrews.

The moment the queen spied Caitrina, she attempted to sit up. "*Ma cousine*," she called.

Caitrina quickly washed her hands in rosewater and joined the queen at her bedside. "My humble apologies, Your Grace. I spent the day in the cellars searching for appointments for the nursery. Had I known you had need of me—"

Yolande's eyes lit up. "Appointments? *Très bien!* What did you discover?"

"Please, Your Grace," admonished the midwife. "You must rest."

A worried frown dulled the excitement in the queen's eyes. "But you assured me the babe was healthy."

"He moves," the midwife said, "but not as vigorously as he once did. You must preserve your strength to ensure a successful birth."

"Am I to remain abed now until the babe is born?"

"Aye," the old woman said. " 'Twould be best."

"I concur." The bishop leaned over the bed and took the queen's hand in his own. "Although the birth is several weeks away, I also think it would be wise to consider gathering the Guardians of Scotland, Your Grace."

The queen lay back against her pillows with a huge sigh. "One simple bout of weariness and suddenly disaster looms."

"Nay," the bishop protested. "God shines his blessings upon thee, but it will take time to send messengers, and the Guardians should be present at the birth."

"Fine," she said. "Send for them. They should bear witness to the event that my dearest Alexander will never know. The birth of his son."

Tears began to leak from the corners of her eyes, a rare moment of weakness from the young royal. To protect her cousin from unwarranted judgment, Caitrina began closing the bed curtains. "Her Grace will sleep now," she said, ushering the bishop and the midwife away. "I will inform you the instant she awakens."

When the room was once again the domain of women, Caitrina carried the wooden baby basin over to the quietly weeping queen. "Look," she said. "Lilies."

Yolande bit her lip and wiped her eyes with a linen and lace cloth. She smiled tremulously at the fine carving that edged the basin. "You have a kind heart, Caitrina. In spite of all that has befallen you and your family, you remain a generous soul."

Caitrina shook her head. "You are a far kinder soul than I, Your Grace. You welcomed me into your entourage when none else would acknowledge me."

"Bah! It is not your fault that your grandfather's titles were seized, or that your father disgraced his family. The blood of kings runs in your veins. You deserved more than to rot away on your uncle's estate."

"Atholl was good to us."

The queen shrugged. "He ignored you."

"He's young, and he has his own battles to fight."

Yolande snorted. "He's an earl. Age has no bearing on obligation." Her expression turned thoughtful and she ran a slow hand over the mound of her belly. "My son will also have battles to fight."

Caitrina set the basin down. "You fear the English?"

"Nay," the queen said. "The Guardians. King Alexander had a strife-torn minority. I do not wish the same for his son."

"Is not the bishop of Saint Andrews one of the Guardians?" Caitrina asked, lowering her voice to a whisper. "Have you reason to doubt him?"

Yolande smiled. "They are all fine men, the Guardians. Strong champions of Scotland. But each has his own vision, and each has a desire to make his mark on history. My son will be pulled in many directions at once, and it will be a challenge for him to find his own way."

Caitrina nodded. But if she feared ambitious men, surely King Edward was worthy of alarm? "Is the lion to the south not a worry?"

"Scotland's relations with England are very cordial. King Edward was fond of Alexander, having once been related to him by marriage. He was most gracious at the state funeral and promised to deliver any aid I might require."

"How very kind of him." He had approached Caitrina at the same time. Offering sweet condolences to the queen one moment and coercing a lass into treason the next. A true paragon.

"I should like to see what other bounty you unearthed in the stores, but not just now." The queen lay back and closed her eyes. "I am truly weary."

"Of course, Your Grace."

Her gut knotted, Caitrina tucked the blankets around the queen and stepped back to close the last bed curtain. How she longed to confess what she knew about the men in the woods and Edward's plans, but that wasn't possible. Not until Marsailli was safe.

All she could do was pray those wicked plans never bore fruit.

She found her embroidery, claimed a chair before the fire, and began adding snow-white stitches to her winter forest scene. The evening meal would take place without her. She wouldn't go hungry—trays were typically delivered to the rooms when the queen was resting. But she *would* be missing an opportunity to see Bran.

A flush rose in her cheeks.

How mad to be looking forward to stolen moments with a wanted thief. But that kiss had been truly marvelous. The intrigues of the past several months were shaping her in ways she could not possibly have imagined. She pushed the needle through the linen backing and pulled the silk thread taut. But her handsome scoundrel would not be pleased to discover that the Guardians of Scotland were about to descend upon Clackmannan.

He'd promptly renege upon his promise to aid her.

Perhaps it might be better not to mention that wee bit of news.

Marsailli's legs shook.

She had not expected to be dragged before the Bear again—Ulric had helped her craft a simple but tasty soup, and the mighty commander had downed several bowls of it at the midday meal. Without a single grimace.

But here she was.

And the dark scowl that distorted his ruined face did not bode well.

"Your sister is a fool," he snarled, seizing her long braid. He tilted her head so far back that she thought her neck would snap. "She thinks to thwart me."

"I don't understand," she whimpered, the words a burning rasp in her throat. What had Caitrina done?

"Have you seen her?"

"Nay!" Much to Marsailli's disappointment. Even a glimpse of Caitrina would have made these last few weeks more bearable.

"You lie."

He dragged her across the tent by her hair, uncaring that her wounded knee slammed into the corner of a table. "But no matter. You are about to learn who truly has the upper hand." With a low growl reminiscent of his namesake, he threw her down on his pallet.

Cruel intent thinned his lips and left deep furrows in his brow. Her heartbeat stumbled. She scrambled to leave the bed, but she wasn't quick enough. He caught her about the middle and flung her back on the sheets.

"You will know what it is to cross me!" Grabbing her

neckline with both hands, he rent her gown right down the middle, splitting it with three decisive yanks.

Now bared to his eyes, Marsailli squeezed her eyes shut.

"No!" she screamed.

Bran slipped through the trees and past Dougal's guard with nary a sound. It was easier than it should have been—the old man was staring into his fire, his ability to see in the dark weakened by the bright light.

It was more of a challenge to bypass the English sentries.

Having learned a lesson from the failures of the afternoon, the guards were now patrolling in pairs. These two were heavily armed, wore solid helms upon their tender brows, and scanned the woods with true dedication. But the night was Bran's ally. A canny sense of timing and dark clothes had gotten him past many a guard in Edinburgh, and they did so now as well.

Each time the men's heads turned, even briefly, he darted to another tree. He made slow but steady progress through their line to the edge of the clearing, where he paused to determine his best route into the camp.

That's when his clandestine survey mission became something else entirely.

Down in the firelit center of the camp, Caitrina's sister was dragged out of one tent, across the muddy field, and into another. Bran was too far away to see faces, but the stiff reluctance evident in the girl's shoulders and the sharp yanks the soldier made on her arm put his teeth on edge. Something unpleasant was about to transpire.

He had to get closer.

Bran swiftly counted the men visible in the camp. Five, if he included the fellow who had just escorted Marsailli into the tent. Six others were patrolling the perimeter. That left one unaccounted for, if Dougal's original assessment was accurate. One soldier who was likely inside the tent with the leader.

A loud male voice raged from the tent.

The words were indistinguishable, but the fury that shook every syllable gave wings to Bran's feet. A man with such anger bottled inside him would find some way to unleash it. Bran dove for the soldier closest to him, unsheathing the dirk at his belt as he ran. A man wearing a mail hauberk was protected against attack, save for in two places: the loins and the neck. Reaching the loins required an adroit knife thrust up and under the hem of the hauberk. The neck was a much easier target.

The man was seated on a fallen log.

Bran swiftly silenced him and dragged his body back into the shadows. Four more to go. The three huddled around the fire would be the true test of his skills. But the one tending the horses would be an easy—

"No!"

The desperate cry froze Bran's blood. He knew that sound—he'd heard it before. Once. In a dark wynd in Edinburgh. It was the hopeless plea of a lass who believed she was doomed. He was out of time. If he didn't intervene right now, Caitrina's sister would be ruined or dead.

He grabbed the dead soldier's sword, spun on his heel, and raced for the rear of the tent where Marsailli was being held. A decisive slice of his dirk parted the canvas, and he stepped inside. The scene was just as he'd imagined—the lass was pinned to a pallet by a very large scar-faced man, who had turned his head at the sound of ripping canvas.

Bran pointed his sword at the man's naked back. "On your feet."

The lout ran a finger down Marsailli's tearstained face. "I do not answer to nameless curs, especially in my own tent."

"As long as you are on Clackmannan land," Bran said, "you answer to me. My name is Marshal Gordon, and my soldiers surround your camp even as we speak."

The man made no attempt to stand. Instead, he kissed the lass's cheek. "You overstep your bounds, Marshal. Even the king has no right to interfere in the matters between a man and his wife."

Marsailli's pale, thin arm, visible beneath the man's large body, trembled violently.

"The lass appears unwilling," Bran noted. "You've proof, I trust, of this union between you?"

The man threw him a scowl. "I have twelve men who will vouch for me."

Eleven men, actually. Bran shook his head. "I'll need more than statements from your men. This lass is a Scot, and as such, is owed my full protection. I assume the vows were made before a church?"

Rising to his feet, the big man faced him, quite unabashed by his state of undress. The scar across his cheek formed a ragged line from the edge of his mouth to his mangled ear. Caitrina's Giric, no doubt. "Nay, they were made here, just moments ago."

Bran grabbed a blanket and tossed it to Marsailli.

"Moments ago, I heard a man's voice raised in anger and a woman's plea for rescue."

"A marriage in Scotland is made by mutual consent," Giric said, dismissing Bran's comments with a wave of his hand. "By law, the word of a man and his wife is proof of the union. So, ask the girl to verify my tale. Ask her to confirm that we are wed."

Bran glanced at Marsailli. The girl was cowering beneath the woolen throw, still shaking badly. Her word *should* be enough—but her fear made her an unreliable witness. She was a captive in Giric's camp, surrounded by his soldiers. What would she say if he asked? "I should like a moment with her alone."

A thunderous frown descended on Giric's brow. "Absolutely not. No man shall be alone with my wife, save I."

There it was, then—Bran had no choice but to ask Marsailli for the truth and let her words fall where they may. He crouched beside the pallet. "Lass," he said softly. He tried and failed to meet her gaze. "I swear I will protect you with my life, should you need it. Tell me the truth. Did you willingly wed this man, or no?"

It was late when Caitrina descended the stairs to the great hall. The evening meal had been cleared away and only a handful of gillies remained at work, banking the fire in the hearth and dousing most of the candles. Bran was seated near the hearth, with an ale in hand and a heavy frown upon his brow.

As she approached, he stood and poured her an ale.

"What did you determine?" she asked, accepting the cup he offered.

"The situation is complicated," he said.

"How so?"

"Sit," he said, tapping the back of a wooden chair.

She sat. His frown had knotted her belly. He looked far too serious. "Is it not a matter of sneaking into the camp and stealing her away?"

"Nay," he said, shaking his head. "Sir Giric is claiming Marsailli is his wife."

"That's preposterous! My sister would never agree to wed that wretch." And Giric despised Scots. He'd never marry one. Of that, Caitrina was certain. "It's a lie."

Bran nodded. "I've no doubt of that. The problem is, your sister will no speak against him. Indeed, she won't say aught at all." He paused. "Unfortunately, this matter is no longer a quiet affair, to be handled by you and me. I was forced to involve the constable."

Her heart sank. If the queen caught wind of her involvement, all her efforts to redeem her family's honor and restore their place in society would be for naught. "Why?"

"When I arrived at the camp, Giric was attempting to force himself on Marsailli."

Caitrina went cold all over. "Dear god."

"My entrance was timely," he said hastily. "She is safe, for now."

Her hand flattened against her chest, a rather pointless attempt to calm her fluttering heart. "Thank heaven." Her gaze lifted to his. "Or rather, thank *you*. If you'd been even a few minutes later—"

"She is safe," he repeated, with a faint smile. "Dougal has placed two men in Giric's camp, tasked with ensuring her safety until we resolve the matter of his claim."

"Does Dougal know Marsailli is my sister?"

"Nay, Giric said nothing of her relation to you. He claims she is the daughter of a Lowland cottar and that she ran away with him."

A convenient lie. For both of them. "What shall we do now?"

"We need Marsailli to speak. To dismiss Giric's claim."

Caitrina briefly closed her eyes, imagining her sister's sweet disposition and the effect Giric's attack would have had. "I'm sure she's too frightened to speak. She believes he will kill her if she dares to naysay him."

"Aye."

Caitrina grabbed Bran's hand. His warm, strong, reassuring hand. It didn't bear imagining what would have transpired had he not aided her. What would have happened to Marsailli. "I must meet with her, convince her to utter the truth. If she tells Dougal she's not Giric's wife, she'll be free."

He gently squeezed her fingers. "It won't be that easy, lass. Giric will no allow you to walk into his camp and take Marsailli back, no without a fight. If he loses his hold over you, he fails King Edward. From what I've heard, incurring the wrath of Longshanks is a sure way to see your head roll. Giric will do everything in his power to prevent that."

Caitrina swallowed. The situation had swiftly spun out of control, much faster than she could have imagined. She had hoped to steal Marsailli quietly from the camp and then renegotiate her terms with Giric. But now disaster loomed on all fronts. If she left her sister in Giric's hands, Marsailli faced rape. If she set her free, Giric would retaliate and a bloody battle would ensue. Men would die. And even if Dougal's men triumphed in said battle, there was a very good chance the Bear would name Caitrina as an accomplice in his crimes.

Dear lord. What was she to do?

She offered Bran a teary smile. "Then what?"

He cupped her chin and wiped her tears away with his thumb. "Let me dwell on it. Marsailli is safe for now. I vow that I will find some way to set her free. Just give me time."

She leaned into his hand. Now would be a fine moment to tell him about the Guardians, but losing Bran would destroy her. When her maither had passed, the burden of making a life for her and Marsailli had fallen upon her shoulders. And that burden was overwhelming now. "You have my faith, and more."

The gillies had all bedded down for the night, and the great hall was a dark haven save for one torch bracketed on the wall next to the door and another next to the stairs. The banked fire in the hearth gave off only the faintest orange glow, and Caitrina took advantage of the soft lighting. She slid to the edge of her seat, moving forward until their knees touched.

Layers of cloth separated them, but that didn't stop hot tingles from running up her legs to her most private parts. By god. Even his knees felt strong and sure. "You are a much better man than you would have the world believe," she said quietly, brushing an errant lock of his hair away from his face so she could better gaze upon his firm cheekbones and deep brown eyes. He had remarkably long eyelashes for a man. "In the space of a day, you've twice saved me from harm and once thwarted an attack on my sister."

He stayed the movements of her hand with his.

"Lass," he said, his voice a low rumble. "I'm not the man you think me to be."

The warmth of his hand on hers was quite enjoyable, but she found herself wanting more. Much more. Starting with another kiss. Strangely, the knowledge that someone in the great hall might wake up and notice only added intensity to her desire. "So it wasn't you who did those things?"

"My sins far outweigh what few good deeds I've done."

Caitrina leaned in, breathing deep of his male scent—a heady mix of pine and leather and that spice that was uniquely Bran. "I'm well aware of your sins. I know, for example, that they include kissing unwed ladies in dark places." She pressed her lips against the corner of his mouth, tasting the slight saltiness of his skin and the rasp of his growing beard.

He grabbed her arms and pushed her away.

"Cease," he said gruffly. "That kiss was an error in judgment. One I do not intend to repeat."

"Why not?" she asked. "It was quite delightful."

"Because sinful men don't stop at kisses."

Caitrina's pulse quickened. "Perhaps I don't want you to stop."

"Your future husband surely does."

She sat back, smiling ruefully. "That future husband does not exist. No man is interested in wedding the daughter of a man outlawed for murder, especially one with no lands or title to her name."

Bran arched an eyebrow. "Your father murdered a man?"

"Not just any man," she said, with a short laugh. All she had of her father were a few hazy memories, but her chest still ached when she spoke of him. "A favorite cousin of King Edward. Inside a church, no less. My papa managed to enrage the crown and the pope with one single act of revenge." There'd been no safe place for him then. Forced to abandon his family, he'd wandered the world until the day he died. But that was not a tale for tonight. She tilted her head and smiled at him. "So, there is no husband waiting for me to arrive chaste and pure at the church door."

"Your reputation cannot be as poor as you say," he disputed, rising to his feet and walking around to the back of his chair. "The queen appointed you lady-in-waiting."

She shrugged. "She is my cousin, and she took pity on me."

"Surely she has the power to make a marriage for you?"

"Had King Alexander lived," she said, "she might have arranged a union. Now? Her only thought is for her bairn." She got to her feet and followed him. His proximity to the chair prevented her from getting too close, so she sidled up to his arm. "Queen Yolande is content that I shall never wed. A husband and bairns of my own would distract me from my duties as lady of the nursery."

He frowned.

Caitrina put a hand on him, relishing the rippling sinews beneath his linen sleeve. "I am honored to be appointed lady of the nursery, and in the queen's court I will enjoy a full and purposeful life. But when it comes to bliss, I am master of my own fate. I will make it where and when I can. And I choose now, Bran. With you."

Bran stared at the dainty hand on his sleeve. Pale and lovely, the nails neatly trimmed and smooth. The hand of a lady. "Why me? Why now?"

Her fingers clenched briefly. "Does it matter?"

Surprisingly, it did. He rarely denied himself a moment of pleasure, but this lass was unlike any lass he'd ever tupped before. In two event-filled days, she'd seduced him with a dizzying blend of courage and fear, strength and vulnerability, confidence and hesitation. Every sweetly feminine feature—her nose, her lips, her glorious hair—teased him mercilessly. He wanted her so surely, he could not sit next to her or endure the touch of her hand on his skin without envisioning her beneath him, moaning in ecstasy. And, damn his soul, he needed to know if she felt even a mote of the same desire.

"Aye, it matters."

A smile came and went on her face. It was gone so swiftly it barely had time to light up her eyes. "Well, then. I suppose a moment like this is best served by honesty." She chewed her delicious bottom lip. "Your fine looks are a consideration, of course. My eyes are drawn to you the instant you enter a room."

A problem he shared.

"But I've met many a braw fellow in service to the

queen and never yet been tempted to cast away the moorings of my maidenhead. So it's clearly more than that. That smile of yours plays a part. You know the one—the devilish curve of your lips that is half wry humor and half suggestion of wickedly sensual secrets. When you turn it upon me, I cannot help but wonder what those secrets might be. I find you very distracting."

Bran blinked. The lady was far more observant than he gave her credit for. His smile was a tool he wielded every day in the streets of Edinburgh. Many a rich lass had lost coins from her purse while dazzled by his suggestive grin.

"But again," she said. "Too simple a reason. The truth lies deeper." Her gaze met his. "It lies inside the heart of the man I *know* you to be—the man I'm not certain you see when you look in the still waters of the pond." She slid her hand across his chest, flattened her palm right over his heart. "You call yourself a despicable thief, and I do not doubt that you are, to some measure. But the man I wish to tup is the honorable fellow who saved my sister from a fate worse than death. Who knocked a young lad on the head rather than run him through. Who urged me to run away when I willingly offered him my body."

His heart thumped like a drum. What honor he possessed was threadbare at the moment. Every hot pulse through his body was telling him to snatch her up and carry her off to his room. Instead, he gripped the top rail of the chair with both hands and managed one last burst of reason.

"I'm also the man who betrayed the faith of a valued

friend by stealing a family jewel. The man who slit the throat of drunken sot in a dark Edinburgh wynd. The man who left his own brother to rot in a prison cell, making no attempt to save him."

Her smile turned sad. "All tales that I hope you'll share the truth of one day."

He stared at her, unable to fathom her belief in him.

She pressed her lips to the corner of his mouth, soft and sweet. "Perhaps I trust too easily. I've certainly been disappointed by the actions of others in the past. But you've had numerous opportunities to take advantage and have taken none."

"I kissed you in the cellars," he pointed out.

"I recall that," she said, laughing lightly in his ear. Stirring the hairs at his temple and sending a wave of molten need rushing to his loins. "Hardly what I would label as taking advantage, however. It was quite delightful, but far too short."

It *had* been short. By necessity. He'd been dangerously close to losing control—but nowhere near as close as he was this moment. The lass had no idea how desperate his desire was, but if he turned to face her, she'd know in an instant.

Her hot, wet lips found his earlobe, suckling. "Would you kiss me again?"

Dear god. Only a saint would be able to resist such a plea. And he was no saint.

Bran grabbed her shoulders and hauled her against his body, relishing every soft curve and gentle mound that met his press. He claimed her mouth with a kiss that was half raw hunger, half frustration. She had driven him to the edge of reason—and beyond. All he knew was the fierce pound of blood through his body and an unrelenting need. A need that could be slaked only by Caitrina de Montfort.

He mashed his lips against hers, demanding everything she could give him.

And she gave. Willingly.

Her arms wrapped around his neck, holding him tight, inviting him to deepen the kiss. Which he did. With a sweep of his tongue, he parted her lips and drank of the nectar that was her mouth. She tasted like honey, faintly spiced with mead, and it was all too easy to imagine tasting another part of her. A low groan rumbled in his throat.

She stiffened in his arms, no doubt shocked by the intimacy, and he gentled his assault. She was a maiden, after all. And if she decided she wasn't ready for more, then he would back away. Using every scrap of his willpower to withdraw, of course. He would need it.

But his intrepid young lass did not break off the kiss.

She thrust her fingers into his hair, angled her head to get even closer, and parried the invasion of his tongue with her own. Bran's eyes closed. Sweet heaven. He was done for. His knees actually wobbled, which he could safely say had never happened before. All his life, he'd been the one to do the charming, the one who beguiled. Now the boot was on the other foot. Caitrina made him feel like a wee lad receiving his first kiss. And lord, what a kiss. The mating of their mouths was spurring his desire into an insatiable hunger. With one hand on her back and the other splayed over the tender curve of her rump, he pulled her even closer, determined to claim her as surely as she was claiming him.

The press of her feminine body up and down the length of his was delightful. The short, quick rasps of her breath in his ear and the perfumed scent of her heated skin drove his excitement to a fevered level.

But none of it was satisfying. Every inch of his skin craved her touch. He wanted her naked and writhing beneath him. He wanted to bury himself deep inside her and show her every delight of the flesh. But those were impossible needs. Despite her pretty pleas, Caitrina was not a woman to be used lightly. And a few days was the best he could offer. There were people in Edinburgh depending on his return.

But he wasn't quite ready to let her go, either.

His body—and hers—still demanded some degree of satisfaction.

He lifted Caitrina off her feet and, in two broad paces, backed her against the stone wall. Grabbing both of her hands, he thrust them over her head, pinning her. Confident now that they were both fully supported, he proceeded to ravish her. He rained kisses upon her face and neck, nipped at her earlobes, devoured her sweet lips.

Had she shown even the slightest resistance, he would have pulled away. She did not. Her head lolled back on her slender neck, inviting him to take all she had to offer, and tiny whimpers of delight escaped her throat. But perhaps the most telling response was the slight rocking of her hips against his pelvis. She wanted him as much as he wanted her.

Bran struggled to keep his passions under control.

He positioned his knee between her legs, burying it deep in the folds of her gown. Visions of taking her to the floor assailed him and his arms quivered with the

effort to restrain himself. She was a lady, and an innocent one at that. She did not deserve a rough introduction to the carnal arts.

Gently, oh so gently, he moved his thigh against her
mons. Up and down.

Almost immediately, her faint whimpers deepened
into moans. Her fingers clenched around his hands and
her head thrashed from side to side. Were the lighting
better, he knew he would see a rosy flush upon her
cheeks and a plumper fullness to her lips. The telltale
signs of excitement. It would have been an added thrill
to see them, but his imagination would have to suffice,
as making love to Caitrina in the light of day was a gift
only some other man would enjoy.

Bran leaned his forehead against the cool stone wall
and closed his eyes.

Bringing the future to mind left a hollow ache in his
chest—one he dared not explore. Better to lose himself
in *this* moment, to slake whatever need he could, than
to dream of a future he could never have. The exhila-
rating press and release of his body against hers, the
dig of her fingernails in his flesh, and the sound of her
ragged breaths were the extent of his entitlement. A
man with a blackened soul could never claim a fine lass
like Caitrina.

And his soul was as black as they came.

No matter what she thought to the contrary.

Bran pressed his lips to the damp, delicate skin beneath her ear. Fine hairs that had escaped her braid
tickled his nose, and with surprising ease he lost himself in a picture of them lying upon a feather-ticked
mattress amid sweaty, tangled sheets. Her limbs en-

twined with his, her long brown hair binding her to him like satin ropes.

His breath quickened.

He would trade everything he had for that moment.

But it was not to be. Instead, he did what any rogue worth his salt would do—he tossed aside his chivalrous airs and deepened his embrace. He rocked against her hip with the firm evidence of his desire, at a pace guaranteed to make his blood pound and make his foolish thoughts disappear in a haze of lust.

No past. No future. Just now.

And he might have succeeded, had Caitrina not turned her head and found his lips with hers.

It was her faith that ruined him—her clear and utter acceptance of his wretched behavior. She showed no fear, no worry. She had placed herself wholly and completely in his hands, and trusted him to treat her well. She believed him to be a good man. A *better* man.

Bran reined in his desire.

As their lips meshed in a tender kiss, he slowed the tempo of his presses to a soft grind. The unfulfilled ache in his groin left him bordering on delirious, but it was the right thing to do. And Caitrina inspired him to do the right thing. Even when it hurt.

With sweat beading on his brow, he broke off the kiss.

"You, lass," he said gruffly, "are more dangerous than a double-edged dirk."

She looked at him with eyes that were dark pools in her oval face. "Is that it, then?"

He released her hands and stepped back. "Aye."

A frown creased her brow. "I didn't find that nearly

as satisfying as I'd hoped. My belly is quivering like I am on the brink of experiencing some momentous event. And my blood is hot and hungry with something I cannot name."

That made two of them. The only difference was that he could name the hunger.

"Those are discoveries to be made on another day. 'Tis time to get some rest. Tomorrow will come all too soon, and I must yet determine a way to free your sister."

She nodded slowly, but made no effort to retire.

"Go, lass," he urged, a little more forcefully. His willpower was ebbing. If she didn't go soon, he might rethink his decision to let her escape.

Her lips pressed against his in a fleeting kiss. "Tomorrow, then."

His fists clenched at his side. "Tomorrow," he agreed.

She darted off, finally, leaving him alone in the dark with his thoughts. Dark, delicious thoughts in which he was able to do all the sweetly depraved things to Caitrina that time and his honor would never allow.

Chapter 6

Caitrina rose the next morning bleary eyed and unrefreshed. She had not slept well. After her midnight tryst in the great hall, it had taken her an age to fall asleep. And when slumber had finally claimed her, her dreams had been filled with lusty images of Bran kissing every part of her naked body. The night had been far from restful.

Normally, she was a cheery sort in the morning, rising before dawn and dressing before the others awoke. Today, it was the hushed chatter of the other ladies that prodded her eyes to open. Her maid looked at her with concerned eyes as Caitrina slid her feet to the floor and stood.

"Are you feeling poorly?" she asked.

"Nay," Caitrina answered, forcing a smile.

"Good," the girl said quietly, as she helped Caitrina remove her night rail and don a fresh sark and gown. "I was fearful that you had the same illness as the queen. She looked much as you do when she woke during the night. But she was soon shivering and crying out for more blankets."

Caitrina's gaze flew to the queen's bed. Her Grace's physician, Chevalier Rodan, was at her side, applying leeches to her bare arms and neck. "A fever?"

The maid nodded. "And a dry cough."

Caitrina slipped her feet into her silk shoes and waited impatiently for the maid to brush her hair. When the ribbons were finally tied, she scurried across the room to the queen's bed. Yolande lay limply on her pillow, her eyes closed.

"Is there aught that I can do?" she asked Gisele.

The French noblewoman turned to her with a frown. "Several of the other ladies have adjourned to the chapel with the bishop. He has agreed to hear their prayers. You may join them, if you wish."

Caitrina nodded. But she could not simply leave her cousin, even when she was in the good care of her physician. She edged a wee bit closer to the bed and took hold of Yolande's hand. Giving the young queen's fingers a light squeeze, she leaned in close and whispered, *"Retrouver la santé, ma belle."*

Then she stepped back.

Although the queen could not see her, Caitrina offered her a respectful curtsy and then turned and left. She was expecting the great hall to be hushed out of respect for the queen's illness, but instead it was a hive of busy activity. Soldiers were rushing about, gathering weapons and shields, and donning mail with the help of their squires.

Bran was nowhere in sight, but the constable stood by the hearth giving orders.

"I want every able man attired and ready in the close anon," Dougal barked, his bushy red eyebrows angled sharply.

She crossed to his side. "May I ask what's going on?"

"Nothing that need concern you, my lady."

Caitrina glanced at the two guards positioned at the bottom of the stairs, both armed with poleaxes. They had not been there the night before. "I think anything that poses a risk to the queen concerns me, Constable."

His lips flattened into a thin line. Then, with a heavy sigh, he nodded. "Several of my men were slain during the night. In a clearing northwest of here."

Caitrina's heart skipped a beat. Northwest? Was that not where Giric and his men were camped? "Do you speak of the two men posted in the English camp?"

His frown deepened. "Aye."

An ice-cold chill ran down Caitrina's spine. Dear god. If the two men guarding Marsailli had been slain— "What of the lass who was held there? Is she safe?"

Dougal's eyebrows nearly knit together under the force of his frown. "How did it come to your attention that I had men posted in the English camp? They were assigned there long after sundown."

"The marshal told me," she said grimly, well aware that she was tarnishing her reputation with every word. The only time that Bran could have told her was late at night, when respectable ladies were long abed. But her reputation was meaningless in the face of Marsailli's danger. "Where is the girl, Constable?"

"Gone," he admitted. "Along with all of the English soldiers. They've disappeared."

A wave of nausea rolled over Caitrina, and she

closed her eyes to compose herself. It was the very worst of her imaginings. Giric had Marsailli firmly in his clutches once more, and he could punish her any way he saw fit.

"I've not the time to address your concerns further," Dougal said, with surprising kindness. "I must see to the manor defenses."

Caitrina opened her eyes and nodded.

As he turned to march off, she caught his sleeve. "Where is Marshal Gordon?"

"In the forest," he said. "It was he who found the bodies of my men, shortly before daybreak. He's taken my best tracker with him on the hunt for the Sassenachs." He spit the word "Sassenachs" as if it were a vile epithet.

"He went out with just one guard?"

Dougal smiled faintly. "Aye, but have no fear, my lady. The man he's with is a very capable fellow. The best with a dirk I've ever seen."

As he walked away, Caitrina grimaced. The best he'd ever seen might not be good enough. The assassin who had attempted to carve Giric's throat had likely been a talented knife handler, as well. But, in truth, it mattered naught. Bran was already beyond her reach. She would have to pray that he didn't run afoul of the huge Englishman.

Just as she would have to pray that Giric's anger had been assuaged by the death of the two Scottish guards. She buried her face in her hands briefly. Only then could there be any hope for Marsailli's safety, because he was not a man to show mercy.

Aware that the gillies must be eyeing her with curiosity, she straightened her shoulders, pasted on a neutral face, and headed for the kitchens. Although prayer was a fine endeavor, good deeds were a better means of keeping the devil at bay. If the queen was suffering from a fever and a dry cough, a cool broth might be just the thing to set her humors aright.

And even if it wasn't, the task would give her less time to worry.

She pushed open the big oak door and descended the steps to the close. Dougal's archers were thick upon the walls—all facing outward, quivers full, eyes alert. Another dozen men stood at the ready in the courtyard, but the bulk of the soldiers had marched out the front gate. As Caitrina made her way to the kitchens, the guards closed the gate and laid a heavy timber bar across the latches.

With the gateway sealed, Caitrina had little fear for the queen. Giric's men numbered only a dozen, and the queen's garde du corps was made up of seasoned warriors. Combined with the soldiers Dougal had left behind, Her Grace was well protected.

She ducked into the kitchen, a small square room with a large hearth at one end and a work table in the middle. On one side of the room, the baker and his apprentices were busy kneading, rolling, and baking fresh loaves of bread. On the other, the two cooks were doing silent battle, each with his own small group of gillies. One was preparing venison, the other a trio of fat fall hares. Caitrina could tell by the vivid flush on Master Andre's cheeks and by the glares the little man kept shooting over his shoulder that he was very unhappy.

"What goes on here?" she demanded.

Master Andre spun around and, upon recognizing her, cast a triumphant smile at the other cook. "See? I told you *le lapin* was an unacceptable choice. A queen does not eat rodents."

The other cook scowled. "Did she say that, you bloody French capon?"

"You dare to call me a castrated cock?" Andre's cheeks flushed an even deeper scarlet. He lifted the large, sharp blade in his hand. "You, whose eyes are like currants in a bowl of suet? *Cochon!*"

Caitrina quickly stepped between the two men. "Cease."

Although his eyes glittered and his arm shook with rage, Andre subsided. The other cook was less accommodating. He came toe-to-toe with Caitrina and pointed over her shoulder. "Let me at that wee bastard," he snarled. "He's been baiting me for days."

She met his gaze evenly. "Are you aware, Mr. Murtagh, that using the term 'bastard' in the presence of a lady is inappropriate?"

His gaze dropped to his toes. "Aye. My apologies."

"Accepted," she said. "Now, what exactly is the problem here?"

"This is my kitchen," he said hotly. "And I know what stores and what spices we have available." He pointed to Andre. "He does not."

"True," she said, offering him a smile. "But he knows the queen's tastes. Can not the two of you work together? Surely that would produce the best results?"

Murtagh wrinkled his nose, clearly not enthused by that option.

"Do not make me seek out the marshal, Mr. Murtagh. I doubt his decision on who rules this kitchen while the queen is in residence would go in your favor."

He blanched.

Apparently, Bran had already shared words with the cook on this subject. Words that closely matched her own. She smiled. Even in his absence, he supported her.

"Now," she said. "If you can put aside your differences, I would like you to produce a broth for Her Grace. It must be cold, with no lumps, and both of you must taste it and agree that it is worthy of the queen."

She stared at Murtagh until he nodded. Then she turned to Andre. He nodded, too.

"Perfect. Bring it to me promptly, as soon as it is ready."

Bran and young Robbie tracked Giric and his men for hours without success. The English soldiers had traveled light, leaving behind the wagon and the tents, taking only what they could pack on the horses. They had followed the burn in an easterly direction for quite some time, then cut across Clackmannan lands toward the northern boundary. Robbie did a fine job of picking up their trail until they entered a deep burn at the base of a crag. Where the waters ran rough, all evidence of the soldiers' passing was lost, and although they searched the shoreline, they could find no sign of exit.

"Did they swim?" Bran asked.

The lad lifted his gaze from the turbulent eddies. "They must have."

Bran watched a waterlogged branch shoot down the

burn. The water here ran swift and deep, swirling and burbling as it sluiced between the rocks. It hardly seemed possible that eleven men on horseback, plus one lass, could have made the journey downstream in safety. But what other explanation could there be?

"Then I suppose we must follow."

Robbie shook his head. "I cannot swim."

Neither could Bran. It had never been a concern before today. He stared into the foam-flecked water. Danger lurked in those depths, without a doubt. But if he didn't make an attempt, how would he face Caitrina? How would he explain that he'd given up the search for her sister?

"Wait for me here," he told Robbie. "I'll return anon."

He urged his horse forward. The edge of the burn was rocky and narrow, quickly dropping off into murky oblivion, but his mount faithfully followed his guidance. Until another branch came sailing down the burn and whacked the horse's foreleg. Then it snorted and fought the bridle.

Bran soothed the animal with quiet words of encouragement that he did not believe. "Easy, laddie. All will be well."

The stallion snorted one last time and then stepped forward. One pace. Then two. The water rose steadily higher, lapping at the toes of Bran's boots. He wrapped the reins around his fists and held on tightly. Every step was shaky, and the cold chill of the burn eventually crested the top of his boots and filled them, but the journey was not as precarious as he'd feared. Assuming the horse could swim, he should arrive downstream cold and wet, but in one piece.

Or so he thought. But with the next step, disaster struck.

The horse completely lost its footing, tumbling into the water and sinking beneath the surface. Bran was swept from the saddle and carried away by the swift current. Frigid water filled his nose and mouth, choking him, and he struggled for breath. The only thing that saved him was the tight hold he had on the reins. The horse's head burst into the air, its eyes wild and wide. It whinnied in shrill panic, but immediately struck out for the shore, pulling Bran along.

As he bobbed uncontrollably, spun by the eddies in the current, he lost all sense of time and distance. His throat was raw, his chest tight. All he knew for certain was the feel of wet leather wrapped around his hands.

Strangely, as he prepared to die, he did not give any thought to the long, eventful years he had spent in Edinburgh. To the many friends and companions who'd shared his life. Instead, he called an image of Caitrina's face to mind—the pale oval of her face, the bright sparkle of her eyes, the full lips of her mouth, all framed by her glorious dark hair.

It was a sweet image to take to his watery grave.

And then, as suddenly as it began, the wild ride was over. He felt a sharp yank on the reins, and then his boot struck a rock—a slimy, growth-covered rock, but most definitely a rock. And he was grateful for that slime when the horse began to drag him over the rocks. First his hip, then his elbow took a sharp whack against a boulder. Although it was tempting to let go of the reins, he did not. Not until the water was shallow enough for him to push his head free and take a sweet, dry gulp of air. Then he unraveled his hands and dragged himself to the shore, where he collapsed, utterly weary.

Lying on his back, drawing in slow, deep breaths, he stared up at the sky.

Never the sort to depend on anyone but himself for life's fortunes, he nonetheless found himself thanking the lord almighty. It was surely a miracle that he'd made it to shore. Pushing to his elbows, he looked around. His horse had gone no farther than a choice field of grass. Saddle askew and soaking wet, it grazed nonchalantly a few feet away. Rowan trees and blackthorn bushes grew along the rocky edge of the burn, their leaves the tired green of late October.

Even here, there was no sign of Giric and his party.

His treacherous adventure had been for naught. The canny Englishman had managed to make good his escape, and Bran would be forced to face Caitrina with the unpleasant fact that he'd lost Marsailli.

He got to his feet. His boots were ruined, but they were stolen anyway, so he could hardly bemoan their loss. It was his hands that had suffered the worst. The wet leather had rubbed his palms raw and the rocks had ripped several deep gouges across his knuckles. A small price to pay for his life, however.

Whistling softly, he called his horse.

The great beast pricked his ears, but did not stop eating. Having saved Bran's life, it certainly deserved a fine meal, so Bran slowly crossed the field to the horse, his feet squishing in the wet boots. As he neared, the stallion lifted its head and looked at him, its eyes bulging slightly. It seemed to be considering a quick jump sideways or a flee into the brush, so Bran halted and spoke gently to it.

"There's a good lad," he said. "You're a fine swimmer, you are. Saved us both, and I'm grateful. But now we must be away back to the manor."

The horse settled, and Bran was able to approach and reposition the saddle.

When the trappings were once again snug and well fitting, he leapt upon the horse's back and headed upstream. It took him well past midday to circle the huge slate crag and make his way to the spot where he'd left Robbie. As his mount picked its way over the rocks, Bran scanned the outcrop for any sign of Giric and his men, but all was quiet.

Slate was a common roofing material, valued for its hardiness and its ability to resist fire. The manor at Clackmannan had a fine roof fashioned from dull gray slate, but this stone was blue-green in color, quite vividly so down by the water's edge. Several of the finer houses in Edinburgh had slate roofs with distinct colors, some from as far away as Ballachulish, but he'd never seen a roof quite this shade.

Bran ducked under the low branch of an elm tree and came upon Robbie lounging against a moss-covered fallen log. The lad did not look surprised to see him.

He leapt to his feet and dusted off his arse. "Did you spy them?"

"Nay," Bran said. "They're well and truly gone."

Robbie nodded. "Whilst you were abroad, I searched the shore high and low in both directions and found nary a flash nor an overturned stone. 'Tis like the washerwoman made off with them."

The washerwoman was one of the fairy folk—a hag typically found knee deep in a burn, washing blood from the grave clothes of men about to die. Bran gave no credence to such tales, but neither did he have an explanation for Giric's disappearance. So he simply shrugged.

"Mount your horse," he said. "Let's away to the manor."

It was a long journey over rolling braes, through trees clinging to the last of their fall leaves, and across windswept moors. Holding the reins loosely in his battered hands, Bran used his knees to guide the horse. He was seriously considering stealing the valiant beast—a braver, more well-trained steed would be difficult to find—when they topped the ridge overlooking the manor. It was obvious in an instant that the manor was still on high alert. Dougal's men had surrounded the village, and Bran and Robbie were met by armed soldiers long before they reached the manor walls.

Dougal himself rode out to greet them.

"Are all inside safe?" Bran asked.

The constable nodded. "There's been no attack on the manor."

A relief, to be sure, although he'd been reasonably certain that all of the English soldiers had departed together. When they had examined the deserted camp, Robbie had found no hoofprints leading toward the manor.

"We chased them north to the boundary marker," Bran said, "before we lost them."

Dougal grimaced. "Wretched bastards. They should

meet the point of my blade for what they did to my men."

The two guards had been decapitated, castrated, and then strung up feetfirst in the trees—a brutal and insulting message. Neither of the men's missing parts had been found.

"If they return," Bran promised, "you'll get your chance."

The heavy wooden gate swung open and they entered the close. Bran scanned the faces of those gathered in the courtyard, hoping to spy Caitrina's dark hair and delicate features. But there was no sign of her. He dismounted and handed off his horse to one of the stable lads. "Have you made an accounting to the queen?"

The constable shook his head. "Her Grace has taken ill."

"Let us not share the details," Bran said. "No need to worry the queen needlessly. It's possible we've seen the last of those Sassenach scum." Unlikely, given that Giric's interest lay in Caitrina and the queen, but possible. "But keep the watch on the wall until we're certain."

Dougal nodded. "You should have one of the ladies see to those hands, Marshal."

The constable's face was bland, but Bran had a sense that the man knew exactly which lady would be willing to offer her services.

"Indeed."

With a sharp nod to the constable, he climbed the stairs and entered the great hall. Supper was still hours away and the room was largely empty. Two of the queen's ladies were seated before the hearth, working on their embroidery and chatting in hushed tones. Neither was the lady that he sought, but a cask of ale stood on the table behind them and his throat was parched, so he crossed the wooden planking in their direction.

"Marshal Gordon?"

He halted and turned. At the bottom of the stairs, looking slightly disheveled but sweeter than a ripe pear, was Caitrina. The look in her eyes was heartbreaking—a mix of deep fear and faint hope. She clearly knew her sister was gone. It took every ounce of his willpower to remain exactly where he was. The urge to run to her and gather her in his arms was so intense, his arms trembled. "My lady?"

She walked hesitantly toward him, almost as if she expected the worst.

"Have you any news?"

"Nay," he said. "The Englishmen have escaped." He didn't add, *I failed you*, but those words hung in the air between them. He had underestimated Giric, just as she'd urged him not to, and Marsailli's loss lay squarely on his shoulders.

Her gaze met his. "I heard that bodies were found."

"The two guards. No women."

"You're certain?"

"Aye." She had stopped far enough away that even a surreptitious brush against her hand was impossible. "They decamped swiftly, leaving most of their belongings behind. We had the opportunity to do a thorough search."

"Then we must hope for the best." She turned to walk away.

Unable to help himself, Bran reached for her arm. "My lady—"

She halted, her gaze dropping to his hand. "By the saints, Marshal. Those wounds are most unpleasant. What befell you?"

"Nothing more than would befall any nobleman who forgot his gloves," he said dryly.

She guided him to a chair before the hearth and encouraged him to sit. "Well, whatever the cause, they are in need of bandages."

Bandages? Was she mad? "Absolutely not," he said, with a scowl. Every gillie in the hall would think him a faintheart.

"Fine," she said. "No bandages. But we cannot allow those wounds to fester. Give me a moment and I'll return with some salve."

He would have refused, save for one thing— allowing Caitrina to care for his hands would give him a legitimate reason to bide awhile in her company. "I'll wait," he agreed. "But be quick about it. I've tasks that I must see to."

She smiled and darted for the stairs.

Bran stretched out his legs, aiming his still-damp boots toward the fire. By god, how did noblemen survive long hours on their arses? He was bored already and Caitrina had only just disappeared up the stairwell. The life of a gentleman was definitely not for him. He glanced at the two ladies quietly plying their needles. At this time of day in Edinburgh, he'd be fleecing wealthy men and women headed home from the market.

He frowned.

He'd been gone far longer than he had intended. Ularaig would be taking advantage of his absence, making life miserable for the citizens of Lowertown. The filthy wretch had almost every castle guard in his pocket and had begun to demand a portion of all coin earned by nefarious means. Any who refused were threatened with the full weight of the law.

"Well," said Caitrina, sliding onto the chair next to him. "Let's have a look at those hands."

She took one of his big hands in hers and laid it palm up on her knees. Using the knife at her girdle, she pried off the thin layer of wax that covered her jar of unguent. Then she slathered the foul-looking stuff all over the deep chafes on his hand. A ridiculous bit of nursing, to his mind, but he would never tell her so. Her tender ministrations were more of a balm to his soul than to his flesh.

As she switched her attentions to his other hand, he said softly, "I will find her and bring her back. I swear it."

She lifted her gaze and smiled sadly. "There isn't time."

"We've no cause to believe Giric has slain her," he said, praying he was right. "And Dougal has assured me that Marshal Finlay is unlikely to return before Samhain."

"That may be so," she said, as she packed up her pot and wiped her hands on a square of clean linen. "But this place will soon welcome the four Guardians of Scotland. Messengers left this morning, at the behest of the bishop of Saint Andrews. It is their duty to be present at the birth of the new king."

Bran sat back in his chair.

William Fraser was himself a Guardian, as was Robert Wishart, the bishop of Glasgow. Religious men he could sway. They concerned themselves more with god than with the law. Earl Buchan and the high steward? They would not be easily fooled by his charade.

"James Stewart resides in Edinburgh," he said. "He can journey here in less than two days."

She nodded. "You should leave now, while your identity is still unquestioned."

The large manor door swung open and a soldier ran into the great hall, his boots heavy on the planking. "Marshal Gordon! The constable requests your immediate presence on the wall!"

Bran shot to his feet. "What is it?"

The lad simply shook his head and ran back the way he came.

Bran grabbed Caitrina's arm. "Gather the other ladies and withdraw to the queen's chamber. Open the door to none but I." When she hesitated, he looked her in the eye and urged, "Go. Quickly now."

Only when he was certain she was in action did he march out the door.

There was no need for Caitrina to prod the other two ladies from their chairs—both women had taken note of the panicked guard and were bundling up their embroidery. As she hastened to their side, they turned to her with worried frowns.

"Is the manor under attack?" Etienne asked.

"I don't know," she said. "But the marshal is a very capable man. He and the queen's guard shall see to our safety. *Allons*. Let us not make his task any more challenging."

The plump woman put a shaky hand to her throat. "No matter how capable the soldiers, we are *sans défense* in such a *manoir piteux*. Why did Her Grace not return us to Stirling Castle?"

A rather pointless question, at this stage.

They scurried up the stairs to the third floor. The queen's guard ushered them into her chamber and then barricaded the door with two heavy chests stacked one atop the other. The physician and the midwife were seated beside the bed—everyone else stood at the narrow arrow loops overlooking the close. A low rumble not unlike a cart bumping along a rutted path vibrated through the air. Other than that, the close was somber and silent.

Although curiosity nearly got the best of her, Caitrina ignored the crowd hovering at the windows and crossed to the bed. Yolande was awake, but pale and weak. The fever had abated during the night, and although her cough lingered, she breathed easier. She smiled halfheartedly as Caitrina approached.

"We are experiencing some excitement, *non*?"

"Not the sort of excitement we typically enjoy," she responded dryly.

The rumbling abruptly ceased, and for a moment there was only silence. Then a quiet male voice ordered, "Open the gate."

Caitrina couldn't be sure, but it sounded like Bran. Why he would choose to open the gate in the face of danger, she had no clue. But she had faith in his decisions. The risk must be minimal.

"Fetch me a cup of wine, *ma chère*," the queen requested, pointing to the decanter at her bedside.

Caitrina poured a small amount of red wine into Yolande's silver cup and then lifted her head to help her take a sip. As the queen lay back against the pillows, the cart rumbled again, louder this time and accompanied by the creaks and groans of an empty wooden wagon.

A few moments later, it stopped, and one of the ladies at the window gasped in shock. Another sank to her knees, genuflected, and began to mutter a prayer.

"*Mon dieu*," said a third, turning from the window. "*C'est barbare!*"

Caitrina's throat closed tight and a wave of dizziness washed over her. What was so terrible that it shocked women who'd seen almost everything?

Yolande grabbed her hand, squeezing it. "A queen cannot shy from that which offends others. Be my eyes and ears—go look for me. Tell me what barbaric display has appeared in our courtyard."

Caitrina swallowed the lump in her throat. The women were not weeping; they were flinching with disgust. Surely that meant the cart in the close had nothing to do with Marsailli? She nodded to the queen, then crossed to the window, knock-kneed but determined.

The group around the window parted to let her pass.

Taking a deep breath, she peered through the cross-shaped hole in the thick stone wall.

The ox-drawn cart stood in the center of a group of

soldiers. Three wooden hay forks had been planted in the flatbed of the cart, two of them acting as poles for the severed heads of the two murdered guards. But the heads were not simply staked—the eyes had been gouged out, the skin flayed, and the mouths stuffed with what could only be the guards' genitals.

Caitrina's mouth soured.

The third fork carried a message meant only for *her*. It was a torn white sark, rent right down the middle and emblazoned with a dark red-brown bloodstain. Bile rose in her throat. It was Marsailli's sark. The blood was Marsailli's blood. Another wave of dizziness struck Caitrina and her knees gave out. With a low keen of despair, she slid to the floor.

Her worst nightmare had come true.

Giric had raped her wee sister and was proudly displaying the evidence.

Chapter 7

Bran glanced up at the narrow window slits on the third floor. He could only hope that Caitrina wouldn't recognize the significance of the torn kirtle. But given the age-old tradition of hanging the bridal sheets after a wedding night, that was a slim hope.

"Depole the men's heads and bury them with the bodies," he ordered crisply. "They deserve an honorable burial."

Dougal met his gaze, hard and meaningful. "What of the gown?"

"Burn it."

The constable directed his soldiers and then returned to Bran's side. "The men are angry. They know the Sassenachs are out there somewhere, taunting us."

Bran eyed the flushed cheeks and clenched fists of the men around him, and he nodded. "Their anger is justified. Gather a troop of your bravest men and mount them on your fastest horses. Let us run these scurrilous rats to ground."

Dougal smiled thinly and turned to make good on the request.

"But, Dougal," Bran said, halting him in midstride, "take care. These men are black-hearted knaves, and we cannot afford to bury any more men."

The constable nodded. "Aye."

With leaden feet, Bran mounted the steps and reentered the manor. Caitrina was due an explanation, but he was not looking forward to the conversation. How could he comfort her when his assurances had thus far proved false at every turn? He had not kept Marsailli safe. He had not even kept her close. Now her sister was in mortal danger and the culprit responsible was waving gruesome banners under their noses. Any vows Bran made would be meaningless.

He rapped his knuckles upon the door to the queen's chamber.

"Who goes there?" her guard demanded.

"Marshal Gordon," he responded. He slid his ring under the door as proof of his identity. "All is safe, for now. You may move about freely."

From within, he heard the scrape of moving furniture, and then the door unlatched. Two stern-faced guards wielding sharp halberds greeted him when the door swung open. "He is alone," one of them confirmed.

"That is indeed the marshal," Caitrina confirmed, stepping into view.

He eyed her carefully. Pale face, dark eyes. Her hands were clasped tightly in front of her, the knuckles white, and a small piece of rush from the floor was entwined in her hair. He did not need to ask her if all was well; the answer was obvious. Giric's message had been delivered straight to her heart.

"A word, if I may," he beseeched her quietly.

She nodded to the guards, who lifted their halberds and let her through.

They walked to the end of the corridor and Bran waved her onto a small wooden bench under a window. This close, the damage was even more clear. There were streaks of salty residue on her cheeks and the faint beginnings of a bruise on her chin. His fault, all of it. He'd fallen into the worst trap of all: getting too comfortable in his stolen clothes. He'd begun to believe he was actually a marshal, a chivalrous knight capable of defending innocent young lasses. But he was not. He was a charlatan. Still, he was a man of his word, and he clearly owed Caitrina his best efforts to right this wrong.

Although his arms itched to gather her to his chest, he did not touch her; he dared not breach the stiff wall of resolve she had erected around herself. It looked too fragile to withstand a kindness, and given the words he was about to speak, she would not thank him for the gesture.

"I think," he said slowly, "that there is more to this tale than you have yet shared."

She stared at him, bleak and unspeaking.

There was no censure in her eyes, but he felt it anyway.

Although it pained him greatly, he continued, "You told me that Giric was only interested in information. That he was simply spying upon the queen and reporting back to his liege lord. As late as this morning, when I entered his camp and saw that he had fled, I believed your tale to be true. It made sense that a spy would flee the instant our suspicions were pricked."

Caitrina sat perfectly still. Waiting.

"But the wagon in the close tells a different story. It's quite obviously a warning. A threat."

What little color there was in her cheeks drained away.

"He wants something from you," he said. "And I must know what it is."

Caitrina glanced away. Her clasped hands parted and she smoothed her palms over her azure skirts, the movement a little shaky. "You say that as if I could know what horrible thoughts a monster such as Giric would contemplate. I do not."

If there was one thing that Bran knew well, it was a lie. And Caitrina was lying.

"He has asked you to perform some reprehensible deed," he guessed matter-of-factly. "And he has threatened to slay Marsailli if you do not bow to his will."

She leapt to her feet, bristling with indignation. "Why would you think such a thing? Only a traitorous wretch would give in to such demands."

"Or a person willing to risk all for someone they love."

"I am *not* a traitor."

"Did I call you that?" He shook his head. "You are simply trying to save your sister."

"It does not matter what you think," she said hotly. She pointed down the hall at the closed doors of the queen's chamber. "It matters what *they* think."

Bran sighed. "Traitor, thief, liar—they're all just words. Labels do not define us; our actions do. Tell me what Giric has demanded of you."

"Gah!" She threw up her hands. "You've no understanding at all. They are *not* just words. My father was named a traitor, and it destroyed our family. His intentions were honorable; he was avenging the murders of his father and brother, but in the end that mattered naught. We were stripped of our title, cast from our lands, and forever shamed by that word: *traitor*."

He folded his arms over his chest. "You think you are the only one with a sorry past? My father loosed his bowels upon the gibbet, strung up by his neck for thievery. I know full well the power of such accusations. But his actions do not define my own."

"So says the man who makes his living as a thief."

He nodded. "Aye, to the casual eye it may appear that he and I are of like mind. But we are not. His only motive was greed. Mine is . . . a story for another day. Today, our priority must be your sister. Tell me what Giric wants, Caitrina."

She turned away, shoulders bowed, arms wrapped around her waist.

"What does it matter what he wants?"

Mostly, it was a matter of trust. Bran needed to be able to trust Caitrina, and as long as she was lying to him, he couldn't. But there was a practical reason as well. "To thwart him, I must understand how far he will go to get what he desires."

She slowly spun to face him. "If I tell you, you will despise me."

"Nothing you say can make me despise you," he

said softly. "My belief in your good nature is unshakable."

A short, bitter laugh escaped her lips. "You are doomed to be disappointed, I fear."

He watched the war of indecision play out upon her face—in the worry of her teeth on her bottom lip and in the lines that came and went upon her brow. Truth or lie, it did not matter. He would help her, whatever she said. He owed her that much. But he still prayed for the truth.

She heaved a sigh and he held his breath.

"He means to steal the queen's babe."

Bran almost swallowed his tongue. Satan's ballocks. Perhaps it was his personal leaning toward coin and gems, but he had assumed Giric's interest would lie in the queen's bounty of copious jewels, not in the politics of the Scottish crown. "Are you certain?"

"Aye." Her gaze met his. "It is *my* task to snatch the child."

In her role of lady-in-waiting, Caitrina would certainly have opportunity, but it would not be easy to steal a royal bairn. "So, it is King Edward's intent to confine the lad as he has confined Gwenllian of Wales?"

Caitrina grimaced. "I know not what his intent is. Save for one brief audience several months ago, I've not had words with Longshanks."

"Raising the Scottish monarch under an English roof would certainly serve him well. A lad who looks to him like a father will be quick to swear fealty."

"Well," she said, her cheeks flushing. "If he succeeds, it will not be on me. I will not betray my queen."

Bran brushed a thumb over the ruddy crest of her

cheek. "As long as he holds Marsailli, your will is not your own. Giric knows full well that if it comes to a choice between your sister and the queen's babe, you will choose your sister."

She wanted to deny it, but she couldn't.

"I do not fault you that choice," he said. "In your shoes, I would make the same decision."

She grabbed his hand with both of hers. "Now you see why I forced you to aid me. If I can free Marsailli, Giric will have no hold over me. He will fail."

It was true. The key to everything was finding and freeing Marsailli. "Dougal is searching for her as we speak," he told her. Not precisely true; Dougal's men were looking for Giric. But if they found the murderous Englishman, they would also find Marsailli.

She frowned. "Did you not say they had eluded you?"

"Aye," he said. She released his hand and he immediately missed her touch. "We lost them near the northern border, but they clearly circled back. The oxcart belongs to a nearby tenant."

A sad smile flitted across her face. "I'm sure Dougal will do a fine job, but you will be sorely missed."

Ah, yes. His imminent departure. He'd almost forgotten about that. The Guardians of Scotland would soon be descending upon Clackmannan, and it would behoove him to be gone when they got here. But the moment that bloodstained gown had fluttered into view, leaving the manor had ceased to be an option. A young lass had suffered because of him. If he turned his back on her now, it would be like abandoning his brother all over again.

He couldn't do that.

Not even to save his own skin.

Nor could he abandon Caitrina and the queen, not while wicked plans were afoot. The future of his country would be decided here, in this very manor, within the next month. And only he and Caitrina knew the full extent of the danger. No one else had a hope of mounting a defense against Giric—it would have to be him.

"I'm not leaving," he said.

Her eyes opened wide. "But the risks of remaining—"

"—can be minimized," he said. "If I acquire forged credentials."

"Can you do such a thing?"

The scandalized note in her voice amused him. He smiled. "With enough coin, sweetling, you can do anything."

But it wouldn't be easy. The timing would be the greatest challenge. The only man he knew who could forge documents well enough to hoodwink the high steward lived in Edinburgh—a day and a half's ride from Clackmannan. And the lad would need time to craft them. Even if all went smoothly, Bran could not acquire papers in anything less than five days.

He just had to hope that James Stewart was not in a hurry to answer the queen's summons.

Magda handed Marsailli a fresh pad of linen and moss. "Place the bloodied one in the bucket," she said. "I'll burn it in the fire later."

"I'm grateful for your assistance," Marsailli said to the midwife, blushing. "Before you arrived, dealing with my menses was a mortifying experience. Men have no knowledge of such things, and during my last monthly time the soldiers treated me as they would a leper."

The older woman shrugged. "They believe what the priests tell them—that a woman's flux is a punishment for her sins. That it is somehow wretched and filthy. But we know better. It is merely the body's way of preparing you for motherhood."

Marsailli adjusted her dress and then pushed aside the curtain to join Magda in the larger part of their tent. "Is it not a punishment? The nuns at the priory said Eve did not bleed before she was cast from the garden."

The midwife grunted. "Believe what you will. I follow the old ways, not the new."

"Are not midwives granted license by the village priests?"

Magda laughed, a deep, hearty chuckle. "Do you think our captor cares whether a priest has blessed my skills or not? Nay. All he bothered to verify was my ability to keep a newborn babe alive."

The midwife snatched up the bucket and left the tent.

Marsailli studied the fluttering tent flap with longing. As autumn advanced, the days grew crisp and short, and the opportunities to enjoy fine weather were limited. Sir Giric refused to look upon her face while her monthly blood flowed, and he would not allow her to step outside. Indeed, he blamed her for the need to pack up and pitch this one small tent—all the others had been abandoned. With a grimace, she picked up her sewing and sat on a stool before the small brazier that kept the chill at bay. The hems and cuffs of her dresses were wearing thin and required constant mending. Best she keep herself busy until her time was ended.

She sighed heavily.

She missed Caitrina. After their mother had passed, they'd become closer than most sisters, sharing every thought, every laugh, every fear. It was Caitrina who had taught her a proper running stitch and how to use embroidery to strengthen a fraying edge. Marsailli studied her mending efforts with a frown. She hoped her sister was having an easier time than she.

Giric was a cruel man, and one day he would make good on the villainous threats he heaped upon her. He would either rape her or kill her, of that she was certain.

What had Caitrina been thinking to send her off with King Edward and his brutish henchman? She must have known it would be Giric who would be tasked with returning her to Scotland. How could she imagine Marsailli would be safe in his care? Had she believed, as Marsailli once had, that his disfigured face was deserving of sympathy rather than fear? If so, she'd been a fool. He was every bit as wicked as his scar suggested. Sometimes— late at night, as she cried herself to sleep—she hated her sister for that lapse in judgment.

But not right now.

Right now, she just wanted to feel the warmth of her sister's arms around her.

Marsailli tossed aside her sewing and leapt to her feet. A braver girl would have long since made her escape, stealing a horse and dashing over the moors in the direction of Atholl. She had been happy there, for a time. But she had never been anywhere alone, and the very thought of striking out in a vague direction without a companion made her stomach heave. She could imagine what horrors would befall her.

She pushed back the sleeve of her linen sark and stared at the bruises on her arm.

Of course, the risks in remaining were high.

She closed her eyes and let the sleeve slip back into place. As evil as Giric might be, he was still the safer option. Here, she had food and clothes and fire. Here, she had the promise of seeing Caitrina and feeling her sister's arms wrapped around her once more. The road to Atholl held only danger.

Still, she could not ignore the warning signs.

Over the past month, Giric had completely transformed. When he had first retrieved her from the priory, he had been quite pleasant and polite. But as time passed and the inconveniences of living in a tent wore on him, all efforts to appear charming ceased. Now he was vile and vituperative. All too quick to raise his voice and his fist. She needed some form of protection, some method of staving off the inevitable. But what? She wasn't strong enough to wield a sword, and the dull eating knife at her belt would barely pierce his thick skin.

Marsailli cast about for a possible weapon.

It had to be small enough to be easily hidden, yet sturdy enough to inflict damage. Her sewing needles failed that test—even if she jabbed them in his eyes, they were unlikely to save her from a punishing blow.

She slowly spun around, mentally itemizing the goods stored within the tent. Several chests full of clothes, three small stools, and a stack of folded blankets. Nothing useful. Her gaze lit upon the wooden crucifix hanging from the tent pole near the exit. Except perhaps that.

She lifted the cross and examined it.

The rood was carved from a single solid piece of oak wood, and if the long end was whittled into a sharp point, it would make a formidable weapon. She mimicked the act of stabbing and grimaced. It would be effective only for someone with a stronger arm than hers. Jabbing such a thick object into Giric would take a great deal of force, more force than she could hope to muster. With a sigh, she hung it back on the pole.

She needed something long and thin, preferably steel.

A blade of some sort.

But Giric was careful—he did not allow her near the weapons or the horses. All she could hope was to spy something useful once she was free to roam the camp once more, something he wouldn't immediately think of as a weapon. In the meantime, she would prepare as best she could. She retrieved the discarded bundle of her sewing, separated the needles, and tucked them into her purse. Anything was better than nothing.

Peering through the narrow gap in the tenting, she studied the soldiers milling about in the camp. What she needed now was opportunity . . . and a wee bit of luck.

Caitrina favored Bran with a heavy frown. "You need *what*?"

"Gowns," he said. "Two of them. Large ones." He used his hands to suggest hips of sizable girth. "And a pair of those white headdresses the ladies wear."

"Brèids?"

He nodded.

What a curious a request. Caitrina struggled to find some reason that he might require ladies' attire and failed. "What purpose will these items serve?"

He tossed her a bold grin. "I have a rather unusual plan to rout our malefactor."

Her eyebrows lifted. "I think an explanation is due."

"Dougal's men had no better luck tracking Giric than I. He's hiding somewhere in the northern forest, but we have yet to determine where."

Disappointing news, to be sure, but not unexpected.

"To capture him," he said, "we'll need to draw him out in a purposeful manner. To a place and time of our choosing, not his."

She nodded.

"I can think of only one way to do that: offering him an opportunity to press his cause with you. His success is entirely dependent upon your support. If you do not steal the bairn, he will return to King Edward empty-handed."

While she agreed with his assessment, the thought of meeting Giric again face-to-face was troubling. And she still did not understand the need for the gowns. "Aye," she said slowly.

He smiled. "Obviously, I cannot give him any opportunity to injure you. It is my intent to disguise one of Dougal's men as a woman."

Caitrina choked out a laugh. "A man dressed as me? That will never work. Giric knows my face."

"It need only work from a distance. By the time Giric is close enough to Dougal's man to realize he has been duped, the game will be up. We will have him surrounded."

"How will you explain your plan to Dougal? Will he not wonder why the English would be interested in a message from me?"

"I've already enrolled Dougal in the plan," Bran said. "Initially, he rejected the charade and protested the use of a white flag to entrap the Sassenachs. Very unchivalrous, he said. But he is so enraged over Giric's desecration of his men that I was able to convince him to set aside the niceties. I've told him the note is a sham, a mock missive from the queen."

Still not convinced, she stared down at the map Bran had spread out on the table. "And where were you planning this auspicious meet to occur?"

He pointed to a small X that marked the location of a farm just north of the manor. "Here," he said. "This is the bothy from which he stole the oxcart. He is clearly familiar with the area, so we shall plant a white flag of parlay in the roof and leave a note written in your hand requesting a rendezvous."

"He will not come unprotected."

"And neither shall we." His gaze met hers, warm and intimate. "Can you find me the gowns?"

"I'm sure I can," she said. Wishing they were anywhere but in the busy great hall, where a bevy of soldiers and gillies played witness to their every move, she brushed her hand lightly over the top of his. He had quite elegant hands, for a man. Large and masculine, but with lean fingers. "But I fear that he will see through your efforts."

"It's a possibility," he allowed, lifting his smallest finger and grazing it along the trailing edge of her hand. A shiver of sweet longing ran down Caitrina's spine. "But the risks are low. If he suspects a trap, he will not come, and we will be forced to devise another plan." He shrugged. "So be it."

She lifted her hand to her lips and kissed the spot that he had touched. "Your request was for two gowns, not one. What is the other for?"

Bran's gaze was locked on her hand and her lips. "Me."

"You?" Her eyebrows soared.

"I'm no more eager to endanger the couple who farm the bothy than I am to endanger you, my lady. They, too, will be replaced by fighting men. Namely, myself and one other fellow."

Unable to help herself, Caitrina grinned. "That will be quite the sight. Will I have the opportunity to assess the strength of your disguise before you head for the bothy?"

"If you wish," he said, giving her a smile and a short bow. "Have the gowns delivered to my chamber within the hour and I'll see to it that you get your opportunity for amusement."

He rolled up the map and strode across the room toward the stairs.

Everything about him bespoke blatant masculinity—the breadth of his shoulders, the heaviness of his thighs, the span of his step. Imagining him draped in a gown, attempting to appear a lady, made Caitrina laugh. He hadn't a prayer of pulling off such a disguise. Even if the crofter's wife was a sturdy lass, she couldn't be more than half his size. Despite her concerns for her Marsailli, she found herself chuckling at the lengths to which he was willing to go in order to secure her sister's safety.

She would find the gowns.

And let out the seams as required.

Bran was standing next to Dougal in the close when Caitrina descended the narrow steps from the great hall. He tightened his brat about his shoulders and bent his head as if to study the muddy ground beneath his boots.

She strode up to them and addressed Dougal. "Have you seen the marshal, sir?"

The constable wasn't much for playing games, and he quickly stepped to one side and pointed at Bran. "The fool is right here."

Bran lifted his head and stared into Caitrina's lovely brown eyes, which widened as she recognized him. A fine reward for the effort he had put into donning his disguise. He smiled. "Elsie Drummond, at your service, my lady."

Caitrina shook her head. "I'd never have thought it possible, Marshal Gordon, but you look quite feminine. Were it not for the dark shadow of beard on your chin, you could pass for a lady."

"A little thick around the middle for my taste," said Dougal, with a snort.

She laughed, a sweet burble of joy that echoed through the close and drew the attention of almost every man. "Aye, but surprisingly bonnie, wouldn't you say?"

"Make sport, if you wish," Bran said. "I'm man enough to endure it."

She acknowledged the truth of his words with a smile. "And what of my replacement? Where is he?"

Bran glanced around. "Yet to appear, it would seem. No doubt a tad reticent to subject himself to ridicule. But he has more time to prepare than I—we must search the farm and find suitable hiding spots for Dougal's men before planting the white flag."

"We may have to remain in place for some time before the Sassenachs appear," Dougal reminded him.

"Aye," Bran agreed. " 'Twill be hardest on your men. You and I will be free to move about."

"Fear not," Dougal said dryly. "My men have plenty of experience with sitting on their arses. But I'll have words with them nonetheless." He bowed to Caitrina. "Excuse me, my lady."

She smiled at Bran. "You have a talent for disguise. I was quite convinced you were a woman until you looked up."

"It's a skill developed by necessity."

"Necessity?" Her head tilted, and she lowered her voice. "Are you not a cutpurse?"

"Nay," he said, equally quiet. But he wasn't particularly worried that someone would overhear them. Dougal had hailed his men and their attention was already engaged. "A cutpurse cannot return to the same corner day after day. He is doomed to cut and run, or face nabbing by the castle guard. I am that more notorious creature: the pick thief."

"And what is that?"

"A thief who uses distraction to lighten a purse or snatch valuables."

Her eyes narrowed. "A distraction such as a charming smile?"

One corner of his mouth lifted in a smoothly practiced arc. "Exactly."

"So the heed you have paid me these past few days has merely been . . . distraction?"

A fair question. He tossed his smiles often, most times without thought. Charm was a tool of his trade, after all. Quite likely, the first smile he'd sent her way had been a meaningless one, but it hadn't taken long for her quiet beauty to shake the genuine smiles free. A minute, or perhaps two.

"Lass," he said softly. "Given that I'm the one who finds himself lighter by one crown, who would you suspect is distracting whom?"

She blushed.

"This is a discussion I would very much like to continue," he said. "But it will have to wait until I return." He smiled. "And frankly, I think it should wait until I am no longer attired like a woman. The skirts are a tad disconcerting."

"Indeed," she said, with a laugh.

He nodded, preparing to step away.

Her hand brushed his sleeve. "Do take care, Marshal. Giric is a villainous man."

Their gazes met and held for a long moment.

"I will," he promised. It was foolish, but his heart skipped a beat, much as it might if he were truly a marshal with enough social standing to court a lady like

Caitrina de Montfort. But he was not. And he should remember that. Even with everything that was at stake, all this could ever be was a game.

Bran turned and mounted his horse.

A very dangerous game.

Caitrina remained in the close long after Bran and Dougal had departed, and the manor had returned to quiet industry. She sat on the stone steps, watching the stable lads mucking out the stalls, and eyeing the cooper as he made new barrels. It was quite inappropriate to sit and do nothing, but her mind was in a state of turmoil.

Bran was nothing like any man she'd ever met before.

He was charming and competent and completely disreputable. She knew nothing of his past, nothing of his family, and nothing of his reasons for choosing a life of thievery. And yet she was quite certain she was falling in love with him.

Not that she'd ever been in love before. But the fluttering of her heart and the tight squeeze of her chest every time she looked at him were a perfect match to the descriptions of love her mother had given her. Back when Caitrina had begged for an explanation for the loyalty her mother still showed to her father, even after he'd deserted them.

But falling in love with a thief was a grave mistake.

There was no common ground on which to build a life. He could not join her in her world, nor could she join him in his. In truth, joining him on the streets of

Edinburgh was *possible*, just not very appealing. She would have to give up all of the finer things in life and learn to survive amid thieves and cutthroats. Even if she was willing, how could she ask that of Marsailli?

She blinked back tears.

Assuming Marsailli was ever returned to her.

And there it was: the very reason her heart beat an uneven rhythm whenever he was about. He was no ordinary thief. He could have taken the crown from her rooms and run off. Instead, he was risking everything to save her sister. Knights and constables and marshals did that. Not thieves.

"Lady Caitrina?"

She looked up.

Standing before her was a lad dressed in a purple gown. It was easy to see why Bran had chosen this young man to masquerade as her—he was short and slim. But, sadly, even in a dress, he looked nothing like a woman. He had a wild, scruffy beard that grew halfway to his belt.

"I can't do it," he said miserably. "The marshal told me I must scrape the whiskers from my face, but I can't do it."

Caitrina stood. "Can't?" she asked. "Or won't?"

His gaze dropped to the ground. "A man's beard is his manhood, my lady. I'm a wee man, and if I lose the beard, I'll be a mockery."

"The marshal and the others are depending on you," Caitrina said fiercely. Marsailli was depending on him. "You must be a man of your word."

"Nay," he said, pulling the gown over his head. "I can't."

He pressed the gown into her hands and stalked off in nothing but his lèine.

Caitrina stared at the soft puddle of purple silk, wondering what to do. Was there another man of a similar size that she could convince to don the dress? A gillie, perhaps? But how could she ask a man unfamiliar with a sword to step into battle? What use would such a man be to Bran and the others?

And how sure could she be that Giric would fall for the ruse?

She couldn't, of course . . . unless *she* was the one to attend the meet. But when it came to sword arms, she would be even less useful than a gillie. Unless she brought a guard. A gentlewoman did not typically travel anywhere unaccompanied, even for short distances. Giric would expect her to bring a man along.

She would not be abandoning the queen. Although she couldn't be certain the broth made by the two cooks deserved the credit, the queen's health had improved to the point that she was once again spending time seated before the fire. Caitrina was free to spend longer periods away from Her Grace's side. The more she thought about it, the more sense it made that she be the one to go.

But the truth was, Caitrina did not want to go. The very thought of climbing atop a horse and facing more of Giric's men cinched her throat so tight she could barely breathe. If Bran's entire plan did not hinge upon the arrival of a woman purported to be her, she would not consider it, not even for an instant.

Her fingers clenched the silk gown.

Someone had to go, and she could not ask some innocent gillie to do what she was too craven to do her-self. She lifted her gaze to the door of the barracks where her bearded young soldier had disappeared. So it would be her, and she knew just who to conscript as her guard.

Chapter 8

It was tedious, waiting for Giric and his men to appear.

Bran and Dougal played the roles of the crofter couple, threshing the fall grain harvest in the barn with flails. They kept the doors, both front and back, wide open to reduce the chaff dust and keep a clear view of the surrounding countryside. The soldiers had found a variety of suitable places to hide, some distance from the bothy. Some were in evergreen bushes, some in tall brown grasses, and some beneath piles of fallen leaves.

The hours passed slowly and uncomfortably.

Bran was confident that Giric was coming, however.

Not long after Dougal had planted the white flag in the roof of the bothy, a lone rider had stopped by to ask what it was for. When Dougal explained that it was a message from a lady at the manor, the rider had collected the note and immediately headed north at a gallop.

The sun was on its descent, the shadows reaching

across the fields, when he spied horses approaching from the manor. It surprised him to see two horses, when he was expecting only one. The lass in the purple dress was obviously young Jamie, but who was the second? He squinted into the setting sun. A bearded fellow; beyond that, he was impossible to identify.

Dougal nudged him with his elbow.

Bran looked north. Sure enough, a group of horses had left the trees and were crossing the field toward them. Giric had taken the bait.

"Wait until they are nearly upon us before you give the signal," he said to the constable.

Dougal nodded. "Who is that with Jamie?"

Bran's gaze again turned west. The lass in the purple dress looked surprisingly bonnie. He frowned. Nay, it couldn't be. Caitrina would never take such a needless risk. But the longer he looked, the more he became convinced that it was indeed Caitrina mounted on the small bay mare. In part, because the bearded fellow began to look more and more like Jamie.

"I think it's Lady Caitrina," he said with a heavy sigh.

"Bloody hell."

There was no time to consider the implications or recalibrate their plans. Giric and his band of helmeted soldiers galloped into the yard, and Dougal ran for the bell they had hung at one end of the barn. With several sharp tugs on the rope, he signaled his men to attack.

Bran flung off his disguise, leapt on his horse, and drew his sword. Hoping that Jamie had the good sense to turn Caitrina around and head back to the manor, he dove into the fray. His swordsmanship was a wee bit rusty—it had been years since he had been called upon to do battle with a long blade—but he successfully dispatched one of Giric's men and moved on to a second.

Dougal's men rode in from all directions, surrounding the Englishmen, and the clash of sword on sword rang through the clearing.

They outnumbered the Englishmen and the fight was going well. Bran was winning his battle against a second soldier when he caught a glimpse of purple silk in the corner of his eye. He prayed desperately that it wasn't what he thought it was, and parried a jab from his opponent. But it was—he spied Caitrina race into the yard a moment later, urging her escort to join the fracas. Despite the distraction, Bran defeated his foe with a swift downward slice. He paused, weary but triumphant.

Only to hear Caitrina scream, "Behind you!"

He spun around just in time to block a bone-rattling blow from Giric's sword. The Englishman was a full head taller and at least four stone heavier than he, and although Bran attempted to angle his edge away, Giric's sword bit into the steel of Bran's weapon. Normally, such edge-on-edge swings were avoided—the damage to fine swords too severe—but Giric didn't seem to care.

There was murder in his eyes.

He swung again and again, raining blows upon Bran's blade.

Bran's sword arm began to weaken under the unrelenting attack, and he knew he wouldn't last much longer. Not in a traditional fight. He palmed his dirk in his left hand and looked for opportunities to break through the huge warrior's defenses. But Giric was not an easy man to study—his fighting style was erratic and punishing. He left little room for any kind of opportunity, and Bran began to worry that the end was nigh. His arm ached and throbbed with such ferocity that could only mean it was about to collapse.

And then, just when he thought all was done, his opportunity came. For the briefest of moments, Giric paused and glanced over Bran's shoulder.

Bran took advantage. He ducked under the big man's sword and slashed his dirk along the back of one thigh. It might have been a defining blow, except for the terrified shriek that rose into the air as he swung in for the final attack.

Caitrina.

He pivoted and spied one of Giric's men hauling Caitrina out of her saddle. And as quick as that, Giric no longer mattered. Bran raced across the yard, reaching the English soldier just as the fiend struck a vicious blow to her chin. She slumped and Bran saw red.

His blade had slipped between the man's ribs before Bran had consciously decided the fellow's fate. He caught her before she hit the ground, then turned to face the battle, his knife at the ready. But Giric had not followed him; the big Englishman had seized the moment and hobbled for a free horse. As a growl of frustration rose in Bran's throat, Giric spurred the horse into a gallop and took off for the northern forest. Only one of his men followed suit—the others all lay dead or injured.

"Go after them," he ordered several of Dougal's men. "He's holding a young lass in need of rescue. Do not rest until you find her."

They took off after Giric.

Bran sheathed his blades. Crouching, he brushed a stray tendril of hair from Caitrina's face. A second bruise now marred the tender flesh of her jaw. He was doing a rather poor job of protecting her.

A firm hand patted his shoulder.

He looked up.

"'Tis but a matter of time before that timorous knave is captured," Dougal said.

Bran wished he could feel as confident. While the bulk of Giric's men had been defeated, there were others hiding in the northern woods, and the big Englishman was still a formidable opponent. It wasn't cowardice that had sent him scurrying, but rather a deep-seated determination not to fail his liege lord—of that he was certain. Giric would not give up. Not before Queen Yolande's bairn was born. But he could not share that reasoning with Dougal.

"Likely true," he agreed. "But I recommend we remain vigilant, in case he mounts a secondary attack."

Dougal shrugged. "As you wish. Shall I send for a cart to transport the lady?"

"Nay," Bran said. "Darkness will be upon us soon. Better that we return her to the manor as quickly as possible." He lifted Caitrina into his arms. Her limpness knotted his gut, especially when her head rolled back, exposing the pale flesh of her throat. Helpless was not a word he would normally use to describe her. And it was his fault that she'd been so sorely abused.

He handed her to Dougal while he mounted, and then took her back into his arms.

Cradling her in the curve of his shoulder, he made

her as comfortable as he could manage as he rode. But that comfort was fleeting. Once the sun slipped toward the horizon, the autumn air grew cooler and she began to murmur incoherently against his collarbone. Only when he wrapped his brat about the two of them, lending his heat to her body, did she settle into a quiet sleep.

Bran held her close to his heart the entire ride home, and enjoyed every moment of her nearness. The soft sighs, the warm press of her body, the complete dependence on him for her safety. He found renewed strength in his sword arm and had almost convinced himself he was champion material by the time they rode through the manor gate.

He wasn't sure what Dougal thought of the arrangement, nor did he ask.

But the look he got from Lady Gisele when he carried Caitrina into the great hall was quite telling. "Put her down immediately, monsieur. It is inappropriate to hold an unmarried woman so intimately."

"She is injured," he explained.

"Put her down," she repeated.

"Where?" he asked, glancing around. "I cannot simply lay her on the floor."

Gisele pointed to a chair in front of the hearth.

He frowned. "But she cannot sit without support."

"Then we will support her," the lady said. "But if you do not release her promptly, Monsieur Marshal, her reputation will be in tatters." She lowered her voice to a whisper. "Her undergarments are on display."

Bran peered over his arm. "Oh."

He deposited Caitrina in the chair. Almost immediately, he was pushed aside as the ladies-in-waiting took over her care. He stood there for a moment, feeling distinctly bereft, but could find no reason to remain. Indeed, he appeared quite unneeded.

Quite the opposite of what he'd felt on the journey home.

But accurate.

He had once again fallen into the trap of believing his own ruse. He was *not* Marshal Gordon. He had no right to inject himself into Caitrina's life, no right to direct her care, no right even to inquire about her health. He was merely a thief, and she was a lady.

Bran backed away from the little group in front of the fire.

No matter how right she felt in his arms, Caitrina de Montfort was not for him. Once Marsailli was recovered—which could be at any time now—he would depart for Edinburgh and that would be the last they would see of each other.

Why did he keep forgetting who he really was?

Before he'd met Caitrina, he'd been rather proud of what he'd accomplished. He'd started with nothing, after all. After his father had met the rope, Bran, his mother, and his brother had escaped to Edinburgh, hoping to make an honest wage. But jobs had been scarce. And then his maither took ill. It was while stealing food that he discovered he possessed unusually clever fingers. A useful skill for a wee lad from the country trying to make his way among toughs born and raised on the streets.

But not a useful skill for winning the hand of a lady.

He grimaced.

It would be best if he stayed away from the lass as

much as possible. She had a soft heart, and as surely as the law would one day catch up with him, he would end up breaking it.

He offered Caitrina the smallest of bows, then turned and strode for the stairs.

She woke up hungry and sore.

It was dark as sin when Caitrina opened her eyes, the only light a flickering torch near the door. Soft snores filled the air around her, and it swiftly became clear that she was lying on her pallet in the queen's room. Safe and secure. The battle that had been raging when she fell was apparently over, and, judging by her current location, the outcome had proved favorable for Bran and his men. Which meant that Giric had been defeated.

Fingering her bruised jaw, Caitrina sat up.

But if that was true, what of Marsailli? Was her sister here in the manor?

She slid her feet to the cold floor and snatched up her woolen brat from the end of the bed. There was only one way to find out—she needed to speak to Bran. Now.

It took her a moment to locate her slippers in the dimness, but once her feet were encased, she eased open the door and entered the anteroom. The two guards eyed her with heavy frowns.

"It appears that I missed supper," she said, smiling ruefully. "I'm headed for the kitchens."

The frowns deepened.

"Were the Englishmen not defeated?" she asked.

They nodded slowly.

"Then I have nothing to fear. I shall return anon."

Not giving them any further opportunity to naysay her, she grabbed a candle and left the room. The corridor was equally dim, with only one torch lit at the top of the stairs. Bran's room was at the opposite end of the hall, and she scurried to his door, hoping that the queen's guards were not listening for her tread upon the stairs.

She rapped as lightly as she dared on the door.

No answer.

When a second light knock produced the same result, Caitrina took a deep breath, opened the door, and stepped inside.

She remembered the room well enough from her last visit. A good thing, as the feeble light from her taper did little to brighten the room. She could barely make out the large platform bed and the two chairs standing before the banked fire, but there certainly seemed to be someone asleep under the covers. Tiptoeing over to the bed, she set the candle down on a side table.

"Bran," she whispered.

That single, hushed word got her far more than she'd bargained for.

In a blink of an eye, she was yanked off her feet, rolled onto the mattress, and crushed beneath the weight of a wide-eyed, angry man. Caitrina felt the prick of a sharp blade at her throat, and she swallowed tightly.

"It's Caitrina," she squeaked.

The knife vanished and he released her, rolling to his back. "Bloody hell, lass. I almost killed you. What are you doing here?"

She sat up and, despite her shock, admired the way the light of the candle traced the lean contours of his arm and chest. In her admittedly limited experience, few men looked as good without their shirts. "Looking for answers," she said. "I didn't expect to be attacked."

He grimaced. "If you enter a man's bed in the middle of the night, that's exactly what you should expect."

A rather short-tempered response, which she attributed to his being rudely awakened. "Did you find Marsailli?"

"Nay," he said, turning his head to look at her. "I'm sorry."

Disappointment flooded her chest and she grabbed his arm. "But Giric is dead, aye?"

He ran a light finger over the bruise on her chin. "Nay," he said softly. "He escaped."

Caitrina slumped against the pillows, her eyes closing. She had risked her life for naught—they had failed. "How is that possible? We had them surrounded."

He said nothing, allowing the circumstances to speak for themselves.

For a time, there was only the sound of her heartbeat, heavy and mournful, in her ears. "You are aware, are you not, that he will punish Marsailli for my rebellion?"

"*My* rebellion," he insisted, scooping her into his arms and holding her tight. "And harming her will not win him your cooperation. He will know that now."

She bit her lip and sent a prayer skyward. "Dear lord, I pray you are right."

"Don't lose faith, lass. I'll retrieve your sister. I swear it."

Caitrina laid her cheek against the firm planes of his chest and allowed his warmth to curl around her. Here in Bran's arms, she could pretend—just for a while— that his assurances were true and that Marsailli would not bear the brunt of Giric's anger. It was a powerful magic, and she wished she could lose herself in it for eternity.

They lay like that, quiet and comforted, for some time.

Until the spicy scent of Bran's skin and the smooth brush of his hand on her hair slowly erased her worries, replacing them with a warm tingle of awareness. A hot stirring deep within her belly. And then she did something quite daring—she lifted her head and kissed his chest.

He froze, all movement ceasing, even his breathing.

"Was that unpleasant?" she asked.

"Nay," he croaked. "A surprise, that is all."

Emboldened by his reaction, she lapped at his nipple with the very tip of her tongue, enjoying the slightly salty taste of his skin.

He sat up abruptly, pushing her gently away. "Lass," he said, his voice edged with quiet desperation. "You ask too much of me. I've not the strength to resist you right now."

"I don't want you to resist me."

Indeed, she wanted him to ravish her. To banish all her terrible thoughts, to bury her worries under a thousand delights of the flesh. She wanted to live in the heat of the moment, to feel loved and cherished and beautiful until the sun rose on a new day.

Was that so wrong?

"Nor do I want you to lecture me on the merits of saving myself for some future husband," she said, running a hand down the ropy sinews of his arm. He was smooth and firm, like silk over fire-heated steel. "I could have died today, pure and chaste and unfulfilled. Is that what you wish for me?"

"Nay."

She leaned in, drawing in a nose full of his delightful scent. "I thought not."

"Don't mistake me for a true gentleman." His words rumbled deep in his chest, and she pressed her ear to the masculine vibrations. Lord. Everything about him was a wonder. "My patience is limited. I've given you fair warning, and I won't repeat myself."

"Consider me warned," she agreed, nibbling her way up his throat to his chin. "Now do your worst. Or rather, your best. I expect to end this night weak-kneed and bone-weary."

He snorted. "You have rather high expectations for a first round."

She trailed a finger down the line of dark hair in the center of his belly. "Oh? Why so? I've been told that a skilled lover can make a woman swoon with joy."

In a quick, sudden movement, he captured her wandering hands and pinned her to the mattress. "Aye," he said, tasting her throat with sweet, tender kisses, much as she had just tasted his. "But you are not yet a woman. You're a maiden."

"How is that meaningful?"

He pressed a hot kiss to her lips. "The first time for a maiden can be uncomfortable."

Caitrina considered that carefully. "So, you are already ceding defeat? Admitting that you cannot make me swoon? How disappointing."

He pulled back, staring at her with narrowed eyes. "Do you goad me apurpose?"

She smiled. "Of course."

He shook his head, then, with a low growl, swooped in to bite her earlobe. A shiver of visceral excitement rippled through her. Incredible. If this was what it was like to be eaten, nothing would please her more than if he consumed her, bite for bite, from head to toe.

She tilted her head back to encourage him to sample further, but Bran's attention slipped lower. He parted the lacing at the neckline of her nightclothes, exposing her collarbone and the tops of her breasts to his view. Her breasts seemed to know more about what to expect than she—even before he touched the soft mounds, they grew heavy and full, the nipples budding.

Caitrina moaned in wordless entreaty.

She did not know what she was demanding until he gave it to her—until his hands cupped and gently squeezed. And then her moan became a mewl of desperate desire. She wanted—nay, needed—his mouth upon her breast. She buried her hands in his thick hair and prayed that he would intuit her salacious longing.

And he did. With surprising accuracy, his lips found her left nipple through the loose linen night rail. Her fingers clenched as the warm wetness of his mouth settled over her breast, delivering a torrid wave of pleasure that rolled right to her toes. But not nearly as hard as they clenched when he sucked. And flicked his tongue over the nub.

Caitrina squealed.

Bran immediately released her breast and planted a soft kiss on her lips. "Lass," he said quietly, "as much as I enjoy hearing your sweet responses to my kisses, I'll no allow this night to cause you harm. If you're discovered in my room, there'll be no end to the grief, you ken?"

She blushed. "Aye."

"If you feel the need to scream, just bite my shoulder."

"You're mad!"

He winked. "Aye, a wee bit. But I suspect you knew that already."

No longer embarrassed, Caitrina relaxed against the covers. "Is biting acceptable play between the sheets?"

"Anything is acceptable, as long as you enjoy it."

"The church would disagree," she said dryly. "I've heard many a sermon denouncing unclean acts, even between a man and wife."

He shrugged. "A priest should not dictate what can and cannot be done behind the bed curtains. Only my lover can make that decision."

"And how is your lover to determine what is right and what is wrong?"

He gave her another quick kiss on the lips and then rolled to one side. His hand trailed up and down her body, his touch featherlight and teasing. "It's simple. Anything that makes you feel uncomfortable is wrong. Anything that excites you is right."

Goose bumps rose on her flesh in the wake of his touch.

"Are not the symptoms of fear similar to those of excitement?" she asked.

His hand halted above the crux of her legs. "The truest test is right here," he said. "That which excites you prepares you for the final act." He took her hand and cupped it over her mons. "You'll always know best if you are ready to proceed. Never let a man decide that for you, priest or no."

With his hand over hers, he rocked her flesh.

Tiny waves of sweet pleasure crested over her and Caitrina's eyes closed of their own volition. Her hips lifted into his hand, eager for a deeper, more satisfying rhythm. She was undeniably hot and wet and excited. But Bran seemed determine to torture her. His mouth found her other breast and even as she rocked against his hand, he suckled, driving her to the very edge of reason.

Only when she was keening softly into his pillow and her hands were fisting in the sheets did he slip the night rail from her body and lie alongside her, naked. He rained kisses all over her hot skin, and Caitrina traded her hold on the sheets for roughly admiring caresses up and down his shoulders. She wanted him closer. Deeper. She wanted to be a part of him.

His hand reached between her legs, testing her readiness, and he grunted when his fingers met obvious wetness.

"I'm ready," she told him huskily, opening her knees wide. "Take me."

And he did. Swiftly and surely. When he was fully seated, he halted, his breathing shallow and rough.

"Is all well?" he asked.

Caitrina couldn't speak. Not for a moment. But the sting soon subsided, and she nodded. "Aye. All is well. But a wee bit more joy would be lovely."

A short, gusty laugh broke from his lips. "I can arrange that," he said, slipping his hand between them. "This, lass, is the better part, I assure you."

And with a skillful thumb, ardent lips, and a series of deep strokes, Bran proceeded to take her to the stars. She discovered a myriad of new sensations, not the least of which was the slow build of excitement in her belly—the one that wound as tight as a bow string and then suddenly let fly.

Bran swallowed her scream with a kiss, and found his own release a few moments later.

He collapsed at her side, his arm across her chest, his eyes closed.

He lay so still that Caitrina wondered whether he had fallen asleep. But a moment later he opened his eyes and smiled. "Did I make you swoon?"

She grinned. "Not quite," she said. "But very near. I'm sure you'll improve with practice."

"Practice?" With a low growl, he pounced on her, tickling every sensitive part of her body until she begged him to yield. Then he lay back on the mattress, tucking her close. "Consider yourself fortunate," he said, kissing the top of her head. "I'm not a man to rest on my laurels. I will endeavor to make you swoon each and every time we are together."

"An honorable goal," she murmured, her eyes drifting shut.

He shook her lightly. "Nay, sweetling. Do not succumb to sleep. You must return to your pallet afore your lengthy absence is noted."

Reluctantly, Caitrina forced her eyes open and wriggled free of his warm embrace. A valid point. The guards must already be wondering what was keeping her from her bed. She found her discarded night rail and slid it over her cooling body. Bran wet a square of linen with the pitcher of water next to his bed, then knelt before her and gently wiped her inner thighs. When he was done, he took her hand and brushed a kiss over her knuckles.

"I've never spent a better night," he said, smiling.

"Nor I," she responded honestly, flushing.

Not sure what else to say, Caitrina gave him a quick kiss on the lips and darted for the door. Daylight would return all too soon, and with it, her worries. She did not want to tarnish what had been a truly memorable night with false promises or awkward conversation.

But at the door, she paused and looked back.

Bran was watching her, a faint smile on his face. His dark blond hair was raked off his handsome face, his muscular arms crossed over his chiseled chest. She wanted to remember him just like this, for eternity.

"I love you," she said quietly. And then she closed the door behind her.

Bran stared at the closed door, his gut achurn.

Dear lord. He was the worst sort of fool. He'd done exactly what he'd vowed not to a few hours earlier. He'd ruined a woman he adored, and he was about to double his crime by breaking her heart. And there was absolutely no way to redeem himself. What could he possibly offer her? Marriage?

He snorted.

That would never happen. He had no right to offer for the hand of a lady—ruined or not. If he dared, she would spurn him in an instant, and rightly so. And even if she didn't, he was a poor choice of mate. He was destined for the gallows, just like his father.

It would be kindest to walk away now. Sneak into the queen's room, recover his crown, and be on his way. Caitrina would mourn his loss for a time, true enough. But then she would pick up the threads of her life and go on as before.

Bran lay back on the bed and stared up at the canopy.

But he could not leave. Not while Marsailli was still lost and Giric was a threat to the queen's bairn. Like it or not, he would have to face Caitrina in the morn and deal with her declaration.

Damn it.

What did an innocent lass like her know about love? She thought she knew him, but all she'd seen so far was a facade. A sham. She knew nothing of Bran MacLean, the thief. The life he led in Edinburgh would shock her, of that he was certain. There was nothing good or honorable in the act of stealing, no matter how well motivated. He regularly added to the troubles of drunken sots, especially jilted lovers and cuckolded grooms. Misfortune was his ally. At best, he could say that he never thieved from men so down on their luck that they couldn't rub two deniers together.

At worst . . .

He grimaced. Well, at worst he was a murderer.

Aye, the man he'd killed was an abuser of women, a wretch who had nearly beaten a lass to death for plying her trade, but claiming his death as redress would be a lie. He'd died because he had a fat purse.

There were many days when he hated who he was. But thievery was all he knew, and he was good at it.

Bran closed his eyes. What he *wasn't* good at was telling the truth—and yet that was exactly what Caitrina deserved. It was long past time. On the morrow, he would tell her how he'd come to have in his possession a silver crown set with a large sapphire. And why three fierce MacCurran warriors would willingly chase him to the very ends of the earth to see him punished for it.

Chapter 9

Marsailli was asleep when the Bear returned to the camp, but she didn't remain that way for long. He hauled her from her bed by her hair, snarling incoherently about her sister's betrayal and the audacity of his mount to die during a race for safety. Heart pounding, tears flowing, she watched mutely as he proceeded to destroy her tent in a fit of unholy rage, snapping the wooden poles like matchsticks and tearing great holes in the canvas walls.

She shivered in the center of the misty plateau, wondering whether her time had finally come.

Slipping her hand into the purse she had worn to bed, she felt for the sharp points of her sewing needles. If he came at her, she would use them, puny or not. If nothing else, they might incite him to kill her with a single blow instead of punishing her with a lengthy torture.

But to her surprise, there was no need for desperate measures.

As the tent came apart in his meaty fists, Giric's rage subsided. Only moments after his tirade began, he stood in the center of the destruction with his eyes closed, breathing heavily.

"Bring me some soup," he ordered quietly.

For a moment, no one moved. Not Marsailli, not the midwife, not the few remaining soldiers in the camp. But then Giric opened his eyes and pinned Marsailli with his cold stare. "Bring me some soup," he repeated.

Biting back her fears, she darted for the cauldron hanging over the fire pit. With shaky hands, she ladled soup into a wooden bowl, and then navigated the piles of broken wood, jumbled clothing, and ripped tenting to bring it to him.

He poured the soup down his throat, then tossed aside the bowl.

"Are you still bleeding?" he asked.

She nodded.

"Then get thee from my sight."

Marsailli needed no further encouragement; she quickly backed away. Her bed was gone and she had nowhere to sleep, but she was alive. And for that she was profoundly grateful. She exchanged a look with the midwife, who looked as wide eyed and pale faced as Marsailli felt. The older woman lifted one corner of the blanket around her shoulders, offering a warm retreat, and Marsailli scurried into her embrace.

Giric exchanged hushed words with one of his men, who then saddled a horse and swiftly left the camp. Once he was gone, the Bear settled in front of the fire, staring into the flickering flames with a grim countenance.

Plotting her sister's comeuppance, no doubt.

Marsailli lifted her gaze to the moon hanging like a fat pearl in the night sky. If Caitrina had betrayed him in some way, did that not suggest her sister was nearby . . . and working to free her? She certainly hoped it was so. It would be so much easier to keep the faith if she could believe her sister was staring up at this very same moon, planning a daring rescue.

She and the midwife sidled closer to the fire, remaining out of the Bear's view.

But time was running out. Once her menses ceased to flow, the huge Englishman would have no cause to restrain himself. He would exact his revenge in some truly despicable fashion. The cold look in his eyes said as much.

She scanned the walls of shale that surrounded the camp, trying to spy a path between the loose, uneven piles of rock painted silver by the moonlight. If she knew what direction to head in, she would attempt to reach Caitrina. But she did not—she remembered the climb up from the burn, but not the direction they had traveled to reach it. One dark corner of the woods looked the same as any other. And the previous night, the chilling howl of a wolf had echoed through the glen.

Nay. She was safer here.

For at least one more night.

She leaned her head on the midwife's bony shoulder and closed her eyes. If she was still alive come morning, there would be some difficult choices to make.

Morning dawned with cruel brightness.

Bran splashed cold water on his face and then

headed downstairs to confront Caitrina. But the moment he descended the steps into the great hall, he was accosted by two of Dougal's men. The lads had the weary, travel-stained look of men who had ridden all night long.

"I'm afraid we have disappointing news, Marshal."

He sighed heavily. "You lost him?"

"Aye," said the elder of the two men. "Near the northern border. He entered a deep burn, and we lost his trail."

Bran knew the spot all too well. He could hardly fault them for losing Giric when he'd done the same. Still, frustration gnawed at his belly. Had he not searched the banks of the burn himself and found no sign of the Sassenachs, he'd have called the lads to task.

"Take a short respite," he told them. "When you have eaten your fill, come find me. We'll return to the burn and search again. I know not where, but they must be hiding nearby."

The two men nodded and headed for the kitchen.

He crossed the great hall to the hearth, where Lady Gisele and Lady Caitrina were diligently tending to their sewing.

"Might I have a word?" he asked of Caitrina.

"Now?" Gisele asked sharply. "Lady Caitrina is engaged in a task of some importance. She is making a sleeping cap for the new king."

He took hold of Caitrina's elbow and favored the elder lady with a steely look. "This will take but a moment." Then he guided Caitrina out of her chair and over to a quiet corner of the hall.

"You are concerned about my declaration of love," Caitrina guessed. "But there is no need."

"Of course there is a need," he challenged. "I've misled you."

"Nay," she said. She kept a proper distance, but her gaze embraced him warmly. "You were truthful—about everything—and my expectations were fully met."

"How could they be met if your declaration has not been reciprocated?"

She smiled. "Because you never promised me love. Nor did you demand it."

It was true—he hadn't spoken of love. He hadn't even dared to think of love. Loving Caitrina was a right that belonged to a much finer man than he. But as low-born as he might be, he wasn't the miserable creature she had just described—the sort who debauched virgins without a qualm.

"You deserve better."

She put a hand to her lips and smiled, as if recalling the hot press of a kiss. "I agree, and I'm looking forward to discovering how much better it can be. Tonight?"

"You deserve better than an illicit affair," he said, pointedly. "There will be no tonight."

"Surely you don't mean that."

"I do."

Exasperation warred with disappointment on her face, and exasperation won. She scowled. "This is ridiculous. You are simply being high-handed. How will abstaining now improve my lot?"

"I cannot repair the damage already done," he admitted. Nor, if he was completely honest, would he reverse the sands of time had that power miraculously been given to him. His memories of last night were too dear. "But I can keep you from making an even graver mistake."

"And what mistake is that?"

"Losing your heart to a lie."

Her eyes narrowed. "You are too late. My heart is already engaged."

He shook his head. "You love a man who does not exist."

"Nonsense," she said.

He spoke quickly, knowing she would interrupt him if he gave her the chance. "The crown you took from me is no ordinary jewel. It is the ancient coronet of Kenneth MacAlpin, the last king of the Picts. The MacCurrans—fierce fellows that they are—are descended from his personal guard, known as the Black Warriors, and they were tasked with protecting the crown, which they believe is destined to be worn by the only king who can lead Scotland into a new era."

She stared at him as if he'd lost his mind.

"As men who've sworn a blood oath tend to be, the MacCurrans are thoroughly committed to their cause, and the only way I was able to gain the crown was to exchange it for a hostage."

Her jaw dropped.

"So," he said grimly. Destroying her illusions about him was much harder than he thought it would be. His every instinct told him to stop talking, to fold her into his arms and soothe away the frown on her brow. "I barter innocent lives for artifacts of immeasurable worth. Does that sound like a man you can admire?"

"A hostage? Who did you take hostage?"

"That doesn't matter." He thrust his untrustworthy hands behind him. "You've given your heart under false pretenses. You'd be wise to take it back."

He wanted her to take the lead, to storm off in an angry fit. But she did not. She simply stood there and stared at him with wide, round eyes. As if he were some kind of vermin that had crawled out from beneath a rock. So he did the hardest thing he'd ever done—he turned his back and walked away.

Dougal's two men met him in the close. Still chomping on bread and cheese, they walked with him to the stables. As their horses were saddled, Bran inspected the crofter's oxcart, which still stood in one corner. Three holes had been drilled into the bed of the cart to hold the poles, which had been removed, as per his orders. He crouched to examine the underside of the cart. A small wooden frame had been attached to the bottom, cradling a slab of slate. Suspended several inches below the cart bed, the slate would have provided a simple but effective support for the poles.

He frowned.

The slate was a vivid blue-green—the distinctive color of the crag near the burn at the northern border. If he needed confirmation that his hunch was right, it was staring right at him. Giric was camped somewhere in that pile of rocks. In a cave, perhaps. Or a small hidden corrie.

He stood, suddenly hopeful.

"Gather a dozen men," he told the two who had accompanied him. Giric couldn't have more than three or four men left. "Quickly now. I believe we have a chance to rout this lawless Englishman once and for all."

As they raced for the barracks, Bran glanced toward the manor house.

The steps were empty, but he suspected Caitrina was watching him from a window. She must surely think him a despicable wretch—and deservedly so—but perhaps he could ease her heartache by retrieving Marsailli. With her sister returned to her bosom and Giric's tyranny ended, Caitrina's worries would be far less onerous.

Bran selected his favorite steed, the big gray stallion, and led him out of his stall.

And he would be leaving her something less unworthy to remember him by.

As Bran led a troop of fourteen soldiers out of the manor gate, Caitrina turned away from the window and returned to the writing desk. She truly was a disloyal wretch. The man she loved was riding off to rescue her sister, and here she was, penning a message to the MacCurrans.

It was horribly unfair.

But what choice did she have? If she accepted the basic facts of Bran's story as truth, then keeping the crown from its rightful caretakers was reprehensible. And if she failed to take action, she would be a party to the crime.

She dipped her quill into the inkpot. The challenge

would be returning it without handing over Bran, which she simply wouldn't do. Perhaps she was a naive fool, but the one part of his tale she refused to believe was his heinous hostage taking. He'd had numerous opportunities to show her the ruthless side of his nature, and it had never surfaced. A more honorable and loyal soul would be hard to find. She simply couldn't picture him holding a dirk to someone's throat and demanding the crown.

She penned her message, short and to the point: *The crown is in Clackmannan.*

Waiting for the ink to dry, she stared into the fire in the hearth.

It still felt like betrayal to contact the MacCurrans. Bran would not forgive her easily, no matter how fine her intentions. He'd gone to great lengths to acquire the crown, and great lengths to earn it back from her. He must need it. But for what?

She had no idea.

Yet understanding that was the key to understanding the man himself. He was a good man, undeniably. But without knowledge of his motivations, of what drove him to do the things he did, she was missing a vital piece of the puzzle. Unfortunately, he seemed reluctant to share details of his life in Edinburgh—which left only her imagination to fill in the gaps.

An imagination that, at the moment, preferred to replay all the magical details of their night together. She rolled up her parchment note, tied it with a small white ribbon, and handed it to the young lad waiting patiently by the door. He bowed and left the room.

The queen was napping in her bed, with one of the

ladies seated quietly at her side sewing. Another trio of ladies was seated in front of the hearth, nibbling on candied fruit, sipping mead, and discussing the merits of various small hawks for hunting. Caitrina would have joined them, but she feared the rosy glow of her cheeks and her repeated sighs would draw more attention than she was prepared to handle. She could not stop thinking of her night with Bran.

She had expected to mourn her maidenhood more.

For something she'd spent a lifetime protecting, it had vanished with surprisingly little fanfare. Just a passing soreness. And her body was already craving another dance with excitement—every time she recalled Bran's hands and mouth making merry on her skin, a delicious thrill ran down her spine. Which happened more often than she cared to admit.

Including right now.

Caitrina returned to the window and stared out into the close. Sullen gray clouds had swept in from the west and rain threatened to dampen the daily chores of the villeins.

Of course, Bran was determined not to repeat their tryst.

And if he discovered she had sent for the MacCurrans, she might never feel his hands upon her body again. An unimaginable future—she had never felt more alive than when she was in his arms. Even now, her breasts were budding in hopefulness. Who could have imagined he could coax such joy from her body? That his simple caresses could make her heart leap and her body hum? It would be true shame if she never made love with him again.

Ah, well. Her time was better spent crafting a credible tale to give the MacCurrans as to how she acquired the crown. They would not easily swallow the suggestion that Bran had run off without it. But perhaps they would believe the truth—that she'd robbed the robber.

The young lad with her note rode out of the gate and headed west toward Stirling.

She would rehearse her words well and leave out the part where she identified her thief as the marshal. So long as her tale rang true and the MacCurrans never caught sight of Bran, they would take the crown and depart without their culprit.

All would be well.

Heavy raindrops began to fall, slowly at first and then faster and faster. The villeins below ran for cover. Her fingers trembled slightly, and she wove her hands together to calm them.

It had to be.

They arrived at the deep burn soaked to the skin. The rain had not let up the entire journey, and any glamour Bran had attached to his role as marshal had long disappeared by the time they reached the blue-green crag near the northern border. In Edinburgh, he spent most cold, wet days in a pub, lifting coins from fat merchants who gathered around the fire. He couldn't remember the last time he'd willingly endured the October rains.

Young Robbie rode up alongside him.

"What are you hoping to find?"

Bran pointed to the huge shards of shale looming above them. A low, wet mist had settled across the glen and the higher points of the crag disappeared into the clouds. "A way up into the rocks."

"But we've already examined every inch of the shore," Robbie said, frowning, "and found no sign of a trail."

"We missed something; I'm convinced of it."

The lad nodded, but doubt tugged at his eyebrows. "Then we'll look again."

Bran dismounted and gathered the men around him. Rain had plastered their hair to their faces and droplets dripped steadily from their noses and chins. "Revenge is within our grasp, but it must be claimed with discipline. Leave the horses here and move quietly up the brae. Surprise will be our best ally."

He led them forward over the rocky terrain, showing them how best to travel with stealth—finding the silent, mossy footfalls and avoiding loose slides of shale. The mist worked to their advantage; the slippery rocks did not.

Twice the treacherous terrain brought a soldier to his knees with a loud clatter of stone.

And twice they froze and waited for their foes to race out of the mist with blades held high.

But the blanket of cloud must have contained the noise, because neither fall brought Giric and his men raging down upon them. Bran peered up into the foggy reaches of the crag. Perhaps the huge Englishman had grown so confident of his hiding spot that he no longer posted guards.

At the burn's edge, they again sought signs of passage.

His men spread out along the shore, examining

every turned stone and bent rowan leaf. They scoured the burnside and the base of the rising tower of slate with devotion, as eager to find a clue as Bran was. But as time passed, their enthusiasm slowly eroded. As before, the search met with no success.

Robbie met Bran's gaze with a grim look and a shake of his head.

Bran picked up a stray piece of rose quartz at his feet and whipped it across the swiftly running water. Bloody hell. How could he have been so wrong? Logic told him this was the most likely place for the English to be hiding . . . So where was Giric? The rock bounced off the wall of stone on the other side of the burn and dropped into the foaming water. But it didn't disappear into the depths as Bran had expected. Once the splash receded, he could still see the rock clear as a summer day, its pink shimmer no more than an inch or two below the surface.

He crouched, peering into the dark water as it sluiced through the narrow chasm.

Sure enough, a flat ridge of rock followed the wall of shale just under the surface, wide enough for a horse. If they stayed close to the edge, they could walk around the huge column of shale that hid the rest of the stream from view. As for what lay beyond that? Only discovery would tell.

He surged to his full height.

"Follow me," he said to the men, stepping into the water. As the frigid burn poured into his boots, the memory of being swept downstream assailed him with breath-snatching clarity. But he ruthlessly shoved it aside.

He waded upstream, taking care not to create noisy splashes that might echo off the rocks. His men followed, equally quiet. Just before they reached the stone column, they paused and drew their weapons. A quick glance confirmed that everyone was ready, and then Bran dove around the outcropping and into the open. But he was met with disappointment, not a band of Englishmen—all he found was more rock. And a steep path leading up into the crag.

Bran gritted his teeth and began a slow and careful ascent.

He eyed every boulder and every outcrop above him, looking for sentries. On a clear day, Giric would have had the advantage—it would have been near impossible to approach the crest of the crag without being seen. But the mist limited sight to no more than thirty paces and they were able to climb steadily.

Despite the dampening blanket of fog, it wasn't long before sounds from the camp above reached their ears. The low hum of men talking, the rasp of whetstones on sword edges, and the soft clink of ring mail armor. Bran raised a hand and brought his men to a halt.

He frowned.

The sounds he'd expected; it was the volume that concerned him. Giric should have had no more than half a dozen men left, but this cacophony implied far greater numbers than that.

"Wait here," he said to Robbie.

The young warrior nodded and signaled to the others to take cover.

Bran sheathed his weapon and slipped into the rocks ahead. He needed a higher vantage point to spy upon the camp. As he scaled the wet rocks, a sharp memory returned to him of a similarly misty day twelve years before, when his father had been found and dragged off by Laird MacLean. He'd been only a lad then, but the memory was still vivid. The wails of his mother, the stoic face of his father, the glistening beards of the Mac-Lean warriors, and the bitter ending upon the gallows. He'd vowed then never to return to these miserable moors, and yet here he was.

He grimaced. The amazing part was, he would break any vow to ease Caitrina's burdens.

Pulling himself up the slippery slab of rock, he peered over the edge. A flat, grassy plateau stretched out before him, the bottom of a great bowl in the rocks, with steep walls of shale all around. Tents and groups of men filled up the grassy expanse; a quick count confirmed the presence of at least one hundred soldiers, all intently preparing for battle. Even more concerning, a large group of the men carried unusually long bows, similar in style to those used by the Welsh. Dangerous weapons, they were capable of piercing armor.

Bran slid back down the rock. Giric wasn't planning to run. He was planning to attack the manor. And he was gathering an army to support him.

With his back against the stone slab, Bran grimly considered his options. Dougal's men totaled fifty, and the queen's personal guard added another two dozen to their number. The walls of the manor were solidly built and well maintained, but not intended to repel a lengthy attack. Reinforcements could be drawn from Edinburgh and Stirling if necessary, but it was clear that Giric was anticipating the arrival of even more

men. Additional tents were being pitched and latrines
dug.

Which meant his men on the path were at risk of
discovery.

It was time to move. Returning promptly to the
manor to warn the queen was paramount.

Caitrina was in the chapel attending morning prayer
with the other ladies and most of the queen's court
when the riders arrived at the gate. A young page entered the chapel and reported the news to the courtiers
standing near the door. After that, word spread through
the small room in frenzied whispers, despite glares
from the bishop and his two priests.

"The first Guardian has arrived," Gisele murmured.

Caitrina's heart skipped a beat. "James Stewart?"

The lady of the wardrobe nodded.

Oh, dear. The royal steward's arrival was much
sooner than expected. It was only the eve of Samhain,
and the birth of the new king was not expected for several weeks. The bishop's message must have carried a
note of urgency.

Caitrina waited impatiently for morning prayers to
conclude, then returned to the great hall with as much
haste as decorum would allow. The visitors' horses
were still in the close, being tended by the stable lads—
a dozen fine steeds, including a mighty bay stallion.

The great hall was a hive of activity when she entered, gillies scurrying to and fro with their arms full of
linens or firewood or flagons of wine. The royal steward was seated before the hearth, having his boots
cleaned.

"If Marshal Finlay is away to Oban," the steward was saying in a booming voice, "then who is seeing to the manor affairs in his absence?"

Caitrina glanced at the faces gathered around him. Dougal. The queen's seneschal, Roger de Capelin. The captain of the queen's guard.

"Marshal Gordon," replied Dougal.

James Stewart frowned. "Archibald Gordon? Of Strathbogie?"

It was Dougal's turn to frown. "Nay, Giles Gordon of Feldrinny."

The direction of the conversation was concerning. In no time, the man would be comparing notes on various branches of the Gordon clan and wondering where Bran fit in.

"I don't recall appointing a Gordon as marshal of Feldrinny," Stewart said, as a gillie carved a layer of mud from the bottom of his boot.

Caitrina took a deep breath and crossed the room. She curtsied to the royal steward. "Good day, Lord Steward."

Stewart leapt to his feet and offered her a deep bow. "Lady Caitrina. A pleasure to see you looking so well."

"Thank you," she responded. "I could not help but overhear your query regarding Marshal Gordon. I confess, I had some concerns about the man in the beginning, but he's done quite well by us. Is that not so, Constable?"

Dougal nodded. "He's gone to great lengths to ensure the queen's safety and comfort."

Caitrina smiled at the royal steward. "I don't recall which family seat the marshal said he hailed from—I read his credentials, but I likely reviewed them as I review most official documents." She gave a short laugh. "Swiftly."

"So you saw his patents?"

"Indeed," she said. "And I am sure he'll happily regale you with his impressive lineage when he returns. He is out hunting that deplorable band of Englishmen who slayed several of our guards."

Stewart nodded. "Thank you for your insights, Lady Caitrina. Please inform the queen that I shall request an audience once I have properly freshened from my journey."

Caitrina curtsied again. "Her Grace will be most pleased to see you again, Lord Steward."

She left the men to their discussion. Wrapping her brat tightly about her shoulders, she traded the warmth of the great hall for the chill of a rainy October day. Bran must be warned about the royal steward's presence. He'd made arrangements to have letters patent drawn up, but had there been enough time to receive them?

She frowned.

It was impossible to know. But alerting him to the inquisition he was likely to face when he stepped inside was a necessity. The only question was, how? She could hardly stand here in the close and wait on his return. Such an act would raise all sorts of eyebrows.

Slowly pivoting, she eyed what little activity there was in the courtyard. One sodden stable lad shoveling mucked straw into a cart, a villein rolling a barrel toward the kitchen door, several stalwart soldiers braving the wet weather with impassive resolve. As her gaze settled on the group of soldiers huddled near the steps leading to a wall, she smiled.

What she needed was an ally.

And she knew just who to tap. Someone who, to her mind, still owed her a debt.

Halfway to Clackmannan, Bran and his men were met by a solitary rider cantering hard and fast, despite the steady downpour. Thanks to the heavy mist, he was nearly upon them before they could put the bearded face to a name. Young Jamie. He eyed Bran's party with a frown.

"No English?"

"Nay."

The young soldier shifted in his saddle. "We thought for sure you'd roust him. All the men were eager to be a party to your venture."

Disappointment was a bitter pang in Bran's chest. "What brings you to my side?"

The young warrior stiffened at the sharp tone of Bran's query. "Lady Caitrina insisted that I bring you this message." He pulled a small rolled parchment from the folds of his brat and offered it.

Bran took the parchment.

A message so urgent that it needed a rider could not be good. He untied the delicate ribbon, unrolled the message, and read it quickly. Raindrops smudged the ink even as he absorbed the significance of Caitrina's words. The royal steward had arrived, and he would not be an easy man to gull. He knew almost as much about the Book of Arms as the marischal and he would likely question the heredity of Giles Gordon. Without his forged papers—which had not yet been delivered and could not be expected until after the feast of Samhain—he would need to be quite creative if he wanted to divert the steward's questions.

The other option, of course, was to run.

Bran glanced at the wet, weary faces of the men who'd followed him to the burn. They looked to him for leadership and hope and the promise of justice for their dead comrades. To them, he truly *was* Marshal Gordon, skilled warrior and bastion of lawful right. When he had descended the slate crag path where they had patiently awaited his return and delivered the news of the huge numbers of Englishmen preparing to attack their home, these men had briefly lost hope. It had been *his* words that shored up their faith. It had been *his* oath to see justice served that had erased the bleak looks and rekindled the fires of passion.

If he ran now, it would be a cruel betrayal.

And he would be leaving Caitrina to face Giric's attack alone.

Nay. Running was not an option.

Did he not pride himself on his ability to fool almost anyone? Well, here was his chance to make good on his boasts. If he could convince the royal steward that he was indeed Marshal Gordon—without the support of official letters of patent—he would truly be a charlatan of legend.

Eventually, he would be unmasked—all it would take was the return of Marshal Finlay—but every additional day he spent in Caitrina's company would be worth the risk. And even one more warrior might turn the tide in the battle against Giric.

He tucked the parchment away and twisted in his saddle to face his men.

"The lord steward has joined the queen at Clackmannan," he told them. "Let us ride swiftly to warn them of the English attack and add weight to the manor defenses."

They spurred their mounts and cantered toward the manor, making good time. They arrived at the gates before sunset. As he dismounted in the close, he sent a lad for Lady Caitrina. "Please ask the lady if she would spare me a moment," he told him.

She appeared at the top of the steps only moments later, a worried frown upon her delicate brow. "Did you not receive my message, Marshal?"

"I did," he acknowledged.

Descending the steps, she joined him in the close. "Then I'm at a loss," she admitted.

Although his arms itched with a fierce desire to gather her near, Bran did the proper thing and merely smiled. "Thanks to your message, I am fully prepared to update the royal steward," he said.

Her gaze met his, her eyes suddenly hopeful. "Is the Englishman defeated?"

"Nay," Bran said. "He has gathered additional soldiers, and we found ourselves outnumbered." Knowing the question that must be burning in her thoughts, he added, "It appears he still has several ladies in his camp. We must do what we can to ensure they are not caught in the middle of our conflict."

"Do you have a plan?"

He nodded. "I do, and I promise that as it becomes more firm, I will share the details. You have my word that I will do everything in my power to keep the queen safe."

As one of the stable lads led his horse away, she asked quietly, "What do you intend to tell the royal steward?"

"I will reassure him of my qualifications."

Her eyes darkened with worry. "He has already inquired about your credentials."

"Well," said Bran, smiling faintly, "he has proven himself a very discerning fellow. We would expect that from a man so close to the queen, would we not?" He tucked his gloves into his belt. "I shall find dry clothes and then meet him in the great hall."

She nodded slowly. "As you wish."

He offered her his arm. "Shall we trade this dreich for the warmth of the hearth?"

She laid her hand on his damp sleeve.

"Aye, lead on."

Chapter 10

There was a large gathering of folk in the great hall when Caitrina descended the stairs for the evening meal. Unlike the queen, who had spent the vast majority of her time confined to her bed, the royal steward was eager to sample all of the food and entertainment the custodians of Clackmannan were capable of preparing. The high table was covered in an expanse of white linen and every chair had been assigned. With the presence of additional nobles, Caitrina, being untitled, found herself seated at one of the lower tables, sharing her meal with a handful of senior villagers and their ladies. She had just taken her seat opposite the reeve's wife when Bran entered.

The sight of him stole her breath away.

His dark gold hair, loosely flowing down his back, shimmered in the candlelight—a perfect foil for his strong chin and long nose. With a crimson doublet laced over his cream lèine and a pair of black trews covering his legs, he looked every bit the part of a nobleman. Few men in the hall could compete with his bonnie appearance, including the resplendent royal steward, who wore forest green trimmed with beaver.

Caitrina bit her lip as Bran audaciously stepped to the high table, gave a short bow, and introduced himself to the steward.

"Giles Gordon, my lord." As the royal steward turned to him with a frown, he added, "We met once in Edinburgh, several years ago. I'm not certain you will remember."

The royal steward's eyes narrowed and he peered at Bran closely through the smoky haze of the room. "I don't recall," he said. "Perhaps you would be so good as to refresh my memory?"

Bran smiled. "Of course. It was the Yule after Queen Margaret's passing. A quiet affair in the great hall. My uncle, Sir Thomas de Gordon, introduced us."

Stewart frowned. "I remember the evening and my conversation with Sir Thomas, but I confess I do not recall you, sir."

Bran shrugged. "You may recall his comment upon my introduction. I believe he called me 'a blight upon the Gordon name.'"

Stewart's eyes widened. Then he laughed. "I do recall that comment. Sir Thomas has always lacked a measure of tact. He'd taken issue with your reluctance to take a wife, as I recall. Have you since remedied that?"

Bran shook his head. "Regretfully, I am still unwed."

Stewart patted him on the back and ushered him toward a chair. "That's a situation that swiftly must be set aright. Are there no suitable ladies in Feldrinny?"

"An estate owned by monks suffers a dearth of fine feminine company, I'm afraid," Bran said, taking the seat next to Lady Martine with a smile.

As the tables settled into the meal, Caitrina struggled to keep her gaze on her companions. Even though their histories were intriguing and their travels far-reaching, her attention kept drifting to the high table, where Bran was engaged in avid conversation with Martine. Again, he proved quite the raconteur. His stories kept the table amused for several hours, and his compliments kept Lady Martine in an almost constant state of pink-cheeked blush.

Jealousy knotted Caitrina's belly.

She had never felt such an intense desire to trade places with another woman. But, at that moment, she would have given every jewel she possessed to be seated next to Bran, basking in the warmth of his charming smiles.

How very foolish. She knew he was a fraud—that every word leaving his glib tongue was likely a lie— but that didn't tame the burning want in her gut. Or silence the fierce whispers in her mind that claimed, *He's mine*.

"Have you any children, Lady Caitrina?" her dinner companion asked.

She glanced at him. Sir Murdoch of Inverary. A handsome enough fellow, for an older man. Probably a popular courtier, in his day. If his stories were true, he'd once been captain of King Alexander's guard. "Nay," she said. "I'm not yet wed."

"I have three daughters," he said. "The eldest is eight."

"How lovely," she said, peering around his large shoulders for a glimpse of Bran.

When the meal was finally ended, after a raucous round of toasts to the queen, Caitrina climbed the stairs to her rooms, weary and exhausted. The men had remained behind, still quaffing copious amounts of ale and regaling one another with tales of their conquests, both on and off the battlefield.

Having miraculously passed the royal steward's identity test, Bran was welcomed into the midst of the courtiers with open arms. How he'd come up with that tale of Sir Thomas, she had no clue. Nor did it matter. Apparently, being called "a blight upon the family name" was an endearing feature.

Caitrina stopped by the drapery-hung platform bed to wish the queen a good night, then crossed to her pallet and accepted the help of her maid in exchanging her gown for a night rail.

She had worried for naught, it would seem. Bran was a consummate liar.

She doused her candle and lay down on her pallet, grimacing. What else had the man lied about? His feelings for her, perchance? If he was capable of pulling the wool over the royal steward's eyes, he was surely capable of gulling a simple lass from the Highlands. No one at the high table had doubted his identity, not for a moment.

Lying there in the dark, listening to the soft snores of the other ladies, Caitrina slowly became enraged. She'd given her maidenhood to a silver-tongued bounder—to a man who had just spent the entire night complimenting another woman, never once looking her way.

Did he think so little of her that his attentions could be so easily redirected? She had thought him a better man than that.

Caitrina tossed and turned, unable to sleep. Finally, she threw back the covers and swung her feet to the floor. There was only one way to quiet her turbulent thoughts—she needed to speak with Bran.

Slipping her toes into her silk slippers, she rose from the bed and gathered her brat. Once again, she excused herself to the guards at the door with a tale of visiting the garderobe and scurried down the hall.

There was a light under Bran's door, so she gently knocked and waited. Moments later, the door swung open and he stood before her bare chested and clad only in his braies. She opened her mouth to explain her presence, but he simply yanked her into the room and closed the door. Pressing her back against the thick wooden planks of the portal, he took her head in both hands and proceeded to kiss her as if he'd been imagining this kiss all night.

Caitrina's indignation melted away under the heat of the embrace.

With his lips on hers, his tongue sweeping the inside of her mouth in a daring dance of desire and his hands caressing her curves with light but loving touches, Caitrina lost all sense of time. She found herself hungrily returning every kiss and wanting more. Had he not broken off the embrace and stepped back, she might well have let him take her right there against the door.

He scowled at her. "Who was that large man you were seated next to at dinner?"

Caitrina stared. "Sir Murdoch?"

"Is that his name? Was he truly as entertaining as you made him out to be?"

She blinked. "What?"

"You laughed at everything he said."

Caitrina could barely remember anything the man had said. "He's twice my age," she said, frowning. "And happily wed to a Frenchwoman."

His scowl faded. "Good. I've never been envious of another man, and frankly I do not enjoy the taste."

"You were jealous," she said, on a breathless note of surprise. "But what of Lady Martine?"

"Who?"

She smiled. "The blond woman who sat next to you at dinner."

"Ah," he said. "The woman whose passion is her garden. I find the easiest way to make conversation is to make simple queries of the other person and then let them speak. My dinner companion grows white roses in honor of her dearly departed mother."

"You did more than listen," she said. "You had your entire table laughing at your stories."

Bran's gaze sharpened. "You were as jealous as I."

"More so," she confessed.

He closed the gap between them and feathered kisses along the line of her jaw. "Impossible."

Caitrina's eyes closed and her head rolled back to give him access to the tender flesh of her neck. Showers of delight sprang up in the wake of each delicate kiss, but she needed more. More warmth, more strength, more of Bran. The smooth expanse of his chest was an invitation she could not ignore and her hands went awandering. Under her fingertips, the texture of his skin was like hot silk, drawn thinly over the powerful musculature of his frame. So wonderfully different from her own body.

The hard curves of his chest. The waves of muscle that ran down the middle of his belly.

Bran grabbed her hands. "Lass," he whispered hoarsely in her ear, "I have spent the past few hours imagining every way in which I could make love to your sweet body. I am like a fully drawn bow, ready to send my arrows flying at the slightest twitch of a finger. As much as I enjoy your gentle exploration, I fear I am not man enough to endure it."

She pouted. "You cannot expect me to simply stand here and take your kisses."

A low chuckle vibrated through his chest. "Nay. I welcome your full participation."

"Then what am I to do?"

"Whatever your heart desires. I would only beg you to avoid—for a short time—the area above my knees and below my belt."

Caitrina chewed her lip. Some of his most intriguing terrain lay in the area he had just declared forbidden. "Then let us be fair. For as long as you wish me to abstain from touching you below the waist, you must also abstain from touching me in the same region."

He frowned. "But that will reduce your pleasure."

"I refuse to accept that. The game shall be to see who can pleasure the other more without touching the most private parts." With that, she bent her head and kissed his right nipple, using her tongue to play with the tiny bud.

He sucked in a sharp breath.

"Dear lord."

She released his flesh, reluctantly. "Oh, and I must return to my room within the hour—else the queen's guards will surely think me lost."

Uttering a low growl, he scooped her up and carried her to the bed. He dropped her unceremoniously onto the mattress and then leapt upon her. "There's no time to waste, then, is there?"

He untied the satin laces of her night rail and tugged the linen down, baring her breasts. For a moment, he did nothing but stare, and Caitrina frowned.

"Is there something wrong?"

A slow smile spread across his face. "Far from it, lass. You have beautiful breasts. Just large enough to fill my hand, with pale pink nipples that tempt me to taste."

"And yet you do not."

A truth that he swiftly remedied. He bent his head and captured one trembling peak in his hot, wet mouth and Caitrina gave up a hitched but deeply satisfied sigh. Sweet Jesu. The sensations he stirred within her were incomparable. She'd always known her breasts were sensitive, but this sweet unbearable attack rocked her to the core. No wonder the priests associated such moments with sin—anything that felt so good had to be sinful.

She closed her eyes and let the ripples of pleasure roll through her body, savoring the delicious tingle between her thighs and the slow build of tension in her belly. It wasn't just the way he suckled her breast that stirred her—although that was masterful—it was the soft, glowing warmth that stole over her as she pictured him in her thoughts. He and he alone evoked such tender emotions, such deep desires. She had the strangest urge to grab his hand and run away to some remote bothy and make love until they were finally, completely, utterly sated.

He gently nibbled on her nipple, and she bit her lip to restrain a squeal.

Right now, it was impossible to imagine ever being sated. Every part of her body was burning, and she wanted him so badly that there were stars dancing before her eyes. Going mad with need actually seemed within the realm of possibility. She lifted her hips, trying to press the ache in her nether regions into submission.

But Bran gave her no satisfaction—he shifted his body to one side.

"Do you already forget the rules?" he asked, hoarsely, his hot breath soft upon her breast. "To the game that you created?"

Caitrina groaned. She *had* forgotten. By god, he wiped all reason from her thoughts. What had she been thinking to set such terms? She thrashed her head from side to side. Such *unbearable* terms? And Bran seemed determined to make her pay. The only way he would set aside this foolish endeavor would be for her to drive him as mad with desire as she was.

"This game is very one-sided," she said.

"How so?" His tongue drew a circle around her nipple.

She squirmed with need. "With you atop me, there's little opportunity for me to play."

He buried his face between her breasts, drawing in a deep breath. "You have another position in mind?"

She pushed at his large shoulders. "Aye. You on your back, me on top."

He lifted his head and looked at her. "Truly?"

"Aye."

"But the rules are no touching below the waist," he reminded her.

"I'm well aware," she said archly. "Roll."

Obligingly, he rolled onto his back, a faint smile on his handsome lips. "How shall you proceed, lass?"

In truth, she had no idea. She was unschooled as a seductress. But wiping that smug look from his face was a fierce ambition. His smile suggested *he alone* knew how to win the game, that only he was capable of taunting and teasing and driving his partner wild. Caitrina rose to her knees on the bed, accidentally trapping the hem of her night rail, which pulled the gauzy linen taut against her skin.

His gaze dropped to the newly exposed skin at her neckline, his eyes dark.

Ahh.

He admired her form. Perhaps she should start there. With a series of slow, sensual tugs on the shift, she removed her night rail and tossed it aside. His eyes narrowed, implying an element of self-discipline belied by the flare of his nostrils and the clenched fists at his side.

He wanted to grab her.

But he did not, so she considered her next move. Her long braid had flipped over her shoulder as she removed her night rail, and she lifted it, prepared to toss it back. Again, his gaze closely followed her fingers and, again, she took his interest as a sign. He was curious about what she would do with her hair. What did he think was possible?

She took the wispy end and drew it up the skin of his arm to his chest. Gooseflesh rose in its trail, and she smiled. He thrilled to touch as easily as she did. How wonderful. Leaning over him, she swept her hair over his upper body, along the strong lines of his chin, down his patrician nose, and over his sinfully shaped lips. Her reward was a low rumble of protest in his chest, and she grinned.

She pressed a hot kiss to his lips, as much for her own satisfaction as for his. Thus far, the game was only mildly amusing.

Sitting back on her heels, she studied him. He had closed his eyes, waiting for more. But more what? How does a lass go about seducing a man? What sensations were likely to make him so crazed with desire that he would toss aside her foolishly constructed rules and bed her right and proper?

His eyes drifted open again.

"Do you cede?" he asked.

"Nay," she said quickly. She took her bottom lip into her mouth. Kisses were an option—she could kiss every inch of his skin above his waist—but she was not convinced that would be enough to make him break the rules.

She let her bottom lip go.

His nostrils flared again.

Something about that little movement enticed him. But what? What did he find so fascinating about her lip? She chewed it again, and released it—to similar effect. Was he imagining chewing her lip himself? If so, could she use his imagination against him? Caitrina ran a light finger down her chest to her belly button. His eyes followed the trail of her fingers with avid interest, and she smiled.

Well. This could be quite intriguing.

Her own hand was not as satisfying on her skin as his was, but it evoked sensations nonetheless. Pleasurable sensations that were heightened by the dark glow in his eyes. She took the tip of her braid and traced slow circles on her belly, up her chest, and across her shoulders. Now the gooseflesh was haunting *her*.

His eyes became hotter and a flush rose on his cheeks.

Caitrina grew more daring, trailing the braid over one breast, down the valley, and circling the nipple of the other. As the hairs drifted over the budded tip, a short gasp broke from her lips. Sweet, sweet Jesu. It was all too easy to imagine his lips on her breasts, his fingers doing the delicate dance of the hairs. A hot wetness blossomed between her legs.

Surprisingly, this romp was having a powerful impact—not only did the sight of his obvious enthrallment excite her, but her imagination and the touch of her own hand doubled her pleasure. Caitrina abandoned the braid and placed her fingers directly on the plump flesh of her breast.

Her eyes closed.

She had touched her breasts before, even teased them to a point of gentle awareness. But this was new. Somehow, the knowledge that he was watching her added volumes to her sensitivity, and her skin reacted to her touch almost as eagerly as if he'd been caressing her breast himself. She rolled her nipple between her thumb and forefinger, moaning at the sharp flood of sensations that spun out in all directions.

A low, feral growl escaped Bran's throat.

Caitrina opened her eyes just in time to see him pounce. He leapt upon her with unrestrained ardor, all smugness vanished from his face. His hands were everywhere—not just above her waist—and it was clear that she was the victor of their little game. Not that she gave her win any thought. She was lost in a dizzying cloud of passion—every inch of her alive in ways she'd never been before.

Her world was spinning, her power immense, even as she trembled with weakness.

Armed with a new boldness, she took his hand and guided his strokes to the spots that gave her the most pleasure. Places she had never dared to suggest he go. It felt so good to have his hands cupping her breasts and rubbing the eager flesh between her thighs.

Together, they teased each other to the point of no return. When Bran finally slid two fingers inside her, Caitrina was dripping wet and she nearly found release.

"Take me," she urged, her breath rasping.

Bran shed his braies in an instant, parted her thighs, and thrust into her with a shudder that racked his entire body. "Lord, lass," he said hoarsely. "I thought you'd never ask."

Then he proceeded to take her so deeply and so thoroughly that she thrashed against the sheets and nearly sobbed with the sweet harmony of their movements. When she came, it wasn't a quick flash of ecstasy—it was a rolling storm of release that went on and on until she lay beneath him so spent that she could not move a muscle.

He collapsed on the bed next to her and rolled onto his back.

"The guards will be wondering where you are."

"I care not," she said honestly.

He turned his head and smiled. "You say that now, but you will likely not feel the same come morn." He leapt off the bed, gathered up the cloth in the water basin by the hearth, and returned to gently cleanse her private parts.

"I've never met a lass quite like you," he said.

"Is that a bad thing?" she asked, with a frown.

"Nay," he said with a laugh. He located her night rail in the jumble of his bedding and helped her don it. "Quite the opposite. I think I may be falling in love with you."

Caitrina stiffened, her arms half into her nightgown. "Don't say that."

"Why not?" He shrugged. "'Tis the truth."

She tugged the linen down over her thighs and rolled off the bed. Staring at him reclined upon the mattress with his head pillowed beneath his arm, she scowled. "You are determined to ruin this wonderful night."

His eyebrows rose. "Why does my declaration of love constitute ruin? You uttered the same words to me not a sennight ago."

"But *my* declaration carried no expectations."

"And mine does?"

"It's common knowledge that men do not speak of love unless they mean to make a claim."

"Is it?"

"You know perfectly well that it is," she said hotly. How dare he steal the beauty of this encounter with his brash words. "But we can never be together."

"Aye," he admitted quietly. "I know."

His agreement deflated her anger. "Then why would you echo my sentiments? Where could it possibly lead?"

"Must it lead somewhere?" He sat up and patted the mattress at his side. "I see no shame in admitting that I care for you. Indeed, the shame would be in letting our dalliance end without telling you the lay of my heart."

Caitrina did not join him on the bed. It was far too tempting. If she went to him, she might never leave. "But embracing the totality of our affections will only cause greater pain when the moment arrives that parts us."

He shrugged. "The pain of parting is unavoidable. It will be the memories we make that will sustain us in the future. Why not make them the fullest possible?"

The moments beyond their parting suddenly loomed with a heretofore unimaginable reality. "What awaits you in Edinburgh? You've previously suggested pressing commitments. Do they involve a woman?"

He vaulted from the bed and padded across the cold floor to her side. Gathering the edges of her brat, he wrapped her snugly in the wool. "No woman waits on my return. Not as you imagine, in any case. A street thug threatens many of my companions, and it was my intent to use the crown to buy the loyalty of the castle guards and have him driven off or imprisoned."

Caitrina's heart sank.

This was the moment to confess what she'd done— to explain that she had sent for the MacCurrans. But the words wouldn't form. If she spoke, her confession would dim that warm look in his eyes, perhaps permanently. "A noble goal," she said, her tongue dry as old leather.

"I do what I must," he said. "We're born to a certain place in life, but our choices are thereafter our own."

They were indeed. And the choice Caitrina had made might well change his memories of her for eternity. "We all do what we must," she said. "And I must return to my room."

He bent and kissed her lips—a tender kiss that sent a ripple of warmth to her toes. "Sweet dreams, lass."

She breathed deep of his spicy, masculine scent, then smiled tremulously, spun on her heels, and dashed from the room. He would never forgive her.

Bran posted sentries to the north and west of the manor, armed with warning fires. If Giric decided to attack, they would need at least an hour of preparation to shut the gate and bolster their defenses.

He'd given an accounting of what he'd discovered to Dougal and the royal steward the night before, but the outcome had not been satisfying. Stewart was convinced that Giric was nothing more than an opportunistic bandit—he'd dismissed the possibility that King Edward supported Giric's efforts with an adamant shake of his head—and there had been no way to rattle his certainty without revealing Caitrina's role in the plot.

Bran stared at the western forest, scanning the trees for any movement.

Stewart had promised to send to Edinburgh for additional men, but there'd been no urgency in his words. It would be four days at best before he saw support from the castle—and possibly longer. The royal steward believed the walls of Clàckmannan were highly defensible. Bran disagreed. While it was true that the older man had more experience defending a keep than Bran did, he'd not seen the group of men gathering to the north, or the longbows they wielded. Bran had described the weapons and explained how they worked, but neither Stewart nor Dougal had put much stock in their value. They were convinced that the effort required to draw a bow of such length would exceed the abilities of most men. They were wrong. They'd never seen a Welsh bow in action, but he had. One of the men in his father's band of brigands had been a Welshman.

Bran had underestimated Giric once before; he wasn't about to do it again.

There had to be a way to claim a victory, even against a company of longbows.

The sharp rap of boot heels on the stone parapets behind him turned his head. Dougal joined him at the wall.

"Did you not say the English were hiding to the north?"

Bran nodded. "But the trees to the west allow a closer approach. It's wise to keep a watch in all directions."

"The fall harvest is only recently completed, and an

inventory of the stores suggests we can survive a lengthy siege."

Bran glanced at him. "As long as the wall remains unbreached."

"We have the advantage," Dougal insisted.

"We also have a village to protect."

The older man sighed. "The queen must be our priority, if there is an attack."

"You doubt Giric's intent?" Bran asked. "Even after witnessing the atrocities enacted against your guards, without provocation?"

"The steward is right," Dougal said. "He is a simple brigand."

"No simple brigand would gather troops."

Dougal shook his head, his red beard swaying. "I think you see fire where there is only smoke. Any large-scale attack by the English would be seen as an act of war. King Edward has long been an ally of the Scots. Why would he suddenly seek to sour relations with his neighbor to the north?"

"King Edward once hoped that his nephew would sit upon the Scottish throne," Bran reminded him dryly. "But his sister and all of her issue are dead. The new Scottish monarch will either be half French or half Norse. Edward's influence will be limited. That's reason enough for him to take a hand."

Dougal was silent.

Bran was no royal courtier gifted with inside knowledge of Scottish politics, but he had spent many an hour in an Edinburgh tap house debating the actions of those who were his betters. "The Welsh were independent once, too. When the Prince of Wales refused to swear his allegiance, King Edward rode in with his armies and conquered him. He has imprisoned all claimants to the Welsh throne. Why do you believe he would treat Scotland any differently?"

"The Welsh were rebellious heathens," Dougal scoffed. "Their prince was never truly recognized by the English monarchy."

Bran snorted. "Those are Stewart's words."

"The man was an adviser to King Alexander. Why would we not have faith in his knowledge of King Edward?"

"I've never met King Edward," Bran acknowledged. "But I've met my fill of greedy men, and I can tell you this—they don't cease until they own it all."

"How can you be certain this band of English brigands is under orders from Edward?"

"I can't." Not openly. "But he's shown remarkable dedication for a simple bandit. In my experience, a man in search of easy coin preys on the weakest target. Waylaying a lone merchant, perchance, or robbing a farmer as he returns from the market. He does not attack soldiers."

Dougal tossed him a wry smile. "Perhaps he's learned his lesson."

Movement in the trees sharpened Bran's gaze. An eagle-eyed watchman on the wall trumpeted the alarm an instant later as a long line of men on horseback broke from the trees, each carrying a distinctive black targe. At least two dozen men were visible, and he glimpsed more in the shadowy wood behind them.

Dougal stiffened. "Those look like Scots."

Three large men rode at the center of the line—all

broad shouldered, brown haired, and grim faced. Bran recognized them immediately. Niall, Aiden, and Wulf MacCurran. He drew in a deep breath and slowly released it.

"They are," he told Dougal.

Then he spun on his heel and descended the steps to the close. The time had clearly come to pay the piper.

Chapter 11

When the trumpet sounded, Caitrina ran to the window. Upon confirming that all eyes were facing westward, she begged her leave of the queen and scurried downstairs. The arrival could be another Guardian, but most likely it was the MacCurrans.

They would assuredly demand a meeting with her, and Bran would need to remain out of sight while they collected the crown. Unfortunately, she had yet to enroll him in her plan. She stood on the steps and scanned the faces in the close. Explaining her decision would be a challenge—one that would likely bring an abrupt end to their affair. But if she hoped to save his life, it was a conversation that must be had.

She halted a passing soldier. "Where is Marshal Gordon?"

He pointed to the stables.

Caitrina dried her damp palms on her woolen skirts, straightened her shoulders, and crossed the close to the open arch of the stables. Postponing the discussion would not make it any easier to endure.

Bran was cinching the saddle on his big gray stallion, head bent to the task, his dark blond hair hiding his face.

"What are you doing?" she asked him quietly.

He looked up. His gaze softened as he absorbed the expression on her face—no doubt her worry was evident in every crease and line. "What I must."

"Nay," she said. "They've come for the crown, not for you. Stay in the shadows until they're gone and all will be well."

A heavy frown settled on his brow. "You know it is the MacCurrans who approach?"

Guilt was a cold stone in her belly. "Aye. 'Twas I who sent for them."

"You?"

She nodded, wringing her hands. "I could not continue to keep the crown, not once I knew its importance. My deepest apologies, but it rightfully belongs to the MacCurrans and I must see it returned."

He took a step back. "You sent them a message? When?"

"Two days ago."

Bran stared at her for a long moment. Then he suddenly turned and ordered the other soldiers and stable lads, "Out. All of you."

His voice was cold and hard, quite unlike the Bran she knew so well. Her gaze traced the stiff lines of his shoulders and the angry cant of his head. He felt betrayed. Quite understandable.

She waited until they were alone, and then said

softly, "I will tell them the thief is long gone. That he hid the crown in the stables and I found it. They need never know you are here."

He spun slowly to face her. "You kept this from me."

Caitrina swallowed tightly and nodded.

"Even as we made love."

A point well taken. Intimacy at such a moment implied a certain level of trust—trust she had abused. "I did not know how to tell you. The crown is important to you. I know that."

He shook his head. "You know nothing."

"You need coin to buy the loyalty of the castle guards, not the crown. I can help with that."

"That may be true," he said quietly. "But the point is that you did not trust me with your concerns. You did not believe that a thief could be party to such a decision, and you sent a message in secret. That tells me far more about your true opinion than you likely intended."

"Nay," she disputed. "You judge my opinion unfairly. I do trust you. I swear it."

"It hardly matters now, does it? What's done is done."

"The crown belongs to the MacCurrans."

He nodded. "And it shall be returned to them. Fetch it, please."

She frowned. Perhaps she hadn't been clear. "You cannot be present when I hand it over. They will surely recognize you as the thief."

"Fetch it," he repeated.

Caitrina crossed her arms over her chest. "You're being difficult. I made the arrangements, and I will be the one to relinquish the crown. You'll remain inside. If you'll not agree, then I'll not fetch the crown."

"You say that you trust me," he said. "And yet your actions defy your words."

His comment was a stab to her chest. It was true, at least in part. She wanted to trust him, but she was leery of what he would do if she gave him the crown. There was a chance he would take the crown and run, but she suspected the more likely scenario was that he would do the foolishly honorable thing and take the crown to the MacCurrans. So, nay, she did not trust him. Not to follow her plan to hand over the crown and lie about the thief.

But his words made her sound so cold and cruel. So unfaithful.

"All right," she said. "I will get the crown."

"Be quick," he urged. "The MacCurrans are not known for their patience."

She returned to her room and retrieved a wooden box from the bottom of her clothing chest. It was one of several boxes designed to hold satin shoes without crushing them. Inside the box was a velvet bag, and inside the bag lay the silver crown. She did not open it, or explain to the other ladies what she was retrieving. She simply scurried from the room and returned to the stables.

"Here," she said, thrusting the velvet bag into Bran's hands. "Now we shall see what my trust begets."

Taking the crown, he tucked it into a leather satchel on his mount's saddle. "Some say trust is a weakness."

When he turned to face her, she retorted, "They say the same about love."

He smiled. "Aye, so they do."

Untying the stallion from the iron ring in his stall, Bran led the huge gray beast into the close. "I need you to understand that what I do now I do because my soul demands it. Wounding you in any way is not my aim."

Caitrina swallowed a lump in her throat.

If he thought to reassure her, he failed. There was still a chance that he would run, and she prayed that would be his choice. Better to lose him to the dark shadows of the forest than to watch him struck down by the MacCurrans before her very eyes. But his next words proved that hope false.

"Mount up," he ordered the six soldiers around him. "But leave your weapons sheathed. The MacCurrans are renowned for their battle prowess—let us not antagonize them."

Within minutes, all were ahorse. The gates were opened and Bran led the way out of the manor. Not once, as he rode through the village and across the field, did he glance back at her. Shoulders straight, head high, he approached the band of fierce, dark warriors that awaited him.

Bran kept his gaze locked on the face of Aiden MacCurran, the clan chief. It was better to avoid a chance meeting of eyes with Wulf. He felt the stare of the largest MacCurran drill into him like a hot blade in his chest.

He and Wulf had never seen eye to eye, especially where Wulf's lovely wife was concerned. Morag had befriended Bran several months earlier in Edinburgh, much to Wulf's chagrin. And she had invited Bran to visit her at Dunstoras—an invitation that had led to the theft of the crown. Wulf would surely carve Bran's heart out, given the chance.

Not that Bran intended to give him the chance.

He halted his men one hundred paces from the Black Warriors, instructed them to wait for him, and then rode the rest of the way alone. "I propose a bargain," he said firmly to the clan chief.

"Give us what we came for and we'll let your men live," Aiden said. "That's the only bargain we're prepared to make."

Although the crown was burning against his left thigh, Bran stared straight ahead. "Help me foil a plot against the queen and the prize is yours."

Aiden's eyes narrowed. "What game do you play now, MacLean?"

"No game. The queen is truly in jeopardy. The English are plotting an attack on Clackmannan as we speak." He opened the satchel, drew out the velvet bag, and offered it to Aiden. "You can leave now with the crown." Bran met the chief's gaze firmly and honestly. "But if you do, there is a good chance that the queen and her bairn will live the rest of their days as prisoners of King Edward."

Aiden took the bag, peered inside, and then handed it to his brother Niall. "You are a liar and a thief. No matter how intriguing your tale, I give it no credence." He tugged on his reins and turned his horse northward. "One word to any soul about this crown or where you found it, and you'll die a very painful death."

"I may be a thief and a liar," Bran said sharply, "but I also risked my life to save your kin." He twisted in his saddle and faced Wulf squarely. "You might well have swung upon the gibbet were it not for me. When you ran afoul of King Alexander's traitorous brother this past spring and were sentenced to hang, 'twas I who came up with the plan to save you. I who prepared the disguise for Morag and coached her to enter the castle undetected. Whether you choose to acknowledge it or no, 'twas my efforts that saw you freed from Edinburgh Castle. In return, I only ask that you protect the queen—the very same queen whose ring you wear about your neck."

Wulf said nothing, just stared at him. Hard.

Aiden continued to ride away, his silent Highlander warriors following in his trail, and Bran grew desperate. "Were the Black Warriors not once the personal guard of Kenneth MacAlpin? Is it not in your blood to protect the kings of Scotland?"

At the name Kenneth MacAlpin, the warriors hammered their targes with their fists. But they did not stop.

"If you'll not take me at my word," Bran said crisply, "then see for yourself. Two leagues north of here lies a burn running through a slate crag. The English are gathering there, preparing their attack."

Aiden halted. Without turning in his saddle, he asked, "What is your gain if we aid you, MacLean? What is your prize?"

An honest question. Bran had done very few things in his life that did not earn him a clear reward. He'd helped Morag and Wulf in Edinburgh in exchange for coin; he'd attended Aiden's wedding with the intent of fleecing the man's guests; he'd helped Caitrina in order to earn back the crown. The gain for his actions today? Nothing tangible. Love and pride and honor. Rewards no one who knew him well would believe. He smiled wryly. Except Caitrina. If he spouted such nonsense now, the MacCurrans would ride off and never look back.

But he needed them as allies.

With their help, he could defeat Giric.

"There is a gold cross in the Clackmannan chapel," he said, "encrusted with jewels. If I stave off this attack, it's as good as mine."

Aiden turned and skewered him a thunderous glare. "You are truly a detestable knave." He sighed. "But if there's a chance your words are true, I cannot ignore them. Wulf will ride to the manor and request an audience with the queen. Niall and I shall assess the threat at the crag."

"I'll accompany you," Bran said. "It's not easy to find the English in the rocks."

"Nay, I'll take one of your men. You'll remain with Wulf. He's the only one I trust to resist your dubious charms."

Although he would have preferred to accompany Aiden northward, Bran settled back in his saddle. He'd won their cooperation—a far better outcome than he had expected. As long as Wulf controlled his urge to separate Bran's head from his shoulders, all would be well.

He signaled to Robbie.

As the young tracker trotted forward, Bran said to Aiden, "The English commander is a ruthless bastard who'll not hesitate to sacrifice any and all to get what he wants. If you're wise, you'll let young Robbie here guide your way into the rocks."

Aiden nodded. "So long as you know that if he leads us astray, you'll pay the price, one strip of flesh at a time."

Two thirds of the MacCurrans rode off with Robbie, leaving Bran with Wulf and, by a quick count, a dozen men. "They know me here as Marshal Gordon," Bran said to the big warrior. "I'd be obliged if you would maintain that ruse."

Wulf said nothing. He didn't even acknowledge that Bran had spoken. He simply raised a big hand to signal his men and made for the manor at a determined trot.

Gritting his teeth at the insult, Bran gave chase. He would willingly pay for his crime after Giric was defeated. Right now, his men and the people of Clackmannan were best served by confident, steady leadership—and that did not include Wulf riding up to the gate ahead of him.

Wretch.

When he caught up to Wulf, he tossed the warrior a hard glance. "The archers on the wall await my signal," he said. "Friend or foe, your fate rests in the turn of my hand." Without waiting for Wulf's response, he gave the signal for *friend*. The archers on the wall relaxed their stance, lowering their bows and taking a step back.

Wulf grunted.

"You are not the only honorable man in Scotland," Bran reminded him. "The men of Clackmannan have sworn to keep the queen safe, at any cost. Do not belittle their efforts."

The warrior sliced him a grim stare. "If a man earns my respect, he gets my respect."

The implication being that Bran had done the opposite. Well, Wulf could think whatever he liked about Bran's character. All that mattered was that he had agreed to help protect the queen—and Caitrina.

His lovely lady-in-waiting stood just inside the manor gate as they rode in. She displayed suitable decorum, standing quietly as they dismounted. But he could see the relief shining in her eyes. Clearly, she had been convinced that the MacCurrans would cut him down.

As Wulf handed off his horse, he turned and addressed the group of people gathered in the close. "I seek the lady Caitrina de Montfort," he said boldly.

"I am she," Caitrina said, stepping forward.

Wulf took her hand in his, bowed low, and kissed her knuckles. "Our sincere thanks for your missive. We will forever be in your debt, lass. Should you ever need a boon, and it is within our power to grant it, it will be yours. I swear it."

She blushed furiously. "You are too kind, sir."

The big warrior released her hand and stepped back. "I request an audience with Queen Yolande." He tugged on the silver chain around his neck and produced a ring. Bran recognized it as the favor the queen had bestowed upon Wulf the morning after her husband's death. "If she will see me."

Caitrina studied the ring. The queen's arms were quite distinctive, and she immediately understood the significance of his possession of them. She curtsied. "She is indisposed, sir, but I will make inquiries. Who shall I say requests a moment in her presence?"

"Wulf MacCurran."

He offered no title, no detail, no reason the queen might agree to see him.

But Caitrina's eyes widened with awe. "You are the knight who saved the queen from a death by poison."

He grimaced. "I merely alerted her to the danger. If any saving was done, it was surely done by her guards."

"Nonetheless, it is the greatest of honors to meet you, Sir Wulf," Caitrina said. "I was not yet appointed to Her Grace's service at the time of the attempt on her life, but the events of that morn have oft been retold. You are a true hero."

A flush rose on Wulf's cheeks. "You make too much of it."

"We will let Her Grace decide that," Caitrina said. "I will share the news of your arrival with her anon. In the meantime, I hope you will partake of our hospitality." She opened her hand toward the main door of the manor. "Some ale would surely be welcome?"

"Always," he said, offering her his arm.

As they climbed the stairs, Bran felt a pang in his chest that was swiftly becoming familiar. Jealousy. But this was not the mild indignation he'd felt at supper the other night—it was a deeper-seated ache that he had difficulty putting aside. Caitrina saw Wulf in a light that would never fall on him the same way. As she herself had said, the MacCurran warrior was a hero, a man unquestionably deserving of respect and admiration. Bran was merely playing a part. Even if he played a significant role in Giric's defeat, it would change nothing. At the end of the day, he would still be a thief.

An important fact to remember.

*   *   *

Marsailli found the camp a very different place with all the new mercenaries. It was busy and loud and very dangerous.

"Need a man to fill that ache in your quim, lass?" one soldier asked, as she carried a bucket of water up the path from the burn.

She ignored him. But she couldn't ignore the man who grabbed her arm and tried to drag her off to his tent. The drunken sot made the mistake of accosting her in front of Giric, however, and a moment later he was nursing a bellyful of steel.

"No one touches the girl," the Bear roared.

He tipped her chin up with his beefy hand. "The time has come, I think, for you to make your pallet in my tent. Gather your things."

Marsailli swallowed. "That's not necessary. I'm perfectly safe in my new tent with the midwife. I'll send a lad to fetch water from now on."

"Gather your things," he repeated. "Now."

His voice was deceptively calm, but she knew it would not stay that way. There was a bitter edge underlying his words, a sharp bite that would brook no denial.

Marsailli nodded and then ran for her tent. Her possessions were few, especially now, after Giric had torn apart the old tent. Darting from one corner of the tent to another, she snatched up her comb, her hair ribbons, and her gowns.

The midwife glanced at her. "Where are you going?"

"He says I'm to sleep in his tent from this moment forward," Marsailli said, choking on the words. She was well aware that sleep would be hard to find under Giric's roof.

Magda's lips thinned. "Drink your fill of wine or ale before you settle for the night," she advised. "It will help."

Marsailli shook her head. "I will not let him dishonor me." She pulled her sewing needles out of her pocket and showed them to the other woman. "If necessary, I will stab these in his eyes."

The older woman grew pale. "Those will not stop a man of his size, and he will kill you for daring to defy him. Nay, lass, better that you should submit. Live to see another day."

"I cannot."

In a flash, the older woman had crossed the tent and grabbed Marsailli's hands. "Aye, you can. Drink until you fall asleep. He'll take you anyway, but it will be less painful. He's a very big man, and you're a wee thing."

As well meaning as the midwife's words might have been, Marsailli could not stomach them. The notion of letting Giric have his way, of doing nothing to stop him, burned like a hot rock in her belly. Nay, she couldn't allow it. She would resist as best she could, and with a little luck, she would wound him enough to scurry free. It was the best she could hope for.

"Take care," she told the midwife.

Then she parted the tent flaps and walked slowly toward Giric's tent, her pitiful collection of belongings in her arms.

"I say we simply bide our time," James Stewart said. "Reinforcements will arrive soon enough from Edinburgh."

"The English will not wait for your reinforcements to arrive," argued Bran. "They will attack soon, while they still hold the advantage."

"The advantage belongs to us," Dougal protested. "We're safe within these walls."

"I agree," said the steward. "It's sheer madness to contemplate leaving the manor to field an attack."

"Not while we hold the element of surprise," Bran insisted. "And right now, they are gathered in one spot. A convenient target."

"What is your opinion, Laird MacCurran?" Stewart asked of the man who had just entered the great hall. "Does fortune favor the brave or the cautious?"

Aiden crossed the stone floor to the great wooden table where the council had gathered. Tucking his gloves into his belt, he said, "We are sorely outnumbered. The English have gathered nigh on two hundred men."

"Well," said Stewart, with a triumphant grin. "There's your answer. We haven't the strength of arms to meet the English on a battlefield."

Bran slapped his hands on the wooden tabletop. "We cannot simply wait for them to attack. Have I not made it clear what a formidable weapon the longbow is? They will place their archers out of range and fire arrows at us endlessly, slowly decimating our entire army."

"Bah," said Stewart. "You make the Welsh bow sound like an instrument of the devil, but King Edward conquered the Welsh—with ordinary men."

"Marshal Gordon is correct."

Bran stared at Aiden MacCurran with a raised eyebrow. Support from an unlikely quarter.

"The longbow is a weapon to be feared," said the clan chief. "In the right hands, it could cripple our defenses. I know this because I have several longbow archers among my men." Aiden signaled to one of his men, who jogged forward and placed a five-foot bow in his hand. "It takes skill to draw a weapon of this size, but once mastered a longbow can send an arrow clear over the castle wall at five hundred paces. Or it can pierce and kill a man hiding behind a shield . . . or a wooden door."

One of his men held up his targe, and Aiden launched an arrow at it. The arrowhead drove deeply into the leather-bound wood, ending its journey halfway through the wooden plank.

Stewart and Dougal stared in disbelief.

"But that is not the only argument in favor of Marshal Gordon's plan," Aiden said. "The English encampment lies at the bottom of a great slate bowl, with rock on all sides. Their position is well hidden, and the rocks provide a measure of protection, but they also trap the Englishmen. If we can approach unnoticed and surround them, their greater numbers will not impede us."

Bran sat back in his chair.

Exactly.

Stewart's eyes narrowed. "So you support a preemptive strike? Even though we have no clear indication that the English are planning an attack on Clackmannan?"

Wulf, who had been silent throughout the discussion, stepped away from the wall. "Englishmen gathering in strength a stone's throw from the manor giving respite to our queen must be seen as an act of aggression. She is soon to give birth to a new king of Scotland. We can tolerate no risk."

"Slaying two hundred Englishmen will start a war," Stewart said pointedly.

"The war began when they killed two guards tasked with protecting our queen," Bran said. "We were not the first to draw blood."

Stewart shook his head. "You are convinced that King Edward has a hand in this affair," he said. "But I do not agree."

"Whether he is or is not matters naught," Bran said. "We cannot allow a band of brigands, be they English or Scottish or Norse, to threaten the queen."

Around the table, heads nodded.

"We will give them opportunity to surrender, should that be their choice," Bran added. "I have no interest in slaying men who do not pose a threat."

Stewart eyed him across the table.

"Fine," he said. "But success or failure, Gordon, the responsibility for this decision rests with you."

His pronouncement lay heavily on Bran's shoulders. Was he mad to lead these men into battle when the royal steward contested his decision? He was no seasoned warrior—he was a thief. While he was confident his reasoning was sound, he lacked the benefit of experience to guide his hand. And although it was reassuring to have the MacCurrans stand behind him, they had only recently regained their reputation. Wild Highlanders who had once carried a price on their heads were perhaps not the best judge of character.

But he was committed now.

Bran stood up.

"Let us prepare. We march north within the hour."

Although it was risky during daylight hours, Caitrina took advantage of the somber mood that had settled over the manor and slipped into Bran's room.

He stood beside the bed, clad only in his braies, staring at the clothing laid out before him. When the door opened, he glanced up. "You should not be here."

Caitrina drew up her courage, faced him square, and spoke quickly. "I know I played you false by reaching out to the MacCurrans. My regrets are legion, believe me, but I do not wish our last words before a battle to be bitter ones."

"I cannot condone your actions—"

"Nor would I expect you to," she said.

"But in the end," he said slowly, "I acknowledge that you did the right thing."

She blinked. "You do?"

A faint smile lifted one corner of his mouth. "Taking the crown was a mistake. I plied an old man with wine, and when he told me his secret, I robbed him. Hardly one of my better moments. But I'm a thief, and thieving is what I do." He shrugged. "The opportunity was there, and I seized it."

"Did you truly hold him for ransom?"

"I held no knife to his throat," Bran said. "But I forced him to show me the hidden vault and stole his horse, so the effect was the same."

"Your reasons for taking the crown were fine enough."

He shook his head. "There are other ways to sway

the castle guard. In truth, I was racked by guilt from the moment I left Dunstoras. I could not equate the theft of the crown with lifting a few coins from a wealthy man's purse. But there seemed no easy way to repair the damage I had done."

"You appear to have found a way."

"I'm not so sure." He smiled wryly. "I may lose my head in the settlement."

"Save the queen, and all will be forgiven."

"I will do my best. Is that why you're here? To see me off?"

"Aye." Circling the bed to his back, she wrapped her arms around his waist. "If you think that I shall let you march off to battle without a token of my affections, you are sadly mistaken."

He covered her arms with his, giving her a welcome reminder of his warmth and strength. Just touching him soothed her worries. He was strong and smart and good with a blade. There was a very good chance he would return in one piece.

"I would not go were the odds not in my favor," he reassured her.

"The gossip says the English outnumber us. Is it true?"

"Aye," he admitted. "We cannot leave the manor unprotected, so we must split our forces."

"Why not simply wait for them to attack?"

He turned in her arms and drew her against his chest. "You promised to trust me."

She snuggled deeper in his embrace. "I trust you," she said. "It is Giric I do not trust."

They were silent for a moment, just holding each

other. Imagining a tragic outcome was too painful, so Caitrina held tight to a vision of him riding back through the gate, weary but triumphant.

"You have not asked about Marsailli," he said quietly. "Or my plan to keep her safe."

Her heart thumped heavily. "Do you have such a plan?"

He kissed the top of her head, the warmth of his lips resting briefly against her scalp. "Do you recall what I told you the last time you asked if I had a plan?"

She closed her eyes and drew in an intoxicating breath of his spicy scent. "Only too well. You prefer to think on your feet, and you'll decide your course of action when you get there."

A chuckle rumbled through his chest and into her body. "That's the right of it."

An image of her sister rose in her thoughts—sweet faced and tenderhearted—and her amusement faded. "It will be difficult to keep her safe in the thick of battle."

"It will," he agreed. "But you have my solemn vow that I'll do everything within my power to save her. There are far better warriors than I among Dougal's men and the MacCurrans. I'll leave the bulk of the fighting to them. My efforts are better spent on finding Marsailli."

"Thank you," she said.

He pulled away slightly and looked in her eyes. "Did you truly bring a token for me to carry into battle?"

"I did." She dug into the folds of her brat and pulled out a long strip of white linen. "I thought this would be appropriate."

He stared at the linen for a long moment. "It's quite innocent looking."

She nodded. "No one would ever guess what role it played in my disguise as a lad. How close it bound my breasts." She gave him her best rendition of a bawdy smile. "Save you."

He took the linen and wrapped it carefully about his waist. "I shall treasure it."

Caitrina gathered his lèine from the bed and helped him into it. Then she did the same with the padded cotun and the chain mail hauberk. She felt like a wife dressing her husband for battle, and her hands trembled slightly as she adjusted the weight of his mail. Even if he returned safely, this was likely to be a singular moment, never to be repeated.

Her eyes met his, and she knew his thoughts had traveled a similar path.

"Mayhap there is some way—" she said softly.

He put a finger to her lips. "Nay, lass. Such thoughts will only make the parting more difficult. You and I are from very different worlds. I have only one talent, and it will one day see me to the gallows. Let me play this part today and forget for a time what the future holds in store. Today I'm Marshal Gordon. Tomorrow, who knows?"

Cupping her face in his hands, he pulled her close for a kiss.

A tender kiss, filled with deep longing and promises that would never be fulfilled. Caitrina closed her eyes and let herself succumb to the dream. Today, she was the wife of Marshal Gordon, sending him off with all the love in her heart.

Tomorrow would come soon enough.

* * *

Marsailli claimed a small corner of Giric's tent as her own. She tried to make herself as small and unnoticeable as possible, hoping to escape the Bear's attention. But she was unsuccessful. When he returned to the tent after an afternoon of training his troops, he immediately demanded her presence.

"I want a warm bath," he snarled. "To soak away the knots in my shoulders. And I want wine. And food."

She fetched the wine and the food, doing her best to see him sated and content. But as the evening progressed, she found him staring at her with greater frequency, the look in his eyes dark with intent.

Almost without thinking, she slipped her hand into her purse and felt for the needles. The tips were reassuringly sharp, but they felt flimsy even to her delicate hands. Still, any weapon was better than none.

As the cooking fires waned and soldiers throughout the camp ambled off to bed, fear soured Marsailli's mouth and dampened her palms with sweat. The Bear would soon retire for the night—and would most certainly force her to join him in his bed. How would she resist him?

She could scream, but that was unlikely to gain her anything except an audience.

Giric's tent stood at the edge of the camp, close to the path that led down to the burn. Her only hope lay in making an escape. If by some miracle she could elude the Bear's clutches, she could disappear into the rocks and evade capture. It would be risky, especially in the dark, but navigating the slippery shards of shale would be easier than withstanding Giric's advances.

"Girl," Giric called.

Marsailli lifted her gaze. He was staring at her over the lip of his ale horn.

"Come here."

Several times over the course of the evening, he had called her to his side, mostly to refill his cup. But something about the current look in his eyes made her heart pound. Swallowing tightly, she picked up the jug of ale and took it to him. As she neared, he held out his cup, and the furious pound in her chest abated.

She filled his cup.

As she turned to leave, he grabbed her arm. "You look nothing like your sister," he grumbled.

Marsailli froze. Was it a good thing she and Caitrina had different looks? That she was slim where Caitrina was curvy?

He tugged her hard and she fell onto his lap.

"You're too thin."

Yet his disgruntlement did not stay his hands. One of them latched onto her breast and squeezed. Marsailli set the wine jug on the table and dipped her hand into her purse. The needles slid smoothly into her damp palm. What would be the right moment? Was this it?

Giric pressed his face into her neck and planted a wet kiss against her throat.

Fear and disgust snatched the breath from her lips in a hoarse rasp. She struggled for her freedom, but was unsuccessful. He held her firmly on his lap, the hard rod of his erection pressing against her bottom. His fingers pinched her nipple and Marsailli reacted instinctively. She ripped her hand out of her purse, put her thumb on the dull ends of the needles, and jabbed them at Giric's face.

She was aiming for his eye, but struck his cheek instead.

He howled with rage, leaping to his feet.

Marsailli tumbled to the floor, losing her grip on the needles. She scrambled, trying to regain her footing, but he kicked her. One of his large boots sailed into her gut and she crashed to the ground. Completely breathless.

"Cease!"

Marsailli lay on the ground with her back to the tent entrance, her legs and arms curled around her aching belly, but she recognized the voice of the midwife.

"She is but a child," the other woman shouted. "Leave her be."

Giric spat on Marsailli, then spun and tackled the midwife. He brought her to her knees with a well-placed blow and then relentlessly pursued his advantage. His fists flew with deadly aim, and the older woman shrieked in agony as he struck her repeatedly about the head. Again and again.

Marsailli attempted to stop him, dragging herself across the floor to strike him on the leg. But he shoved her aside with ease and continued to beat on the midwife. With distressing speed and a final, pummeling blow, he silenced Magda's cries.

Marsailli couldn't move. She could barely breathe.

She jammed her eyes shut, dreading the moment when the Bear's fists turned on her.

But he merely leaned over her, grabbed the jug of ale, and flopped down on his bed.

"I'll need a new midwife now," he said grimly. Then he downed cup after cup of ale, until his eyes drifted shut and loud snores fluttered his lips.

Marsailli waited until she was certain he was asleep, and then she grabbed a few belongings, crept from the tent, and slipped into the night. Her gut was bruised and several of her ribs were painful to touch, but she was alive. Which was more than she could say for the midwife. Marsailli said a prayer for the dead woman's soul, and then scrambled over a slide of shale and headed for the bottom of the crag.

Chapter 12

They scaled the crag under cover of darkness. Niall MacCurran, a skilled woodsman with a keen sense of sight, led the Black Warriors up the rocks under a cloudy, moonless sky. Bran found himself climbing alongside a gruff bowman by the name of Cormac.

"Mounting cliffs in the dark of night," the archer grumbled quietly, "is becoming a bloody bad habit."

Bran had no extra breath to spare him a response—Niall ascended the peak at a grueling pace. They reached the summit in record time and took out the posted sentries with little effort.

"Lazy Sassenachs," Cormac muttered as he toed the unconscious body of one of the guards. He unhooked his bow from his shoulders—a smooth curve of solid ashwood—and nocked an arrow. Taking his cue from Niall's hand signal, he led the way around the basin to the other side of the rocks.

Bran had spent most of his early years in the forest, living the life of a brigand. He knew the value of a well-placed foot and a silent approach, but the Black Warriors were in a league unto themselves. They made not a single sound as they traversed the ridge. Every movement was spare and efficient, every boot carefully planted.

In no time at all, they had completely surrounded the English encampment.

Bran peered down through the rocks at the quiet group of tents. Most of the mercenaries were asleep—only a handful of men sat before the fires, keeping watch. The horses at the far end of the plateau were moving restlessly, and they would soon alert the Englishmen to the presence of danger.

It was time to make their move.

With a quick strike of flint, Bran signaled the rest of his men, who waited on the path, and they swarmed the entrance, creating a blockade. The only way out of the basin now was through the rocks, and Niall's men controlled that egress. In unison, the Black Warriors launched their arrows, planting warning shots into the ground at well-placed intervals.

The plateau erupted in a frenzy of fear as the mercenaries realized they were under attack.

"Hold your fire," Bran called to the men in the rocks. To the Englishmen in the basin, he said, "Surrender now and no blood shall be spilled."

At the far end of the basin, near the path leading to the burn, a huge man strolled out of his tent. Firelight flickered over his features, including the rough scar on the left side of his face. Giric. "There will be no surrender—unless it is yours. Archers, to the center."

Some thirty bowmen dashed to the center of the plateau, their longbows at the ready.

"Fire at will," Giric ordered.

And with that command, the battle began in earnest. As arrows flew in both directions, the bulk of Giric's men charged the soldiers blocking their exit. Sword met sword, arrow met arrow. The Black Warriors held the advantage in both visibility and position. Even against the powerful draw of the longbows, they made quick and decisive gains.

Amid the furor, Bran searched the plateau for some sign of Marsailli. But there were no women among the faces he spied, no high-pitched voices amid the sounds below. If she remained in the camp, it wasn't immediately clear where she was.

His gaze fell upon the huge frame of Giric. The mighty Englishman was cutting a swath through Dougal's men. Bran nudged Cormac's shoulder and pointed.

"Take that man down," he said, "and the battle will be won."

Cormac immediately redirected his aim. He sent a flurry of arrows in Giric's direction, but they all fell short. "He's too far away," the bowman reported. "I'll need to move closer."

He slipped out from behind a rock and dashed along the ridge. Although he wisely zigged and zagged as he ran, his luck was in short supply. Just as he was about to dive behind a protective slab of slate, one of the Welsh arrows sang through the air and drove deep into his thigh. He fell hard, sliding a good thirty feet on a loose bed of shale.

In the corner of his eye, Bran saw Giric lay another man low and barrel through the blockade. Once again, the Englishman was making an escape. A low growl of frustration rumbled in his throat. He'd promised Caitrina that he would leave the fighting to more experienced warriors, but all were occupied. No one was giving chase.

Bran eyed the horses tied at the far end of the plateau. There wasn't time to dwell on the likelihood of success. He simply ran. Slipping and sliding on loose shards of rock, he dashed for the bottom of the basin. When he reached the grass, there were other obstacles in his path—bodies felled by MacCurran arrows, dying fires, the trampled remains of pitched tents.

To his amazement, he reached the horses and suffered nary a scratch. Freeing the closest palfrey with a quick jerk on its lead, he bounded onto the back of the powerful beast and spurred it toward the crumbling blockade.

"Duck," he yelled to his men as he urged the horse into a jump. He sailed over the heads of several men and raced for Giric's departing back.

It was only as he gained on the mighty Englishman that he remembered the significant difference in their sizes. Giric was nearly twice the man that he was. And the swing of his sword had enough power to make the air hum. The last time they had met in battle, Giric had very nearly destroyed him. What had possessed him to think he could duel such a mountainous man and come out the victor?

Giric spun around at the clatter of horse hooves on the stone path. His eyebrows clashed as he recognized

Bran. "You," he growled. "I should have taken your head the first night I saw you."

He swung his blade with lethal intent and very nearly decapitated the horse—only a quick jerk on the reins saved the poor beast's life. And even so, the edge of Giric's blade sliced across the horse's shoulder, and it screamed in pain.

Bran slid to the ground and sent the palfrey on its way with a swat to its rump. He gripped his sword in one hand and his dirk in the other. "Only cowards take aim at unarmed horses," he said, with more calm than he felt. Winning a lengthy duel against Giric would be impossible. The man was a giant.

Giric shrugged. "Only a weak-minded man would concern himself with a beast."

Bran studied the huge Englishman with a critical eye, trying to recall every detail of their last meet. Everyone had a weak spot. What was Giric's?

"Where is Marsailli?" he asked as he dodged left to avoid an impressive slice.

"Dead," Giric pronounced. "She was too small to take all of my cock and she bled to death from her injuries."

A crude tale, with just enough fact to make it believable. But Bran knew a lie when he heard one—there was a tad too much glee in Giric's voice for it to be an honest accounting. Which suggested, thankfully, that Marsailli was still alive. All Bran had to do was discover her whereabouts.

"Escaped your camp, did she?" he taunted.

The Englishman growled with rage and swung his sword. Bran ducked—just in time to avoid losing his head.

"A resourceful lass," Bran said. "Just like her sister."

"Nothing like her sister," dismissed Giric. "A scrawny bird with unremarkable plumage."

Bran feinted right with his sword, then spun left, slashing with his dirk. The tip of his blade caught the Englishman's upper arm, and his sleeve blossomed with red. First blood belonged to Bran.

But he paid a price for the maneuver.

Giric came at him with a series of quick, powerful strikes, two of which he deflected with the flat of his blade. The third struck his sword at an awkward angle and left a nasty gouge in the steel.

As he parried and blocked his opponent's blade, Bran continued to hunt for a weakness in Giric's defenses. But the man was surprisingly nimble, leaving very few openings. And he kept the pressure on Bran, forcing him to dart and dash from side to side to avoid the brunt of his blows.

When he finally spied an opening, Bran was nearly exhausted. Rivulets of sweat ran down his back and his hair clung damply to his neck. The moment was now or never.

He raised his sword to parry a blow and ducked under Giric's sword arm to stab the huge Englishman in the chest. It was a well-executed maneuver, and he surely would have succeeded had his damaged sword not chosen that precise instant to fail him. It snapped neatly in half under the force of Giric's strike.

The muscles in his arm were wrenched sideways as the blade gave way, and a paralyzing numbness ran across his shoulder. The pieces of his sword clattered to the ground.

The huge Englishman immediately took advantage, twisting his blade as it swung and clipping Bran's undefended midriff. He planted his feet and prepared to make the killing thrust.

It was a moment of crisis.

And in such moments, Bran's father had taught him to do the unexpected.

He dropped to the ground and rolled.

Once he was clear of Giric's extensive reach, he leapt to his feet. With only a dirk in hand, a hasty retreat seemed wise. But the image of Marsailli, naked and trembling in Giric's tent, surfaced in his thoughts. She had not deserved such treatment, nor had the two guards he had assigned to watch her deserved their cruel and merciless fate.

He could not let this wretched cur walk away.

On the streets of Edinburgh, Bran's most valuable tools were his hands. In the blink of an eye, he could delve into a man's purse, remove a few coins, and pat the fellow gently on the shoulder. Speed and a light touch were his saving graces.

And he put those same skills to work with Giric. With his right hand hanging limply at his side, he stepped deep inside the Englishman's reach, ducked under his swinging sword, and jammed his dirk into the soft skin of the other man's neck.

Giric dropped to his knees, holding a hand to his bleeding wound. "What have you done?" he cried.

"No more than you would have done for me, if given the chance," Bran said. "King Edward's plot is foiled."

"Never," Giric gasped. "My liege is a man of strong

will. Whate'er he desires shall come to pass." He collapsed in a heap on the ground. Dead.

Bran allowed himself a brief moment of satisfaction, then spun around and headed for the plateau. Mercenaries without a benefactor would be quick to lay down their arms.

When morning dawned, Marsailli took stock of her situation.

She lay on the sandy bottom of a ravine, having taken a tumble during the night. Save for some additional bruises, she was uninjured, but the climb to freedom was proving difficult. The walls of shale on either side of her were sheer and slippery with seeping moisture. Every attempt thus far to scale the walls had led to another tumble.

She grimaced. Of all the places to fall, she had definitely picked the worst.

She tipped her head up and studied the clear blue sky. At least the rain had ceased to fall. If she could dry her brat, she might finally be able to get warm. And if the walls dried sufficiently, perhaps her next attempt would be successful.

It would truly be a shame if she had escaped Giric only to meet her maker in some forgotten hole in the earth.

She spread her damp brat over a rock to dry and settled on the sand.

Her mouth was dry as dust, but it was better not to think about a long-term battle with cold and thirst and hunger. She would give the sun an hour to dry the walls, and then she would attempt the climb again.

Because she had no choice.

*   *   *

News of their triumph over the English reached Clackmannan well ahead of the returning troops, but details were sparse. Caitrina paced the floor of the queen's room, impatient for Bran's return.

"Sit down, little cousin," Yolande urged. "You tire me with your endless movements."

"My apologies, Your Grace," she said, reluctantly taking the seat next to the bed. She could see nothing from here. "Would you care for some honeyed mead?"

"Even as you offer that, you look to the window," the queen said, with a light chuckle. "Have you found a suitor among the soldiers of Clackmannan?"

Caitrina blushed. "I would never think to pursue such an interest without first gaining your approval."

Yolande's eyebrows rose. "So there *is* someone."

The trumpets sounded and Caitrina's gaze flew to the window. "It would seem that they have returned." It took every ounce of Caitrina's willpower to remain in her chair.

"Go," the queen said with a shake of her head. "But I shall expect to hear every detail of what transpired when you return to my rooms."

Caitrina stood and curtsied. "Of course, Your Grace. Every detail."

Then she dashed for the door.

Downstairs in the great hall, preparations for the Samhain feast were under way. Trestle tables were assembled, linens aired, candles lit. The two cooks had found common ground and delicacies of every sort were being organized into a series of tempting courses, each with its own palate-cleansing remove. Caitrina's stomach rumbled hungrily at the sight of eel soup, spinach tarts, May eggs, apple muse, poached herring, honeyed capon, caudell, suckling pig, roe deer in almond sauce, roast hare in wine broth, beef and onion pie, black pudding, clootie dumpling, tablet, and of course haggis. But food would have to wait.

She skirted the pair of gillies who were tapping a keg of ale and made her way outside to the surprisingly large crowd in the close.

After a few discreet queries, she located Bran in the infirmary.

"You're injured," she said, staring at the blood-stained bandage wrapped around his middle.

He grimaced. " 'Tis little more than a scratch, but the barber is insisting on plying his needle."

"And how, pray tell, did you acquire this injury?" She bent and lifted the edge of his bandage. "It looks like a sword slice."

"It is," he confessed. "But it was unavoidable, I swear."

The three MacCurran warriors, Niall, Aiden, and Wulf, entered the infirmary and made their way to Bran's side. "A fine bit of swordsmanship," Aiden said. "I confess, I wouldn't have thought you capable. Defeating a man of that size is no easy task."

Caitrina glanced from Aiden's reluctantly admiring face to Bran's slightly guilty visage. "Who did you defeat?"

"Giric."

Caitrina stiffened, afraid to hope. "Giric is dead?"

"Aye."

Her eyes met his. "And Marsailli?"

He shook his head. "There was no sign of her. I think it possible she escaped the camp sometime before we attacked."

"Then she is out there in the wild, lost and alone."

The MacCurran chief frowned. "Of whom do we speak?"

"My sister," said Caitrina. "She was a prisoner in the English camp."

Wulf raked a hand through his long hair. "The body of a lass *was* recovered in the wreckage of the camp."

Caitrina's throat clenched tight and she closed her eyes, refusing to believe. "Nay."

Bran's hand clasped hers, squeezing gently. "Stay strong," he said. "It may not be her. There was another woman in the camp." Turning to Wulf, he asked, "What age would you guess the lass to be?"

"Difficult to tell," Wulf admitted. "She had been beaten."

Caitrina's knees shook and her belly heaved. She knew just what such an injury looked like. She'd seen the broken body of that poor wretch Giric had slain. "Dear god."

Bran tugged her against his chest and smoothed a broad hand over her brow. "Do not assume the worst. In his last moments, Giric implied that she had escaped."

"Then we should search the crag for her," Caitrina said.

"Such was my intent," Bran said. "Had the barber not insisted, I would be there still."

"I'll go with you," Niall offered.

"And I'll go, too," Caitrina insisted. "After all she's been through, she might need a familiar face to set her at ease."

"It's a long ride," Bran warned her. "And the weather is about to turn wet again."

"Then give me a few moments to change my attire. A lad might be better suited to such a journey than a lady."

He smiled at her. "Fair enough. We'll meet you at the postern gate."

They began their search in the basin of the slate crag. Despite the words of assurance he had offered to Caitrina, Bran insisted on seeing the body of the dead woman. To his relief, it was immediately clear that she was a good deal older than Marsailli. Her hands were spotted with age and the skin around her neck was loose.

He pointed to the wreckage of the tent Giric had occupied. "We should assume she began her journey here."

Niall peered up into the misty heights of the crag. "She likely made no attempt to climb higher. Unless she was chased by Giric's men, her goal would have been to descend."

"I agree, but the main path would have carried a significant risk of discovery. We should focus our search on alternative routes to the bottom." Bran turned to Caitrina. "I think it best you remain here. The rocks are dangerous and slides are not uncommon."

She pulled her brat lower over her head as the rain steadily fell from the sky. "The damp chill saps my strength. If Marsailli is without shelter, she too must feel the cold."

He nodded. "The sooner we find her, the better."

"If I call out her name," she said, "perhaps she will hear me and seek us out."

It was possible, assuming Marsailli was uninjured and free to move about. Unfortunately, there were numerous reasons she might not answer. But he did not voice his concerns. Better that Caitrina remain hopeful.

He and Niall split up, each taking a separate path through the rocks.

Bran searched every crevice, every overhang, and every cliff bottom that he came across. It was a perilous task. Every few feet, the shale gave way and slid down the crag in a shower of muddy water and rocks. Several of the crevices were so deep he could not see the bottom. He called down into them with an uneasy sense of dread. If Marsailli had lost her footing, there was a very good chance she lay at the bottom of some hole too battered to move.

All he could do was pray that her slight frame and lighter weight disturbed less loose rock than he did.

As he searched, the faint sound of Caitrina's voice reached his ears.

The steep sides of the slate basin and the low-hanging clouds seemed to swallow her calls.

After several fruitless hours, he returned to the top of the path. Caitrina stood there, shivering in the cold. Using the remnants of the English campsite, he built a lean-to and started a fire.

"Have you heard from Niall?" he asked as she warmed her hands over the flames.

She shook her head.

Her hope was fading; he could see it in her eyes. Marsailli had been out in the wet weather for almost a full day. In the summer, that would have been less of a concern. On the last day of October, with a bitter wind drifting down from the Highlands, it gave him pause.

"Let's hope he's had better luck than us."

Marsailli knew she was in danger when the shivering stopped. Her fingers were a bloodless white, her breaths shallow and unsatisfying. The rain kept her from thirsting, but it also robbed her of warmth. For a while, her brat had been enough to keep her warm. Even damp, it had held her heat to her body. But over time, that heat had escaped.

She peered up at the misty sky.

If it would only stop raining, she might have a chance.

She'd been smart enough to grab a round of bread and some cheese before she ran. And she'd stolen an oilskin of ale from a dozing guard. So it was not lack of food and drink that was her enemy—only the rain and steep sides of the crevice caused her grief.

Even the crevice might be conquerable with a lengthy break in the rain.

It was only about ten feet deep.

She was even lucky that the bottom was sandy—the rain did not accumulate. It quickly drained away. But if she could not get warm, none of that would matter.

A shadow flickered overhead, and she glanced up.

A soaring bird? Or something more promising?

"Hallo?" she called. "Is someone there?"

For a long moment, there was only silence. She sagged against the rock wall.

Then, suddenly, the gloomy sky was blocked by a pair of broad shoulders and a brat-covered head. "Marsailli?"

For an instant, she couldn't speak. Her throat had closed tight, grateful beyond belief that someone had found her. "Aye," she croaked.

"My name is Niall MacCurran," the shape at the top of the crevice said. "Your sister sent me. Hold tight, lass. I'll have you out of there in a wee moment."

"Caitrina sent you?"

"Aye, and Marshal Gordon." The end of a rope dropped down beside her. "Tie that around your waist. There's a good lass."

As soon as she knotted the rope, he began to pull her up. At the top of the crevice, he layered his brat atop hers and rubbed her arms to build some warmth. Marsailli immediately felt the burn of heat returning to her skin, and she smiled at her savior. "Thank you," she said, as her teeth began to chatter.

"I can smell a campfire," he said. "Let's get you back to your sister and dry those damp clothes."

It took them longer than Marsailli thought to reach the basin. Niall tested every route carefully before trusting his full weight on the rocks—a wise decision. Several times, the entire shelf of rock slid off the edge, crashing to the ground some distant drop below. Eventually, though, they reached the sturdy stone path.

At the mouth of the basin, Marsailli hesitated.

"Giric is dead," Niall told her quietly. "Marshal Gordon did what had to be done."

She lifted her gaze to his angular face. "Good," she said simply.

He pointed to a haphazard lean-to and a blazing fire. "I think someone is waiting for you."

Marsailli had endured a great deal in the four months since she last saw Caitrina, and she'd felt a full range of emotions about her sister. But the moment she turned her head and looked into Caitrina's familiar face, all of it instantly fell away. Tears sprang to her eyes and her bottom lip trembled.

She lifted the hem of her gown and raced across the rain-sodden grass.

Hot tears competed with the cold droplets on her face. She threw herself into her sister's arms and released a sob of pure joy. Caitrina's warmth and scent and familiar shape enveloped her, and she closed her eyes.

Finally, she was safe.

Bran rode alone on the journey home.

They waited until daylight, then wended their way south through rain-chilled glens and across gray, somber moors. Caitrina and Marsailli shared a mount, grateful for the time together, recounting in hushed whispers meaningful moments of the past four months.

As he watched them rebond as sisters, he realized the day had come to say good-bye to Marshal Giles Gordon. All he had hoped to accomplish was done. Caitrina was happily reunited with her sister, the crown was back in the hands of the MacCurrans, and the deaths of the two guards had been avenged.

There was nothing left to hold him to Clackmannan.

Except Caitrina.

He took a deep breath and felt a twinge of pain in his chest. It was very tempting to ply his charm and convince her to run away with him. He was fairly certain he could paint a rosy picture of their future together—rosy enough to coax her into giving up the life she currently led, which lacked a wee bit in the promise of love.

But that would be selfish.

Caitrina deserved so much more than a life on the streets of Edinburgh. It was a hard, cruel existence. The law eventually caught up with even the best thieves, and the only thing he could guarantee his wife was that she would one day see him swing.

Only a blackguard would lead a woman down that path.

And he was better than that. Or so Caitrina believed, anyway.

Bran glanced at Niall MacCurran. "I'm ready to return to Dunstoras to face my punishment."

The other man shrugged. "Your fate is in the hands of the laird."

"How did Bhaltair take my betrayal?"

Niall snorted. "As he takes everything. The witless old fool is convinced you were destined to take the crown. That it was a necessary event, predestined by the stars."

Bran chuckled. "I need not hang my head in shame, then."

Niall pinned him with a pointed stare. "You purposely got him sotted."

A tactic he regularly utilized with fat merchants in

Edinburgh, without feeling a single ounce of remorse. But Bhaltair had considered him a friend. Therein lay the shame. Other than Morag, Bhaltair had been the only citizen of Dunstoras to show him genuine kindness.

"My actions were reprehensible," he admitted.

Niall tipped his head toward the now visible walls of the manor. Numerous flags were flying, indicating the presence of yet another senior nobleman of Scotland. "Let us hope you have the opportunity to make amends."

"Are those the colors of the Earl of Carrick?"

Niall nodded. "But more important," he said, pointing to the green and black flag waving just below the queen's banner atop the guard tower, "it appears that Marshal Findlay has returned from Oban."

Bran's heartbeat slowed to a heavy pound in his chest. He spurred his horse forward and snagged the bridle of Caitrina's mount.

He drew the two women to a halt.

This was not the ending he had imagined, but it was the only one possible. He could not enter the gates of Clackmannan and hope to remain a free man. "It appears that Marshal Findlay has returned," he said to Caitrina. "Marshal Gordon must now retreat to Feldrinny."

"But we have much left to say," she protested.

"Nay," he disagreed. "We've said all that needs saying. I suffer no regrets, and I would hope you say the same."

"I will not accept this as the end."

He smiled wryly. "You were always a difficult lass."

"If what we had means anything to you, you will not rest until you find a way for us to be together."

"Lass," he said softly. "Do not make our last moments bitter ones. You've made me a better man, and I'll treasure the memories of our time together for eternity. But there is no hope of a life together. We both know that."

A flush rose on her cheeks. "You give up too easily."

"Nay. For once in my life, I am doing the right thing." He leaned across the horses and planted a firm kiss on her lips. "You deserve better than a thief and rogue."

She smiled. "Then we are in agreement. You are better than a thief and a rogue."

He slipped the ring off his finger and tucked it into her hand. "Don't forget me, lass."

Then he did the hardest thing he'd ever done. He turned his horse and rode off—without looking back.

Marsailli hugged her as they rode through the gate at Clackmannan. "Promise me that when the time is right you'll tell me the entire tale of Marshal Gordon."

"I don't know the ending yet," Caitrina said.

A stable lad grabbed the bridle of her horse and helped the ladies dismount. Samhain celebrations were well under way, with music and dancing and a bonfire in the close. Caitrina spied a young lad watching the merriment with an overly serious expression.

"Who is that?" she asked Niall.

"The Earl of Carrick's son, Robbie le Brus."

As she watched, the lad left the bonfire and crossed the courtyard to a group of horses tied outside the stables. He ran an admiring hand over the withers of a black-and-white stallion, then stopped with his hand atop the leather satchel strapped to the destrier's saddle.

"Is that Laird MacCurran's horse?" she asked.

Niall followed her gaze—and frowned. "Aye."

"Is the crown in that satchel?" she asked, in a hushed voice.

"It may well be," Niall said, leaving her side and striding toward the earl's son. He was quick, but not quick enough. Robbie opened the satchel and stared at the contents with a mesmerized expression.

Marsailli touched Caitrina's sleeve. "Is aught amiss?"

A strange expression settled on Robbie's brow as he stared into the satchel, and before Niall could stop him, he reached in and touched the crown. Had Caitrina not been watching, she might never have noticed the faint blue glow that rose from the satchel and then swiftly faded away.

Something had just happened, although she could not begin to guess at what it was.

As Niall reached young Robbie and yanked the flap of the leather satchel down to cover the crown, she shook herself free of her reverie and smiled at her sister. "Nay, naught is amiss. Let us go inside and partake of the feast. We have much to celebrate."

At the top of the stairs, she paused. Turning to the east, she looked out over the gate. Bran had disappeared. The manor was already abuzz with talk of a charlatan marshal, and in the coming days no doubt much would be said to disparage his actions. But she knew the real man behind the mask of Marshal Gordon.

Bran MacLean. A thief, yea, but also an honorable man who had done much to set her world right.

He had hoped she had no regrets, and she could honestly say she had nary a one.

Except that he was gone.

With a hand to her lips and a smile on her face, she entered the manor.

Chapter 13

The invitation came by courier—a rolled parchment written in a flowing script and signed by the laird. Aiden MacCurran demanded the presence of Bran Mac-Lean at Dunstoras. Immediately.

Seated at his favorite table in the alehouse in Beggar's Close, Bran stared at the parchment.

He had offered to return to Dunstoras to meet his punishment. But that had been weeks earlier. When no demand had come from the laird in the days after his departure from Clackmannan, he had assumed the debt was cleared.

But apparently, he'd been mistaken.

Perhaps the sad events of recent days had stirred the pot. Queen Yolande's wee son had been delivered stillborn and the capital was still reeling from the news that the new monarch would be Queen Margaret, the bairn born to Alexander's daughter and the King of Norway.

What impact that news might have on Dunstoras, he had no clue, but the black crepe that hung everywhere in Edinburgh at the moment was definitely impacting Bran's ability to earn a coin. The market was excessively quiet and pickings were slim.

"Well?" prompted his companion. "What does it say?"

Bran lifted his gaze to the bright blue eyes of Elsie Drummond. Slight of build and nimble as a water sprite, the young lass hid her charms beneath a loose gray lèine and a dull green brat. It was a surprisingly effective disguise, especially when paired with shorn locks and a brash, confident stare. None of the alehouse patrons were aware that the young lad in their midst was actually a woman. "I've been summoned to the Highlands."

She snorted. "Why would ye go? Last time ye ventured north, ye returned with naught but a belly full of twine."

"To repay a debt."

Her frown deepened. "Who could you possibly owe?"

He sighed. " 'Tis a long tale, not worth repeating."

Elsie sat forward, peering into his face. "Are ye planning to leave us, then?"

He said nothing, not entirely sure of his answer.

"Bloody wretch," she muttered, flopping back in her seat and snatching up her horn of ale. "Go ahead, then. Abandon yer mates."

"I've done my part," he said, smiling faintly. "Ularaig is in the dunny, the castle guards are no longer the bane of your existence, and I've taught you every skill I know. What more would you ask of me?"

It was Elsie's turn to be silent.

Bran picked up the jug of ale and refilled her cup.

Five years before, he'd slain the drunken sot who'd near beaten her to death in a dark wynd a few hundred paces from here. Little of the damage done that night remained on her face—just a small bump on the bridge of her nose—but the attack had changed Elsie in ways that could not be seen.

"If you have need, I will return," he promised.

She sent him a hot glare. "I fend for myself."

"Aye." He nodded. "You do." Quite ably, in fact. She carried two very sharp dirks at her belt. "But you're like a sister to me. Whatever the danger, I'll not hesitate to stand for you. You must know that."

Elsie downed the contents of her cup and plunked it down on the oak tabletop.

"Off you go, then. Find yer lady-love."

Bran grimaced. "Now you are just being cruel."

Her gaze lifted to his. "Admit it. That's the true reason ye want to leave. Ye've done naught but plot ways to win the lass back since ye've returned. If the Mac-Currans can offer you the respectability ye need to claim her, then I'll not fault ye for leavin'. Go after her, ye bampot." She flipped a silver denier onto the table and rolled to her feet. "But never forget where yer roots are."

Bran stared at her back as she sauntered out of the alehouse. An unexpected endorsement, that. He'd never told Elsie about Caitrina, but apparently a lack of words hadn't kept his bright little apprentice from discerning the truth. He glanced back at the parchment. There was no guarantee that settling his affairs with the MacCurrans would give him the means to claim Caitrina, but if there was even a small chance . . .

Perhaps a brief sojourn in Dunstoras was called for.

At the very least, he owed Bhaltair an apology. The old man might never forgive him, but it would satisfy Bran's conscience if he had the chance to make his peace.

Bran exited the alehouse, returned to the small hovel he called home, and gathered up his satchel of meager belongings.

It took him several days to make the journey from Edinburgh to Dunstoras, but they were pleasant days. There was something about the Highlands that called to him.

As soon as rolling hills of heather replaced the thicker forests of the Lowlands, his step lightened. And when he caught a glimpse of the creamy tower of Dunstoras through the glen, he smiled. It had the look of a tower that had stood for a thousand years—bold and beautiful against the pale gray sky.

But as he approached the portcullis, a ripple of trepidation ran through him.

What punishment would the laird deem appropriate for his crime?

Lashes? Days in the stockade? He took a deep breath and straightened his shoulders. As long as it didn't involve the severing of body parts, he could withstand whatever humiliation the laird had in store. The portcullis was up and Bran rode into the close with a resolute expression.

Wulf was standing on the stone steps on the donjon when Bran entered the inner close.

"About bloody time," the big warrior said. "Did the invitation not say 'immediately'?"

Bran dismounted. A lad with features similar to Wulf's took his horse. His son, perhaps? "Is there reason for haste?"

"According to the Lady Isabail, aye," Wulf said. "Come, we'll see you properly attired."

"Properly attired for what?"

The big warrior scowled. "You ask too many questions."

"Or not enough," Bran retorted. "Is there to be a public trial?"

Wulf smiled. "In a manner of speaking."

The big warrior led Bran into the great hall, where—to his bafflement—a banquet was in progress. "What is the occasion?"

Wulf pointed to the high table. "Your wedding."

Bran's gaze latched onto the sweetly beguiling face of Caitrina de Montfort. He hungrily devoured every detail of her appearance, from the welcoming warmth in her eyes to the bold blue satin of her gown. "My *what*?"

Wulf prodded him in the ribs. "Take your seat, MacLean. The laird is about to speak."

The chair at the center of the high table stood glaringly unoccupied, and Bran walked to it with a turbulent gut. How could this be his wedding, when he had never asked for Caitrina's hand? And how could Laird MacCurran condone the marriage of a street thief to a lady of the court?

He dropped onto the seat next to Caitrina and offered her a weak smile.

"Are you party to this?"

"Of course," she said. "The arrangements are mostly

my doing. Isabail has provided great support, but the costs are mine to bear."

"Are you mad?" he whispered, as Aiden took the floor.

"Kith and kin, I welcome you. We have gathered here today to bear witness to a wedding that shall take place before the door of the chapel shortly after we feast. I offer my most sincere congratulations to Lady Caitrina de Montfort and her husband, Sir Bran MacLean. Sir Bran was knighted a few short weeks before, in absentia, by the queen, for services above and beyond the call of duty."

There was a round of raucous applause.

Bran simply stared. Knighted? By the queen?

Surely this was some sort of cruel jest.

"What does he speak of?" he whispered to Caitrina. "I refuse to live a lie."

"'Tis not a lie," she said. "Queen Yolande did indeed knight you. Unfortunately, the tragic circumstances surrounding the death of her son made it impossible for her to inform you."

"That's preposterous. I was impersonating a nobleman. Why would she knight me?"

Caitrina took his hand in hers. "Several prominent people stood in your defense. Myself, Laird MacCurran, and Lord James Stewart. The royal steward credits you with saving the life of the queen. It was he who spearheaded the call to knight you."

Bran endured the rest of the speeches, and a rather lengthy wedding ceremony that made him thankful he had eaten beforehand. He was silent through much of it, even the dancing and drinking after the wedding. But when the pipes and lutes were finally put away, and the guests were dispersing, he sent a warning glare to the three MacCurran warriors and then swung Caitrina into his arms. He'd had no say in the making of this wedding, but he'd be damned if another man would have a say in how he bedded his wife.

He mounted the stairs two at a time, his steps sure and determined.

Only when he was alone with Caitrina in a room that had been decorated with candles and flower petals did he tug her into his arms and kiss her soundly. "You, madam, are quite incorrigible," he said.

"Are you unhappy?"

He shook his head. "Far from it." He untied the ribbons in her hair and slid his fingers through her long, glorious tresses. "I am utterly content."

She encircled his neck with her arms and pulled his head down for a passionate kiss. "Laird MacCurran says he is looking for good men to take up the sword in defense of Dunstoras. Do you think we could make a life for ourselves here?"

He cupped her rump and hauled her up his body. He'd forgotten how sweet she felt in his arms. "The wretch would be lucky to have me."

"You would need to give up the thieving," she said, tilting her head back to give him access to her neck. "He was quite adamant about that."

Bran rained tiny kisses up her neck and along her jaw. "Was he?"

"Will that be a challenge?"

"Nay," he said, burying his face against her perfumed flesh. "It seems you've managed to get everything your heart desires."

She smiled.

"Aye. What else could a lass possibly want?"

Favoring her with a wolfish grin, he scooped her off her feet and carried her to the bed. "Ah, sweetling, I think I might imagine a thing or two. Shall I see if I can make the rest of your dreams come true?"

He put his skilled fingers to good use, and her answer was lost to a squeal of delight.

Continue reading for an excerpt from
another Claimed by the Highlander Novel,

WHEN A LAIRD TAKES A LADY

Available now from Signet Eclipse!

The Eastern Highlands
Above Lochurkie Castle
January 1286

Atop a huge black-and-white warhorse, Isabail's view of the destruction was unimpeded. Six of her guards, including the valiant Sir Robert, lay lifeless on the moonlit trail. The others had been forced to their knees and tightly bound like cattle. A pair of chests packed with her belongings had been rifled through and the contents scattered. The reivers had gathered only a few items, mostly simple gowns and practical shoes. The more expensive items—those intended for her sojourn in the king's court—lay in careless heaps, trampled in the snow and mud.

Isabail had no sympathy to spare her fine clothes, however. Fear for what would next befall her and her maid, Muirne, had cinched her chest so tight, there was no room for anything else.

The fur-cloaked Highland raiders who had attacked her party were small in number but large in size—a mouth-souring blur of fierce faces, broad shoulders, and brawny limbs. One of them, apparently the leader, wore a thunderous scowl so dark that her belly quailed each time she spied him.

To her amazement, the attackers numbered only three. How they had succeeded in defeating the dozen guards that accompanied her carriage, she could not fathom. But defeated them, they had. The raiders worked swiftly, their movements spare and deliberate. No pack was left unopened, no chest left unturned. They finished their looting in no time and were soon mounted and ready to depart.

Except for the leader.

He scooped a colorful selection of clothing into a pile, removed a flint from the pouch at his belt, and crouched with his back to the wind. With experienced ease, he soon had the pile in flames. Isabail had to bite her lip to stem a wail. As she watched, a sizable portion of her fine wool gowns, white linen sarks, and beaded slippers went up in a fiery pyre.

Under any other circumstance, Isabail would have burst into tears. But Muirne's pale plump face was turned to her, her eyes a silent plea for hope and guidance. Isabail could not give in to the waves of despair pummeling her body. Not now. Not when Muirne needed her to be strong.

The leader eyed the plume of gray smoke drifting its way into the sky, then grabbed the reins of Isabail's horse and, in a single fluid bound, leapt up behind her. A steel band of an arm encircled her waist and hauled her into his lap. A short shriek escaped her lips before she could tame it. Instinct urged her to fight for release, to wriggle free and run, but fear held her fast. The man was huge. He could kill her with a solitary blow from one of those massive fists.

Better that she wait for rescue.

Surely their intent was to ransom her? If she but braved his inappropriate touch for a short while, Cousin Archibald would pay the ransom, and she would be freed. There was no need to risk life or limb to flee.

Her captor urged the horse forward, leading his small group toward the narrow opening at the end of the ravine. Isabail glanced at the fallen bodies and bound figures of her men, and the words spilled from her lips before she could stop them.

"Surely, you don't intend to leave them like this."

"I do." His terse response rumbled through his chest, vibrating against her back.

"But there are wildcats and wolves in these hills."

He said nothing, just urged his horse into a trot and then farther up the mountain slope. Higher and higher they climbed, the horse picking its way around boulders and thick patches of heather. As they traversed a steep ledge, she got a clear view of the moonlit glen and the mist-shrouded stone castle that was her home.

The folk in the fortress were no doubt going about their usual evening chores, oblivious to the tragedy that had struck her party. How long would it be before the remaining guards were found? Helpless as they were, would they not starve to death or be torn apart by wild animals?

Isabail chewed her lip.

One of the bearded outlaws riding alongside her caught her eye. "You fret for naught," he said. "The smoke will draw notice from the castle. Unless the earl's soldiers are asleep at their posts, your guards will be home by morn."

Her captor released a derisive snort.

Isabail breathed a sigh of relief, but did not relax. She was struggling to retain her dignity. The upward climb made it extremely difficult to hold herself aloof from the warrior at her back. She did her best to maintain a stiff ladylike poise, but every time the massive warhorse surged up a steep incline, she collided with her captor's very solid chest.

It was bad enough that their hips were so intimately connected. She refused to give up any more of her self-respect than was necessary. But as the air thinned and grew colder, the steady warmth he exuded held more and more appeal. Even with her lynx cloak wrapped tightly about her shoulders, the hours in the saddle and the frigid air began to take their toll. She slipped farther and farther back in the saddle. Several times, she stiffened abruptly when she realized her body had slumped wearily toward the wall of male flesh behind her.

Fortunately, her captor did not seem to notice her lapses. His attention was focused on carving a trail through the bleak wilderness that was the Highlands in January. Perhaps fearing pursuit, he kept their pace as hard and fast as the terrain would allow.

Isabail was just beginning to wonder how far he intended to take her from her home when he drew the massive destrier to a halt and barked out an order to his men. "Make camp here."

As he leapt down and icy air swirled around her in his absence, she took stock of his chosen campsite. She considered herself born of much hardier stock than her English cousins, but even to her seasoned Scot's eye, the spot looked anything but hospitable. Barren rock, blanketed by a thin layer of ice and snow. The only break to the north wind was a large boulder and, in the distance, a tall standing stone erected by the ancient Picts.

But the lack of obvious comfort did not dismay his men. They helped Isabail and Muirne dismount, then immediately set about making a fire. Once the peat bricks generated some heat, they tethered the horses and passed around meager portions of bread and cheese. The meal was too late to be supper and too early to be breakfast, but it tasted wonderful just the same.

Isabail and Muirne were left alone as the men went about their tasks. Muirne's thoughts had not eased on the long ride up the mountain. Her eyes were bright with unshed tears. "They mean to rape and kill us," she whispered.

"How can you know that?" asked Isabail. "They've not made any such threats."

"You only need to look at the dark look on that one"—she pointed to the towering shape of the leader as he unsaddled the horses—"to know that we are doomed."

Isabail's stomach clenched. Muirne's assessment had merit. Everything about the man was terrifying, from the daunting width of his shoulders to the grim set of his chiseled jaw. And her maid was correct—the scowl on his face did not bode well. But to admit the bend of her thoughts to Muirne would not calm the maid's fears.

"The only reason for them to accost a noblewoman is to ransom her," she said quietly but firmly. "They will not harm us for fear of losing their reward."

"That may protect you, my lady, but it'll no protect me," muttered Muirne. "I'll no see my Fearghus again. I can feel it in my bones."

"You are seeing a badger where there is only a skunk," chided Isabail. "The possibility of rescue yet remains. We are still on Grant land."

Muirne frowned. "How can you be certain? We've journeyed several hours beyond sight of the castle."

Isabail nodded toward the standing stone in the distance. It was too dark to see the Pictish symbols engraved on its surface, but the shape was very familiar. "I recognize that stone. We are but a short distance from the bothy my brother used as a respite stop during lengthier hunts."

Her maid's face lit up. "Och! Then we are saved. We can escape there and await the earl's men."

"Nay," Isabail said sharply. "I will not risk the wrath of these men by attempting an escape. Our best option is simply to wait. They will ransom us soon enough."

Her sharp tone drew the attention of one of the reivers. The heavyset fellow with the wiry dark beard stopped brushing the horses for a moment and stared at them. Neither woman dared to speak another word until he resumed his task.

"See?" hissed Isabail. "They watch us too closely. Escape is not possible."

Muirne nodded and sat silent for a time, chewing on her bread and cheese. Although morn was surely only an hour or two away, the reivers laid bedrolls near the fire and offered two of them to the women. Isabail claimed her spot with trepidation. She had never passed a night under the stars without a tent overhead. It hardly seemed possible that she would be able to rest here now. Especially with the fierce face of the leader staring at her across the campfire. The flickers of the firelight added harsh shadows to an already grim countenance and left her with the distinct impression that he resented her, though heaven only knew why. She'd seen him for the first time just two days ago in the orchard. At the time, unaware that he was a villain and a cad, she had silently admired his physical form. Few men of her acquaintance sported such a blatantly muscular body, and he possessed a rather handsome visage for a heathen brute—the sort of sharply masculine features a woman does not soon forget.

He stood suddenly, and Isabail's breath caught in her chest. By God, he was huge. Dark and powerful, a veritable thunderstorm of a man. He tossed back one side of his fur cloak, revealing a long, lethal sword strapped to his side. Beneath the cloak, he wore a leather jerkin atop a dark lèine and rough leather boots, which hugged his calves. His clothing was common enough, but there was something decidedly uncommon about the man.

Perhaps it was the intensity of his glacial blue stare— neither of the other two held her gaze for more than a glance. Or perhaps it was the way he held himself, shoulders loose but firm, like he was a direct descendant of Kenneth MacAlpin himself. Lord of all he surveyed.

He glared at her and drew his sword.

Muirne shrieked and Isabail's heart skipped a beat.

But the brute did not advance. With his gaze still locked on Isabail, he returned to his seat before the fire and began to clean his weapon.

It took long moments for Isabail's heart to resume its regular rhythm. Not one word had been exchanged, but she had felt the weight of his blame as surely as if he'd unleashed a furious diatribe. In his mind, it would seem, she was the cause of his troubles.

Perhaps Muirne was right. Perhaps he had no intention of ransoming her. If his intent was vengeance for some imagined slight, he would be far more interested in extracting his pound of flesh than in keeping her safe and whole. Perhaps escape was a wiser option after all.

Isabail dove beneath the blankets provided by his men and lay on her side with her back to the fire. She could still feel the cold gaze of her captor, but she did her best to ignore it. The hunt camp was so very close. Yet how could they hope to reach it while under such intense scrutiny?

"The women are slowing us down," one of the men muttered. "At this pace, it'll take another full day to reach Dunstoras."

Isabail froze. *Dunstoras?*

"That assumes the earl's men don't catch us first," retorted another.

"You worry for naught," said their leader crisply. "The earl's men are a league behind us. They think we're headed south. We'll lose them when we turn west and descend into Strath Nethy."

Nausea rolled in Isabail's belly. Dunstoras was home to the MacCurrans—the clan whose chief had robbed the king and murdered her brother. The same chief who had escaped Lochurkie's dungeon and absconded to parts unknown. If the man seated across the fire was Aiden MacCurran, she was in far more dire straits than she thought. A murderous traitor to the Crown would hardly follow the unwritten rules of hostage taking.

She lay stiff and silent, unable to sleep.

MacCurran deserved to pay for his crimes. John had been a fine man and a good earl. Far more noble and worthy than her father had been. If only she could escape to the hunt bothy, she could ensure MacCurran was brought to justice. From the standing stone, she could find her way to the hut with ease—she and John had stopped there a dozen times over the years.

The challenge was getting away from MacCurran and his men. It might be possible for one of the women to sneak away, but two? Unlikely. Yet she could hardly leave Muirne behind. No, if an escape was to be made, it would be both of them or neither of them.

ALSO AVAILABLE FROM

ROWAN KEATS

TAMING A WILD SCOT
A Claimed By the Highlander Novel

Wrongfully accused of murder and left to die in a hellish
Highland dungeon, Ana Bisset has lost all hope of
freedom. But the beautiful healer's luck takes an
unexpected turn when a hooded stranger appears as her
rescuer. After a harrowing escape, Ana settles alone in a
quiet village where no one knows her past or her
reputation. And the last thing she ever expects is to meet
her mysterious savior again…

Niall MacCurran is no hero, but a warrior on a dangerous
mission to expose a threat to the realm. After his decision
to free Ana, he now realizes that it is he who needs her
help—willing or no—to advance his quest. But his
growing feelings for the delicate yet resilient beauty soon
jeopardize their safety—and not even Ana's healing gifts
may be enough to protect their love, or their lives.

"A rich, exciting new voice in Scottish
historical romance!"
—*New York Times* bestselling author Monica McCarty

Available wherever books are sold or at
penguin.com

S0582

ALSO AVAILABLE FROM

ROWAN KEATS

TO KISS A KILTED WARRIOR

A Claimed By the Highlander Novel

Shunned by her village, weaver Morag Cameron lives a solitary existence in the woods—until the night she finds a sorely wounded Highlander by the loch. Under her care, the handsome warrior slowly recovers his strength, but his memories have disappeared. Morag is torn. For if she helps him regain his past, she may sacrifice a life with the man she has come to love.

Wulf MacCurran wants nothing more than to claim Morag as his own, but his past holds too many dangerous secrets—secrets that put them both in mortal danger. He must discover who attacked him and left him for dead. Traveling to Edinburgh, Wulf and Morag find themselves swept into a mystery with the power to determine the fate of their passions—and change Scotland forever...

"[Keats is] a master storyteller and a force in Scottish romance."
—*Romantic Times*

S0584

ALSO AVAILABLE FROM

ROWAN KEATS

WHEN A LAIRD TAKES A LADY

A Claimed By the Highlander Novel

Isabail Grant has had to be strong all her life. Over the years, she has lost everyone close to her, and now she's seeking justice for her brother's murder. But en route to Edinburgh to petition the king, she is kidnapped by a fierce warrior—and is shocked to find herself irresistibly drawn to her captor.

Aiden MacCurran is an outlaw. The laird of a small clan, he's been falsely accused of killing the king's courier and stealing the Crown's property—and the key to clearing his name and redeeming his clan lies in Isabail's memories. But Aiden and Isabail must first weather deceit and treachery before they can find the truth and claim the love that's growing between them.

"A rising star of medieval romance."
—*Romantic Times*

Available wherever books are sold or at
penguin.com

S0583